"You're taking my plight awfully seriously. How about *you* help me?"

With a little laugh Fiona backed away. "I'm not qualified to do more than get you another coffee."

"Have dinner with me," Marc said.

"No. Thank you. I have other plans."

Marc wheeled after her. "Tomorrow?"

"I can't."

"Why not?"

"I just can't."

"*Won't*, you mean," Marc said bitterly. "Because I'm in a wheelchair." In his heart he couldn't blame her. What woman wanted to go out with a cripple?

"It's not because your legs don't work. Your real handicap is your attitude."

Her challenging gaze held his until Fearless Marc Wilde had to look away.

Dear Reader,

Writing *Family Matters* required me to "take a giant step outside my mind," as the saying goes. Timid ol' me had to delve into the psyche of Marc Wilde, whose greatest thrill is meeting physical danger head-on. When Marc ends up in a wheelchair not knowing if he'll ever walk again, once more I found myself in foreign territory, navigating by empathy, imagination and a lot of help from people who'd been there.

When I began writing this book I worried that a story about a hero in a wheelchair might be depressing to readers. Through my research I learned not only the hardships and difficulties paraplegics face, but about their ability to achieve rich, full lives. These men and women are true heroes whose stories are a triumph of the human spirit and a tribute to the joy of simple things.

Marc's recovery is assisted by Fiona Gordon, whose combination of tough love and compassion raises his spirits and helps him find meaning in his new life. Ultimately Marc must face his demons alone and find the courage to let Fiona go to live the life she's always longed for.

For me, *Family Matters*, the second book in THE WILDE MEN trilogy, became an uplifting story of moral courage and the healing power of love. Does Marc walk again? You'll have to read the book to find out—no peeking at the final pages, please! I hope you'll agree that by the end of Marc and Fiona's story (which is really just the beginning) whether he walks or not truly is irrelevant. One thing we can always count on in a romance is a happy ending, and *Family Matters* is no exception.

I love to hear from my readers. Please write to me at P.O. Box 234, Point Roberts, WA 98281-0234, or e-mail me at www.joankilby.com.

Sincerely,

Joan Kilby

Family Matters
Joan Kilby

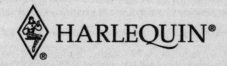

HARLEQUIN®

TORONTO • NEW YORK • LONDON
AMSTERDAM • PARIS • SYDNEY • HAMBURG
STOCKHOLM • ATHENS • TOKYO • MILAN • MADRID
PRAGUE • WARSAW • BUDAPEST • AUCKLAND

ISBN 0-373-71224-3

FAMILY MATTERS

This edition published by arrangement with Harlequin Books S.A.

® and TM are trademarks of the publisher. Trademarks indicated with ® are registered in the United States Patent and Trademark Office, the Canadian Trade Marks Office and in other countries.

www.eHarlequin.com

Printed in U.S.A.

I would like to thank physiotherapist Clifford Leckning and Dr. David Brumley for their invaluable advice and information regarding the nature of spinal injuries and their treatment and recovery. Any errors are mine.

My thanks and admiration go to a certain paraplegic young man—who prefers to remain nameless—for his humor, courage and insight.

My thanks, also, to Sheena Gibbs for introducing me to her beautiful alpacas and telling me all about these fascinating creatures.

Books by Joan Kilby

HARLEQUIN SUPERROMANCE

777—A FATHER'S PLACE
832—TEMPORARY WIFE
873—SPENCER'S CHILD
941—THE CATTLEMAN'S BRIDE
965—THE SECOND PROMISE
1030—CHILD OF HIS HEART
1076—CHILD OF HER DREAMS
1114—CHILD OF THEIR VOWS
1212—HOMECOMING WIFE*

*The Wilde Men

CHAPTER ONE

He soared off the jump on his snowboard, looping through the mountain air, the sky a brilliant blue against the diamond-white glacier. Legs braced, he landed with a satisfying crunch on the sparkling ice and, with a rush of adrenaline, whooshed at breakneck speed down Whistler Mountain....

"Another drink, buddy?" the barmaid asked.

Marc opened his eyes to find an empty glass clutched in his fingers and his dead legs draped uselessly over his wheelchair.

The Pemberton Hotel pub in midafternoon swam back into his consciousness—glasses clinking, pool balls clunking and football on the big-screen TV in the corner. Home after a month in a rehabilitation hospital in Israel, Marc spent most of his time either lying in bed staring at the ceiling or here at the pub. This vast room with its clientele of truckers, loggers and laid-off railway workers was preferable to the fancier drinking establishments in Whistler, frequented by skiers and mountain climbers who reminded him of everything he'd lost.

He swirled the ice cubes melting in a pool of diluted bourbon at the bottom of his glass. Fearless Marc Wilde they used to call him. Hah!

"I'll have 'nother Jack on the rocks. Make it a double." He could hear himself slurring his words but who gave a damn? Not him. He didn't care about anything anymore except escaping the tedium of life in a wheelchair. His days of snowboarding and rock climbing were over and his career as a foreign-war correspondent at an end. What was left to live for?

"How about a coffee instead?" the barmaid suggested. "I put a fresh pot on."

Marc peered up at her through bleary eyes. Her thick curling mass of strawberry-blond hair, tied loosely back, framed an oval face with the type of pale pink skin that blushed easily. She looked fresh and pretty, making him even more aware of his unwashed hair and dirty fingernails. At one time he'd taken pride in good grooming but what was the point when people he passed in the street averted their eyes and even his old friends avoided his company?

The barmaid's voice might be soft but that steady gaze looked anything but timid. Just to test her, he repeated his order. "Jack on the rocks. Double."

He lifted his hand to place his empty glass on her tray and missed. The glass fell to the floor with a quiet thud and the remaining liquid soaked into the carpet.

"No more booze for you," she said firmly.

They bent simultaneously to retrieve his glass. The scent of roses wafted toward him, faint and delicate amid the stale odor of cigarette smoke and beer. His hand fumbled, hers grasped the tumbler securely. Coming up, they bumped heads.

"Sorry." Rubbing his temple with one hand he stretched shaky fingers toward her smooth forehead.

Before he could touch her, she pulled away, her eyes filled with disgust. "I'll get you that coffee."

Swiveling on her low heels she was gone, leaving him with a back view of well-toned legs in a short black skirt. Her fitted white blouse with three-quarter sleeves emphasized a slender waist. Once upon a time he'd had his pick of diplomats' daughters and foreign beauties. Now not even a small-town barmaid wanted to know him.

Weeks of frustration exploded inside his booze-addled brain. *If he wanted to walk badly enough, he ought to be able to do it.* He planted his hands on the arms of his chair and pushed with all of his strength. The effort propelled him forward only to send him sprawling facedown on the carpet, his cheek in the wet patch where his drink had spilled. He closed his eyes as a wave of self-loathing engulfed him in blackness.

Dimly he heard the clatter of a coffee cup as the barmaid set a tray on the table. Small hands reddened by hot water crept under his armpits and tugged. She was surprisingly strong but not strong enough to lift his dead weight.

Marc struggled to push himself up, cursing his use-less legs. The barmaid gave up trying to lift him and held the wheelchair steady while he dragged his sorry carcass back into a sitting position with the help of a burly logger from the neighboring table. Behind the bar, the sandy-haired bartender polished glasses and kept a wary eye on him.

Too ashamed to look at the barmaid, Marc reached for his coffee with a mumbled thanks, hoping she'd just go away.

No such luck. Sitting down at his table, she said, "Aren't you Marc Wilde?"

"Used to be."

"I recognize you from TV," she went on. "You were reporting from a war zone in the Middle East. Bullets were flying past your ears, buildings blowing up behind you. I thought you were so brave."

Marc squinted in her direction. Her delicate fea-tures, so sweet and lively, made him feel one hundred years old. He recognized her expression, having expe-rienced it a thousand times in the past month. Pity.

"Your point?" he demanded. He hated pity even more than he hated the wheelchair.

She tilted her head forward and a mass of glowing hair spilled over her shoulder. "You've got guts. You're not the type to waste your life in a bar."

"You don't know the first thing about me." Marc sucked back the coffee, burning his tongue and not caring. Pain felt good. At least some part of his body was alive.

"What happened out there?" she asked.

"Bomb explosion threw me against a brick wall," he said mechanically, weary of repeating the same information to everyone he met. "I fractured two vertebrae and my spinal cord was compressed from the inflammation."

Once upon a time he'd believed in the adage "live hard, die young." No one had told him he'd one day find himself in the devil's waiting room, trapped in an existence that was neither life nor death.

"I'm so sorry. What's the prognosis?"

The compassion in her voice was seductive but he *did* have guts and he was strong enough to resist. He hadn't forgotten the disgust she'd displayed moments ago. *That* was real, not the compassion, and at least he knew how to deal with it.

"Another month 'n I'll be walking," he blustered. "Hell, I'll be running. Straight onto the next plane outta here."

"That's wonderful," she said, nodding. "You'll be one of the lucky ones."

"Right," he snorted. "Lucky is my middle name."

The doctors hadn't guaranteed he'd get his life as he knew it back. They weren't guaranteeing him anything. If cortisone, physiotherapy and the most maddening treatment of all—time—proved successful, he would eventually be back on his feet. Big *if*. As much as he tried not to think about it, the possibility he might never walk again constantly occupied his tortured mind.

"If you were going to kill yourself how would you do it?" he mused, rubbing his unshaven jaw. Some perverse core of him wanted to shock her.

She eyed him, an uncertain smile pulling at her lips, then apparently decided he was joking. "You could always drink yourself to death."

"Nah, it'd take too long. Pills, slit wrists, a bullet to the temple… What do you reckon would be easiest? I'm serious." He was taunting himself as much as her. In many ways it would have been better if he'd died in that bomb blast.

"Don't talk like that." She rose abruptly and wiped the table with jerky movements. "You said the doctors gave you a good prognosis."

He'd said nothing of the kind but he couldn't be bothered arguing.

"A man with your talent and experience has so much to contribute to the world," she went on.

"Another lecture," he groaned. "I get enough of those from my physiotherapist."

"Life is too precious to squander," she persisted. "Think of your friends and family…" She paused, the empty tray balanced on her cocked hip. "There's a Wilde Construction company in town that makes log homes. Any relation?"

"Jim Wilde is my uncle." Jim and Leone had raised him and the thought of them suffering over his suicide was enough to make him think twice. His cousins, Nate and Aidan, whom he regarded as brothers, would *kill* him if he tried to pull such a stunt. He spared a chuckle for his own dark humor. Who knows, even his father might be upset, although Marc wouldn't know since he hadn't seen his dad on more than a handful of occasions in the past fifteen years.

"Don't you have a counselor or psychiatrist on your rehab team you can talk to, help you come to terms with your changed situation?" the barmaid asked.

"Nurses, shrinks, doctors, they all try hard but they don't understand." His gaze slid down her smooth legs and the tendency to flirt that used to be second nature to him surfaced, "You're taking my plight awfully seriously. How about *you* help me?"

With a little laugh she backed away. "I'm not qualified to do more than get you another coffee."

"Don't go. What's your name?"

She hesitated. "Fiona."

"Fiona." Her name slipped off his tongue like a breath of spring air. "Have dinner with me, Fiona."

"No. Thank you. I have other plans." She started walking toward the bar.

Marc wheeled after her. "Tomorrow?"

"I can't."

"Why not?"

"I just can't."

"*Won't,* you mean," he said bitterly. "Because I'm in a wheelchair." In his heart he couldn't blame her. What woman wanted to go out with a cripple?

"It's not because your legs don't work." She closed the hinged length of bar, placing a physical barrier between herself and him. "Your real handicap is your attitude."

Her challenging gaze held his until Fearless Marc Wilde had to look away.

FIONA SHUT THE BACK DOOR of the pub behind her at the end of her shift and breathed in a lungful of crisp September air. Free at last. For a brief interval between work and home she could pretend she had no responsibilities.

Dodging puddles in the gravel parking lot, she wove her way toward her one-and-only extravagance, a near-new Honda Prelude. Her "real" job as a substitute primary teacher took her anywhere from Squamish to Lillooet, both drives of over an hour, often through torrential rain or deep snow. Safe and reliable transport was a necessity not a luxury.

Unfortunately being a substitute teacher didn't cover all the bills for her and her younger brother, Jason; hence the job at the pub. She'd enrolled in a correspondence course in early-childhood education, hopeful that the extra qualifications would help her get a full-time position; so far that hadn't happened.

Two blocks took her out of town and onto a straight country road through flat pastureland nestled between fir-clad mountains rising steeply on three sides. The few deciduous trees dotting the lower slopes had taken on a yellow tinge, heralding the change of season.

Fiona turned in to the driveway of the modest white-and-brown timber home on half an acre she shared with Jason. In the field beside the house her three alpacas were crowded atop the mound of dirt she'd christened Machu Picchu. Their long necks swiveled toward the sound of her car.

Her brother's wheelchair ramp zigzagging up to the front door reminded her of her encounter with Marc Wilde. Jason, confined to a wheelchair since he was eleven, had had seven years to get used to not being able to move freely and independently. Marc, she'd read in a magazine article, had been into extreme sports; being immobilized would be a lot harder for him.

He was lucky he had family to care for him because as surly as he was, who else would take him on? Before her shift ended, Bill, the bartender, had made a phone call and two men bearing a family resemblance to Marc had arrived to take him home.

Fiona walked through the barn and scooped up a handful of pellets from the barrel before going out to see the alpacas. Ebony, Snowdrop and Papa John walked daintily down the mound single file to greet her at the fence.

"How are my babies today?" she crooned to Ebony while Papa John sniffed at her hair and Snowdrop nudged her for treats. Holding her hand flat she fed them each a handful, smiling as their muzzles tickled her palm.

Some of the pellets fell into the grass and as Snowdrop dipped her head to nibble them, Fiona recalled how Marc had fallen out of his wheelchair. She cringed with embarrassment for him. Had he been joking about killing himself, or not? It didn't make sense if he was assured of recovery, but he wouldn't be the first paraplegic to suffer denial, especially shortly after injury. Maybe she should have spent more time with him.

No, she was not going to feel sorry for him.

"I don't need another lost soul to care for, do I?" she asked Papa John. The cream-and-brown alpaca hummed softly and bobbed his head.

"Fiona!" Jason called from the open back door. From the low deck, another ramp slanted down to a concrete path that branched off to the driveway and the barn. "Dinner's almost ready."

"Coming." She made sure the alpacas had water, tossed them each a flake of hay, then turned toward the house as the setting sun streaked the western sky with pink and orange above the mountains. As usual, a few minutes with the animals had turned into half an hour without her being aware of the passage of time.

The kitchen was full of light and warmth and the

spicy aroma of beef burritos. Travel posters from Greece covered the walls with images of blue sky and whitewashed villas cascading with hot-red geraniums. Bilbo and Baggins, stray dogs of indeterminate parentage she'd rescued from the pound, came to greet her, tails wagging.

Jason was positioned before a section of benchtop specially constructed at a lower height, slicing lettuce and tomatoes. A long lock of fine straight hair the same hue as hers fell over his hazel eyes.

Fiona hugged him in greeting. "How was your day?"

"Pretty good." Jason smiled up at her. "I linked the electronic circuitry of the sound system in my bedroom to a switch operated by the front door. When the door opens, music comes on. It's my own invention."

"Great. What do you call it?"

He looked at her pityingly. "A burglar alarm, of course. Oh, and I taped the noon movie for you. Gregory Peck and Audrey Hepburn."

"Thanks, Jase." She ruffled his hair. "You're due for a cut. I'll make you an appointment in the morning."

Jason pushed the hair off his face. "I'm not totally helpless. I can make my own appointment."

"Of course you can," Fiona agreed. Except that it wouldn't have occurred to him and they both knew it. "Just check with me about a time when I can drive you there."

At just-turned eighteen, her brother was the same

age she'd been when she'd become his carer. He was more than a boy but not yet a man. She, on the other hand, had had no choice but to grow up quickly, going from sister to surrogate mother overnight when their family car had collided with a logging truck, killing their parents outright and paralyzing Jason. Only she had come out of the accident unscathed. On the outside, at least.

Fiona shrugged out of her navy polar-fleece jacket and crossed the room to hang it on the hook beside the back door.

Jason spun his chair to face her. "Dave called today from Vancouver."

Jason's best friend from high school. "How does he like the university scene?"

"He loves living on campus and his profs are great." Jason paused. "He says the wheelchair facilities at UBC are excellent."

Fiona, leafing through the mail, froze, her back to him. She and Jason had been having an ongoing "discussion" all summer over when he would start university and how. He wanted to study electrical engineering, but she didn't think he was ready to make the adjustment from living at home to being on his own in a big city. Despite being a whiz at electronics he was young for his age and shy. She hated to think of him struggling with the pressures of university as well as those of a disabled student. And then there were the financial considerations.

"You'll go someday, Jase," she assured him. "Have you read those books I got you?" She'd bought sec-ondhand text books for first-year math, chemistry and physics, as well as a third-year lab book titled *Methods in Electronics,* hoping they would help slake his thirst for knowledge.

"Yeah, they're good," he mumbled. "But it's not the same as working toward a degree."

"You could do courses by correspondence like I am, and work for a year. University costs money, you know."

Never having been responsible for paying the bills, Jason was blithely ignorant of the cost of living, aside from the often expensive electronics bits and pieces she bought him. Maybe she shielded him too much but he was still so young and he'd been through a lot, los-ing his parents and the use of his legs at the same time.

"What about applying for a job at the Electronics Shop here in Pemberton?" she suggested. "You know Jeff, the owner, and I could drive you to work."

"It's a dead-end position and Pemberton is small potatoes compared to Vancouver." Jason scooped the chopped lettuce into a bowl and sprinkled on the other salad ingredients. "I don't want to get old before I start living."

Like *her,* in other words, although she knew he hadn't consciously meant it that way.

The pot of spiced beef bubbled on the stove, creat-ing condensation which fogged the darkened windows and gave a homey atmosphere to the small cluttered kitchen. If only their parents hadn't died. If only Jason hadn't been paralyzed. If only she hadn't had to give up her dreams of career and travel— Guilt abruptly put an end to these unproductive thoughts. She was alive and whole and she could never allow herself to forget that.

"I saw a funny thing on the way home from work," Fiona said to change the subject. "You know that garden gnome at the corner house? Someone propped it behind the steering wheel of that old car in the driveway. It looks as though it's trying to escape."

Jason laughed and the tension was broken. As their chuckles faded, Fiona became aware of another noise— a whining from behind the closed door of the laundry room.

"What is that?" Fiona said, rising to her feet.

"I forgot to tell you." Jason's face became animated as he wheeled across to the laundry room. "Mrs. McTavish from across the road was walking by the river and she found a burlap sack. It was moving so she investigated. Inside she found—" Jason opened the door "—a puppy."

A skinny white pup with brown markings cowered in the doorway, his ears flattened against his head and his fearful gaze darting from Jason to Fiona. Fiona dropped to the linoleum and held out a hand. The dog approached slowly, shivering and trembling all the way from his pointed muzzle to his docked tail.

"Poor thing," Fiona murmured as the dog cautiously sniffed her fingers before retreating a few paces. "He's so scared. I wonder if he was abused."

"He's half-starved, too," Jason added. "You can see every one of his ribs."

Fiona stayed in a crouch, waiting patiently while the dog gathered his courage to creep forward again. "He looks like a Jack Russell cross. How could anyone get rid of such a cute dog, especially in such a cruel way?"

"Can we keep him?" Jason asked eagerly, looking exactly like the kid he claimed he wasn't. "He could be my dog. I'd take good care of him."

"Oh, Jason, you know we can't. We've already got more animals than we can afford to feed." The dog came close and she picked him up, tucking him securely in the crook of her elbow. "We'll just have to try to find him a good home. I don't suppose Mrs. McTavish would take him?"

Jason shook his head. "She said she's a cat person."

Fiona scratched the puppy behind the ears. A small pink tongue emerged and began lapping at the base of her thumb. "Surely we know *someone* who would enjoy having this little rascal—" She broke off as a thought struck her, which she immediately dismissed. "Nah, forget it."

"Who?"

"Do you remember that war correspondent who reported the latest conflict in the Middle East—Marc Wilde?"

"He grew up in Whistler. Mrs. McTavish told me last week she'd heard he'd been injured and flown home. I mentioned it at the time but you were working on an essay and weren't listening. What about him?"

"He came into the pub today. He had a spinal-cord injury that left him in a wheelchair."

Jason let out a low whistle and sat back. "I didn't know that. Do you think he'd like a puppy?"

"He'd snarl at the mere suggestion, but I think it would be good for him." Whether he would be good for the dog was another question but Fiona had a hunch Marc wasn't quite as cynical as he made out.

Fiona put the dog in Jason's lap then thumbed through the local phone book for the number of the Wilde residence. Chances were better than even Marc would be staying with his aunt and uncle. If he wasn't, they would know where he was.

She dialed and as the phone began to ring she realized she had another motive for calling—to make sure Marc hadn't done anything to harm himself.

The phone picked up. A woman answered and Fiona said, "Hello—Mrs. Wilde? I'm Fiona Gordon. May I talk to Marc if he's available?"

A moment later, Marc's distinctive, deep voice made raspy by alcohol spoke into her ear. A sudden attack of nerves set her to pacing the floor. "This is

Fiona. From the pub. Can I come and see you tonight?"

"I thought you were busy."

Shoot! The essay that was due tomorrow. "I—I am. I meant just for a few minutes."

"I don't know. I've got a hell of a headache—"

"The thing is, I need to ask you a favor."

"What is it?"

He would undoubtedly say no to giving a home to a stray dog over the phone but if he saw the puppy, surely his heart would melt just as hers had. "I have to ask you in person."

There was a long silence. At last, he said, "All right. When?"

She needed time for a quick bite to eat and to bathe the dog. "I'll be there in forty-five minutes."

CHAPTER TWO

"FIONA'S COMING OVER," Marc announced as he hung up the phone.

A favor, she'd said. What could he possibly do for her?

Leone smoothed back a curving lock of chin-length auburn hair and glanced up from her book. "Is she a friend of yours? You've never mentioned her."

Marc wheeled into the space created for his wheelchair between Leone's new ivory-colored sectional sofa and Jim's worn Naugahyde recliner, angled for a good view of the TV. The yellow cedar of the log home made a dramatic backdrop to the stone fireplace and Jim's collection of Haida masks.

"She's a barmaid at the Pemberton Hotel." He was curious to know if she would seem as captivating when he was sober as she had when he was drunk.

Jim and Leone exchanged glances, a fact not lost on Marc. "Was there any trouble?" Jim asked.

"No." Embarrassed at the memory of his drunken behavior he spun away, moving his hands too roughly against the wheels. He winced as the hard rubber chafed the broken blisters on his fingers and palms. He'd racked up a lot of miles in the weeks since he'd been getting around in the chair and had yet to develop protective calluses.

Leone saw his grimace and hurried across the room to turn over his hand. "Let me put some dressings on those blisters. You don't want to get them infected. Goodness knows what muck you go rolling through in those pubs."

"I'm all right," Marc said irritably and pulled his hand away. "I'll put some Band-Aids on later."

"Now, Marc, I'm a qualified nurse—"

"Don't fuss over him." Jim rattled his newspaper open. His dark hair sprinkled with silver could just be seen over the sports section.

Leone withdrew, smoothing down her cardigan and slacks in lieu of her ruffled feelings. "I was only trying to help."

"I'm fine. Thanks anyway," Marc told her in a milder tone. Leone and Jim had taken him in at the age of five after his mother died and his father resumed his pursuit of glory on the pro-skiing circuit. Marc was grateful and loved them dearly; it just rankled that after ten years on his own he was living at home, dependent on them.

He picked up the local newspaper and skimmed through the articles. More controversy over parking in Whistler Village, municipal elections coming up, the rising cost of real estate…. Ho hum.

The doorbell rang. Before he could react, Leone went to answer it.

Marc ran a hand through his hair, still slightly damp from the shower. After he'd sobered up, he'd cleaned up, but he knew he looked far from his best. Giving himself a push he rolled across the polished hardwood to the tiled floor of the entrance hall.

"Come in," his aunt invited Fiona with her customary warmth. "I'm Leone. We spoke on the phone."

"Pleased to meet you," Fiona replied, stepping inside. "I apologize for dropping in on you on such short notice."

"Marc's friends are always welcome," Leone assured her. "Especially now that he's limited in his mobility, it's nice for him to have people over."

Gritting his teeth over his aunt's effusiveness, Marc nodded to Fiona. She had on the same skirt and blouse she'd worn to work, her hair hadn't been combed for some time and her lipstick had long worn off. But there was a sparkle in her eyes, which suggested that whatever had changed her priorities for tonight held some degree of excitement. Over her shoulder, tucked tightly under her arm, she carried a large woven straw bag.

Jim put down his newspaper and rose, his large callused hand extended in greeting. In his early fifties, he kept trim and fit through physical labor. "I'm Jim, Marc's uncle. Can I get you a drink?"

"Thank you, no." She glanced around the living room then said to Marc, "Maybe we should go into the kitchen to talk."

"They want to be alone," Leone murmured to Jim, nudging him back to his recliner.

Cringing inwardly Marc led Fiona down the hall to the kitchen/family room. It was his favorite part of the house, informal and comfortable, with colorful rugs scattered over polished floorboards and dried grasses arranged in large earthenware pots.

"Sorry about my aunt," he said when they were out of earshot of the living room. "She means well but she tends to fuss."

"Your aunt is lovely. Please don't apologize for her." Fiona's straw bag moved suddenly and a bulge appeared in the side. She gripped the bag more tightly.

Marc gestured to one of several cushioned wicker chairs grouped around a glass coffee table. "Sit down."

"I really can't stay long," Fiona replied, not complying. Her bag had gone still.

Marc rubbed the back of his neck, sore from looking up at people all day. "Please. Sit. Down."

His tension conveyed itself in his voice. Abruptly she sat. "Sorry. I should know better."

"You probably think I should apologize for myself," he went on with the lazy cynicism he fell into so easily these days. "I could tell you I'm not really such a jerk as I acted this afternoon but frankly, I'm not sure that bastard isn't the new me."

"I'm quite sure he *isn't*." Her bag started moving again. A tiny whimper came from within and Marc heard the sound of scrabbling claws against the straw. "I think underneath you're a caring man who hasn't yet come to terms with his disability."

Marc winced at the word disability and his hands tightened their painful grip on the wheels of his chair. "You're being a little naive, don't you think?"

"I believe people are essentially good at heart," she insisted over the sounds coming from her bag. "Sometimes though, they're so unhappy the goodness doesn't have a chance to shine through."

"Forget the sermon, Pollyanna. Why don't you show me what's in your bag?"

He thought for a moment she might refuse but the matter was taken out of her hands, literally, when the top of the bag pushed open from within and a small wiry dog leaped out and into Marc's lap.

"What the—!" Marc burst out.

"I'm sorry. He has no manners." Fiona reached for the dog who squirmed out of her hands and tried to burrow under the hem of Marc's sweater. He succeeded in hiding only his head, leaving his rump sticking out. She added hopefully, "Isn't he adorable?"

"I've never seen a more miserable scrap of fur in my life." And yet, when he lifted his sweater, the pooch's woebegone expression made him smile, the first he'd cracked all day. He put a hand out and the puppy cowered away from him, his thin body trembling.

"He was found in a burlap sack by the river. I think he's been abused," Fiona told him. "He's sweet natured, though. With a little TLC he'll bounce right back."

Marc noticed a dark patch begin to spread through the fabric of his blue jeans and his glimmer of good humor vanished. "He peed on me!"

"Oh, I'm so sorry!" Fiona exclaimed. "He's excited after being cooped up too long." She snatched the puppy away, shoved him back in her bag then got the wet cloth sitting by the sink. "I'm *really* sorry," she apologized again and started to scrub at the stain on Marc's upper thigh.

"Stop!" He pushed her hands away. "Why did you bring the damn dog here, anyway?"

"I thought you might like to have him as a pet. He was abandoned and I can't keep him. He doesn't look like much I know but once he's gained a bit of weight—"

The sound of the bag falling over cut her off. The puppy escaped, skittering across the floor to hide behind a large potted plant. Fiona picked him up and held him close to her chest to try to calm him.

"You thought I might like a pet," Marc repeated incredulously. "Do I *look* like I run a lost dogs' home?"

"Pets are good therapy for the elderly and disabled. It's a well-known fact that dogs give patients a sense of well-being." She cradled the puppy protectively against her chest. "Please consider taking him. If your aunt and uncle don't mind, that is. I must confess I didn't stop to consider them. It's their house, after all."

She'd lumped him in with the elderly and disabled. That alone was enough to make him refuse. That he hadn't an ounce of physical or emotional energy to give another living creature, not even a half-dead hound, sealed the dog's fate as far as Marc was concerned.

"They hate dogs," he lied. "Especially rambunctious puppies." He hoped she wouldn't notice Rufus's food bowl near the back sliding doors. Leone and Jim's Irish setter slept outside but evidence of his existence was around. "Besides, once I'm walking again, I'll be back at work. I travel constantly. I can't take care of a dog. So if that's all you came for—" Spinning the chair around, he started back to the front of the house "—I'll see you out."

Fiona's heavy sigh rent the silence. "Poor little guy," she crooned to the puppy. "I'll have to take you to the pound."

Marc glanced back at her. "The pound?"

She lifted her shoulders and let them fall in an exaggerated fashion. "Someone will adopt him. I hope."

Marc's eyes narrowed. He resumed his progress down the hall. "You're just trying to guilt me into taking him."

"Will it work?" Fiona followed with the puppy cradled in her arms.

"No. Too obvious."

"It was worth a try. If you change your mind…"

"I won't."

They passed the living room. Jim glanced up from his newspaper and Leone put down her book to call out, "Leaving so soon?"

"I'm afraid so," Fiona paused to reply. "It was nice to meet you."

"Come again, anytime," Leone said from her seat on the leather sofa. "What a sweet puppy. Look, Jim, isn't he gorgeous? We just love dogs," she confided to Fiona.

Groaning, Marc dropped his head into his hand.

"Who wouldn't love a pup?" Fiona said without a trace of reproach in her soft voice.

Marc escorted her to the door. "So now you know I'm a liar as well as a lush," he said. "Not a fit parent for an impressionable dog. But then, *you* lied, too. You said you wanted me to do you a favor when all the time you were trying to do me one."

"Is that so bad?" she demanded. "Life is a lot easier if people help each other."

Marc had nothing to say to that. Ever since he'd learned to tie his own shoelaces he'd pushed away all attempts to help him. Why should that change just because he was in a wheelchair?

Fiona dropped into a crouch in front of him and put

her hand on his forearm. In a low voice not meant for Jim and Leone's ears she said, "Look me in the eye and tell me you didn't really mean that about killing yourself."

"I didn't really mean that about killing myself," he parroted back, deadpan.

With an exasperated sound, she rose, wincing slightly. Her feet probably hurt after being on them all day, Marc thought. He'd give anything to feel pain in his feet.

From the doorway he watched her walk back to her car and waited until she'd driven off before going back inside. The adrenaline buzz induced by her presence drained away and he wheeled slowly back to his room, brushing off his aunt's suggestion to join them.

His room, virtually unchanged since he'd left home after high school, was plastered with posters of snowboarders soaring above snowy peaks and rock climbers moving like spiders up sheer rock faces and impossible-looking overhangs. The shelves of his bookcase were lined with sporting trophies instead of books and his closet teemed with specialized equipment and clothing he might never use again.

Going to his dresser he opened the middle drawer. Away at the back, beneath his socks and underwear he found the vials of pills he'd been saving since rehab. Pain pills, sleeping pills and God knows what else. They were his safety hatch for that hypothetical day when the doctors told him there was no hope. Without action, movement, adventure, his life would be unbearable.

He opened one vial and let the tablets flow through his fingers. How many would be enough? Leone would know but he could hardly ask her.

Marc put the pills away and shut the drawer. He was feeling low but not that low. *Yet.*

Wheeling over to the window he watched the streetlights wink on in the growing dusk. His unlit room became darker and darker compared to the outside illumination, reflecting his thoughts. For weeks now he'd ricocheted between anger, self-pity and despair.

And worst of all, sheer excruciating boredom.

Imagine Fiona bringing him a puppy. It was a silly, impulsive thing to do. Damn cute little dog, though. He almost wished he'd had the guts to say yes.

Free: Jack Russell–cross puppy to a good home.
Call Fiona 555-6283.

Fiona got permission from Jason's hairdresser to put a notice in the salon's front window when she dropped Jason off for a haircut. She had a whole sheaf of them which she'd photocopied at the drugstore that morning and was now distributing around town. Her heart wasn't in it—she was attached to the little dog already—but she didn't see any other option.

"I'll meet you back at the drugstore in half an hour," she called to Jason who was draped in a black gown that hung down the sides of his wheelchair.

"Make it an hour," he said, twisting to speak to her. "I want to go to the Electronics Shop for some components."

Fiona paused at the door. "I noticed Jeff put an ad in the local paper for help wanted. Why don't you ask him for an application form?"

Shaking his head, Jason turned back to the mirror. "See you later."

Fiona dropped off notices at a half-dozen more stores then picked up a couple of take-out coffees from the café and continued to her friend Liz's yarn shop. As well as handspun yarn and knitting accessories Liz sold sweaters, shawls and scarves she designed and knit herself. She'd made the brown-and-cream alpaca pullover Fiona wore over jeans.

Liz's cropped dark curls were bent over her spinning wheel as her nimble fingers spun a fluffy mass of wool into a lengthening thread. At the sound of the door opening her foot stopped pumping and the wheel slowed.

"Coffee!" she exclaimed with a welcoming smile. "You read my mind. I'm glad you stopped by. I've been going crazy this morning trying to come up with a theme for Jilly's birthday party. She wants to invite her whole kindergarten class. How am I going to entertain twenty six-year-olds?"

Fiona handed her a foam cup and sank onto an armless wooden rocker that Liz called her knitting chair. "That's a tough one. I guess fairies won't work two years in a row?"

Liz shook her head. "She's over that and anyway, there'll be boys at the party."

"If I come up with any brainwaves I'll let you know. Meanwhile, I've been pounding the pavement all morning putting up notices." She handed one to Liz. "Can I tape this inside your front window?"

"Of course." Liz sipped her coffee and scanned the paper. "You shouldn't have any trouble finding a home for a Jack Russell—they're so smart and cute."

"This animal's not a shining example of his breed, unfortunately. In fact, he looks like a drowned rat. I tried to give him away last night but he peed on the guy's lap and that was that."

"Bad luck." Liz paused to pull on the wool in the basket so it fed evenly into the spindle. As she set the foot rocker in motion again, she said, "By the way, I sold the last of Snowdrop's cria wool to a client in Whistler—Angela Wilde."

"Angela *Wilde?*" Fiona repeated. "Is she any relation to Marc Wilde?"

"She's married to his cousin, Nate. Why?"

"Marc is the guy I tried to give the dog to. He— Marc, that is—came into the pub yesterday and got stinking drunk."

"I heard he's in a wheelchair now. He was injured during a bomb explosion, I think Angela said."

"Apparently he's going to recover but in the meantime he's not taking his loss of mobility well." Fiona fingered a soft skein of dark blue wool, remembering the thinly veiled rage and despair in Marc's eyes when he spoke of his injury.

Liz sipped her coffee. "From what Angela told me, those Wilde men live up to their name. Apparently Marc was the wildest of them all when it came to courting danger."

So why had he asked *her* out? Fiona wondered. She was the tamest person she knew, mired in responsibilities she'd willingly taken on but with no life to call her own.

"He invited me to dinner," she told Liz.

Liz's eyebrows rose. "And you said...?"

"No, of course." Fiona put down the skein of wool and rose to pace the narrow aisle between the shelves of yarn. "He was drunk. He probably didn't even know what he was saying. Anyway he's got a serious attitude problem. I don't want that kind of negativity in my life. Plus, he's not sticking around once he's recovered."

"One excuse would have been enough." Liz smiled to herself as the thread slipped between her fingers. "Not because he's in a wheelchair?"

It took Fiona a moment to answer. "No..." she said finally. "That would be pretty insensitive of me."

"He's got a fabulous voice," Liz said. "Is he as attractive as he looks on TV?"

"In a cynical, world-weary sort of way." With his dark gold hair and eyes the color of new denim he could have been very attractive if he hadn't let himself get so scruffy. Fiona noticed Liz watching her closely and turned away to gaze out the front window. "Speak of the devil."

On the raised wooden sidewalk Marc had stopped to read her notice. Seeing her, he motioned for her to come out. Fiona cast an uncertain glance at Liz.

"Go on," Liz urged. "What are you waiting for?"

"I'll see you later." Fiona gathered up her notices and walked back outside under the shelter of the wooden awning that ran the length of the block. The morning clouds were breaking up and the afternoon promised more of the fine Indian-summer weather they'd been having lately.

"Hi," she said to Marc. "I didn't expect to see you again so soon."

"What's this?" he asked, pointing to her notice. His eyes looked even bluer in daylight and his hair glinted in the sun like gold threads. He was wearing a dark green track suit that showed off his broad shoulders. Marc was *more* attractive than he appeared on TV, somehow larger than life.

"I can't keep the dog so I've got to do something," she explained. "Giving him away is better than sending him to the pound."

Marc shook his head, frowning. "You have no idea what kind of people he'll end up with. They may say they'll give him a good home but how do you know he won't be mistreated again?"

"Whoever answers this ad will be someone who wants a pet," she said mildly. "But it's nice that you care."

That brought him up short. His mouth clamped shut and he glanced away. "I don't."

Fiona wagged a playful finger at him. "I don't believe you."

One corner of his mouth twisted down as his hardened gaze swept back to her. "I don't care what happens to the damn dog."

A woman and a small boy about four years old approached, interrupting their discussion. Fiona stepped to the side, dodging a hanging flower basket, to let them pass and Marc maneuvered his wheelchair out of the way behind one of the chunky posts that supported the awning.

The little boy's unblinking gaze fixed on Marc. "Why's that man in a wheelchair, Mommy?" he said in a loud voice.

"Shh, honey." The mother flushed as she glanced at Marc and quickly away. "It's not nice to stare."

"But, Mommy, what's wrong with him?" The boy tugged on his mother's hand to slow her pace, craning his neck to look back at Marc.

Fiona saw Marc's hands tighten on his wheels and felt herself tense up, too. The man was a time bomb waiting to explode. Definitely not ready to handle this.

"I had an accident," he snarled. "What's wrong with *you?*"

The boy burst into tears. His mother stared in shock for a split second before dragging her son away. "That wasn't very nice, mister."

"What a horrible thing to say to that poor kid!" Fiona exclaimed. Just when she was starting to think she'd judged Marc too harshly.

Marc shrugged. "Maybe he'll think twice next time before making comments about strangers."

"He's just a little boy." She shook her head in dismay. "I can't believe you could be so mean. And on such a beautiful day, too."

"Is it? I hadn't noticed."

Fiona remembered the notices in her hand and gratefully seized the excuse to leave. "I've got to take these around." She started to walk up the street.

Marc set his wheelchair in motion, following her. She glared at him and he said gruffly, "Can I help it if I'm going in the same direction?"

Fiona continued in silence, leaving as much space between her and Marc as possible on the wooden sidewalk.

"Are you working today?" Marc asked.

"No," she replied, wishing she was rude enough to ignore him. "I'm off to Vancouver after I finish putting up the notices."

"What for?" he wanted to know.

She threw him an exasperated look. Couldn't he see

she wasn't interested in talking to him? Maybe if she explained he would go away. "I take a class by correspondence and once in a while I go to the university for a tutorial or to use the library."

"What are you studying?"

"Early-childhood education."

"Ah," he said knowingly, "you want to brainwash the little brats before they lose their innocence."

"I'm a primary-school teacher upgrading my qualifications. I only work at the pub because I can't get a full-time teaching job." Speaking of the pub, he was heading in the opposite direction. She hesitated, not wanting him to think she was interested in him but curiosity got the better of her. "Where are *you* off to?"

"An hour of torture, misery and pain." When she raised her eyebrows, he added, "My physiotherapy appointment."

"Why come to Pemberton when Whistler has so many highly trained physios?"

"Val was recommended by my physiatrist in Vancouver. Plus she's conveniently located close to my favorite drinking establishment."

"Why am I not surprised that would figure in your motivation?" she said. Fiona paused to pin one of her advertisements to a public notice board outside the grocery store. Marc waited while she accomplished her task.

"Maybe you could ask your therapist to put a notice in her clinic window," she said, handing him one.

He scanned the contents then let the flyer drop onto his lap. "What happens if no one wants the mutt?"

"Someone will."

"And if they don't?"

The wooden sidewalk slanted down to the pavement as they crossed a side street. Fiona walked a little ahead. "I'll wait till the end of the week then if no one comes forward I'll have to take him to the pound—"

"Damn!"

At first she thought his expletive was a reaction to her plan to take the dog to the pound, but when he gave vent to more muttered curses she turned around. His back wheel had hit a crack in the pavement and swiveled, sending him shooting toward the road. He managed to stop before falling into the path of an on-coming pickup truck but at a cost to the raw, red skin on his hands.

Fiona hurried over. "Are you all right?"

Marc waved her away with a sharp gesture, swearing again under his breath in his efforts to get his wheelchair back on level ground. "Why me?" he muttered fiercely to himself. "Why the hell did this have to happen to me? I've got a life to live, dammit!"

She knew he wasn't referring to hitting a bit of uneven pavement. There was no satisfactory response to his demand, as he would learn eventually. Why anybody? Why not him? She'd been through the whole litany of questions-with-no-answers, the outbursts of rage, with Jason.

"Everything happens for a reason," she told him.

He uttered a scornful grunt. "Bull."

"The reason might not be obvious right away but if you search for meaning in life something good will come from even the worst events."

"Thanks a lot for your comforting words," he drawled derisively. "Probably I'm the butt of some huge cosmic joke and the gods are having a good laugh as we speak."

He must think her impossibly ingenuous and unsophisticated. He couldn't know she had her own demons to face and that her determined hopefulness was how she'd learned to cope with the events of her life. "Give yourself time. Things will get better—"

"Oh, please. Spare me your wide-eyed optimism. I need a drink." Laboriously he turned his chair around.

"Wait, Marc—"

"Go back to your swings and dolls, Pollyanna." He cut her off with the back of a sharply upraised hand as he headed in the opposite direction.

Pushed too far, Fiona ran after him and yanked his chair to a halt. His startled glare didn't stop her anger from pouring out. "Don't be a jerk! Instead of drinking yourself into oblivion you should be glad you're alive. There are a lot of people worse off than you. You know that better than anyone, the places you've been. When someone tries to help you could at least be gracious if you can't be grateful."

"How dare you?" he growled when she paused for breath. "You have no idea what I'm going through."

"Yes, I do. Not firsthand but—"

"Then you *don't* know. You, who can run and walk, dance and jog, don't have any idea what it's like to be conquering mountains one day and having someone wipe your ass the next."

"Oh, you…" she sputtered, fists clenched at her sides. "Why don't you stop feeling sorry for yourself and do something to help someone else?"

"Yeah, right. How can *I* help anyone in my condition?"

"Use your imagination. You've got plenty of time to think. Or is your brain disabled, too?"

At Marc's stunned expression Fiona's anger subsided. *Oh, dear, that was so mean.* "I'm sorry," she said, aghast at herself. "That was totally unlike me. You made me so mad I didn't know what I was saying."

"The truth according to Pollyanna, apparently," he said. His rage seemed to have vanished, replaced by sudden interest. "Anything else you want to say to me?"

She started to back away. The intense curiosity in his gaze was unnerving. "Er… Have a nice day?"

CHAPTER THREE

MILDLY SHOCKED but definitely intrigued, Marc watched Fiona walk away. That sweet nurturing woman had a hidden streak of spit and vinegar. She was completely wrong, of course, but at least she didn't hesitate to say what she thought.

Remembering his physio appointment, he turned around just in time to see Fiona go into another store with her damn notices. He *didn't* care about the dog but for some stupid reason he felt responsible for the animal's plight. And although he hated to admit it, Fiona's comments had stung. The sooner he became mobile enough to get out of town, the better.

The automatic doors to the clinic opened and he wheeled in to find his physiotherapist, Val, at the front desk reading through a patient's file. "Hey, Marc," she said, glancing up. "What's up with you today?"

With her butch haircut and muscular forearms, Val could have belonged to an eastern European shot-put team. Marc valued her because she was the only female he knew who didn't smother him with platitudes and sympathy.

"Nothing," he muttered, trying to rub away the furrows between his eyebrows. There was no way to explain how rotten he felt, and not just physically. He used to be a decent guy who got along with everyone. Now he seemed to snap a dozen times a day.

"Just your usual generic mad at the whole world, is that it? Never mind, it comes with the territory." Val put down the file and motioned Marc through the wide doorway into the workout room. "Come into my parlor. I'll give you something to complain about."

Val was also the only person he allowed to help him move around. With her assistance he transferred to a narrow, padded massage table and lay on his back, hands gripping the sides against the inevitable pain.

"Are you experiencing much cramping?" she asked, raising his straight leg and stretching out the hamstring.

"Occasionally at night I get muscle spasms right down my legs." He grunted as she bent his leg at the knee and pushed it into his chest. "How come the nerves work enough to make me feel pain but not to walk?"

"There are a lot of theories but no definitive answers," she told him. "When the spinal cord is injured, nerve messages get mixed up. Soft muscle tissue is bombarded by stray electrical impulses which can be experienced as pain. Or, you could be feeling referred pain from an injury or sickness somewhere else in your body. You need to do something about those hands, by the way. Leather gloves are essential if you're going to be active." She manipulated his ankle and then his knee to keep the joints mobile. "Any burning or tingling sensations in your legs? Pins and needles?"

Marc thought for a moment. "Yeah, once in a while. It's a pain. No pun intended."

Val let his leg down and picked up the other one. "That could be good. Pins and needles are often an indication of nerve function returning. Not always, though."

"When can I expect to recover nerve function?" Marc asked, ignoring her caution.

Val shrugged. "Spinal-cord injuries are individual and unpredictable. It could be weeks, or months, but Marc, you've got to be realistic—you may never get function back in your legs."

Marc didn't reply. He simply couldn't accept what she was saying. Only at night, when his defenses were low did he fully acknowledge the reality of his situation.

Val finished stretching and manipulating his other leg and came around the table to position his chair where he could get into it. "Time for the race."

"Talk about a misnomer," Marc grumbled as he shed his tracksuit jacket.

Attempting to move his legs while supporting himself inside the "race" or parallel bars was the most frustrating exercise of all, highlighting as it did his inability to control his body in ways he'd always taken for granted.

"Put some weight on those legs," Val barked as she walked slowly along beside him, monitoring his progress. "The nerves in your lower limbs need feedback about what's happening. Don't let your arms do all the work."

Marc clamped his jaw down hard to bite off a sarcastic retort. If he could get his legs to help out, didn't she think he would? No matter how hard he concentrated all his will on making his legs move he ended up dragging them along. He felt like a marionette who'd had the strings controlling his feet cut for the amusement of a cruel puppet master. If this *was* a cosmic practical joke, he didn't find it very funny.

Despite the pain and frustration he forced himself to think about his goal. Normal life. Work and travel. No one feeling sorry for him. Ever. By the time Val suggested he quit for the day, sweat was pouring off his forehead and trickling down his back, soaking his T-shirt. Marc insisted on doing another four lengths before he collapsed, arms sagging against the bars while he waited for her to bring his chair over.

He got back on the massage table, stomach down. Marc gazed through the face hole in the padded table at the stain on the gray indoor-outdoor carpet immediately below. Sweat? Blood? Tears? Maybe all three.

Val squirted peppermint-scented oil onto her hands and began kneading his calf muscles. At least he assumed that's what she was doing; he couldn't feel a thing.

"Do you know a woman here in town called Fiona?" he asked, thinking to do a bit of journalistic probing into her background.

"Fiona Gordon? Not personally. I moved here only a few months ago. Her friend Liz, who owns the yarn shop, has a daughter in the same kindergarten class as my boy, Andy. Why do you ask—because of her brother, Jason?"

"I didn't know she had a brother." Nor did he particularly care. "What's she like?"

"She's nice. Had a tough go of it when her parents died and she was left to care for Jason who was still in primary school. From what Liz tells me she's a sucker for animals and kids." Val moved to the other side of the table and her voice became teasing. "Why, are you interested in her?"

Marc maintained a neutral tone. "I hang out at the pub where she works as a barmaid. She tried to get me to adopt an abandoned puppy. I told her no, of course."

Val paused to apply more massage lotion. Marc heard it squirt from the bottle and imagined he could feel the cool liquid splash onto the back of his thigh.

"A puppy would be just the thing for you," Val said. "Why don't you go for it?"

"I haven't got time for a dog. Once you whip me into shape my producer wants me back on the beat."

"Marc," Val said, a warning in her voice.

"Val," Marc warned her right back. The last thing he wanted was another lecture.

"Okay, okay. Just don't go buying season tickets for the ski lift."

"Does she have a boyfriend?"

"Fiona? Not that I know of."

Val finished the massage, gave him a shot of cortisone next to his spinal cord and sent him back to the front desk to get Cindy to make him an appointment for hydrotherapy at the Meadow Park Sports Centre.

It was only later, after Jim had taken time out of his lunch break to pick Marc up and drive him back to the house that Marc remembered he hadn't asked Val to put Fiona's notice in the window. He pulled the folded sheet from his breast pocket and started to toss it into the recycling bin. He hesitated a moment and for no reason he could think of, tucked it back into his pocket.

Then, ignoring the golden autumn sunshine pouring onto the backyard patio, he wheeled into his room, drew the curtains and shut the door. His energy had drained away and he was left feeling exhausted and depressed. Immobility was easier to handle without the beckoning mountains in sight.

Perversely, he shut his eyes and relived in minute-by-minute detail the last rock climb he'd done on

Stawamus Chief with Nate and Aidan two months ago, before he'd left for the Middle East and his date with destiny. With his near-photographic memory he could visualize every detail. He'd just handjammed an exposed corner crack and was heading up a small chimney when Fiona's trite phrase popped into his mind.

Everything happens for a reason.

Logically, that would include hanging on to her notice about the dog. Had he done that because he was actually considering adopting the pet? Taking on the scrawny mutt seemed somehow like admitting he was as pitiful and needy as the dog.

Or had he kept the notice because he wanted Fiona's phone number? That, he dismissed immediately. There was no point in even thinking about Fiona; as long as he was in this wheelchair he had nothing to offer a woman.

So why did he have this maddening urge to prove he did? He couldn't make love. His future was uncertain. He was a miserable son of a bitch to be around. Even *he* didn't like himself these days.

He'd mulled this over for a full five minutes before a crow cawing loudly in the pine tree outside his window snapped him out of his melancholic brooding. Fiona was right; he did have too much time to think.

But what else did he have to do? At first he'd watched CNN compulsively until he couldn't stand it anymore because it reminded him too much of the life he'd lost. The radio was full of sappy love songs. He got bored surfing the Internet. Books weren't the answer; he'd never been one for reading when he could be out *doing* something.

Frustrated, he left his bedroom and wheeled through the house. Restless with an energy he couldn't expend, he rolled down the long hallway to the kitchen, turned around and rolled back again. He wished he could call someone but his cousins were both working; Nate at his bike shop and Aidan in the ski patrol on Whistler Mountain. As for friends, Marc had lost contact with most of his old buddies over the years and wasn't keen on making new ones in his present state.

He'd told himself he would stay away from the pub, that drinking every day wasn't good for him. But the empty silence of the house began to close in. Before another ten minutes passed he was summoning the taxi for the disabled.

Fifteen minutes later the taxi with the high cab at the back pulled up to the house and a young driver he hadn't had before got out.

"I'm Brent," the driver said with a wide smile as he went around to open the sliding passenger door and lower the motorized lift that always made Marc feel like cargo being loaded onto a truck. "Where are you off to on this glorious fall day?"

Oh, great, someone high on life. Marc could tell right now this was going to be a long trip even though the drive took only half an hour. "Pemberton Hotel."

Brent slid the door shut, got in and started to back out. "What's your name?"

"Marc." He stared out the window and pretended not to hear the driver's friendly chatter as they sped up the highway. How many trees in these forests? Millions? Billions?

"Here you are," Brent announced as he pulled up in front of the pub. He jumped out and lowered the ramp for Marc to roll down. "Enjoy your day."

"Oh, I plan to have a wonderful time." Marc handed him a couple of big bills, overtipping to compensate for his lack of grace.

Inside he went straight to the table in the far corner where he always sat. The big room seemed even emptier without Fiona but sitting at a table listening to the jukebox gave him the illusion he was doing something.

After a couple of drinks his conscience started to work on him. He couldn't stop thinking about that damn dog, imagining the undernourished mutt sitting on a cold concrete floor at the pound, cringing and snarling every time someone walked by. *That's no way to find an owner,* he wanted to shout at it. Wag your tail, look happy to see folks, muster up a little warmth and puppy charm.

He was on his fifth, or maybe it was his sixth, bourbon, his mind flipping back and forth between the dog and his last day in Damascus, when the two images merged. He heard a whimper and instead of an injured boy, he was carrying the abandoned pup through mortar blasts and crossfire. Up ahead was the brick building. If he hurried, he'd make it—

A hand gripped his shoulder. "Wha' the—?" he said, startled into flinging his head up and back.

A familiar chestnut-haired figure in a blue corduroy shirt and jeans stood beside him. Aidan. Marc slumped down in his wheelchair. "You mus' come here 'lot," he joked feebly. "This's the sec'nd time this week you been in the pub."

His cousin took the glass from his hand and set it on the table. "I'm tired of rescuing you from yourself, bud. It's time you found another form of entertainment."

"Stay 'n have a drink," Marc said when Aidan took hold of the hand grips at the back of the chair and pulled him away from the table.

"Can't. Emily's waiting in the car." Aidan waved to the bartender and started for the exit.

"I can push myself," Marc protested but Aidan was walking too fast for Marc to get hold of the turning wheels. He twisted in his chair and squinted up at his cousin. "You're not mad, are you?"

"I'll be mad if you drink yourself to death after surviving that bomb blast." He started to help Marc into the truck and without the coordination to transfer himself, Marc was forced to accept.

Emily, Aidan's six-year-old daughter stared at Marc. "What's wrong with Marc, Daddy?"

"He's drunk," Aidan said bluntly.

Marc winced and turned away from the little girl's expression of pity and distaste. Once upon a time she'd begged for piggyback rides, shrieking with laughter as he galloped her around the yard. Now, God help him, even the child could see he was sinking.

He stayed away from the pub the next day, and every day that week. But although the hangover wore off, he found he was still thinking about the pup. On Friday after his physiotherapy he checked and discovered that Fiona's notices were still up in store windows. That meant she hadn't found a home for the pooch. Marc tried to reason with himself—it was just a dog, for goodness' sake—but by four o'clock the unfairness of the animal's fate had him agitated.

"You're going to wear holes in my carpet wheeling back and forth like that," Leone complained. She'd just walked in the door after making her rounds as a public-health nurse and was still in her navy blue skirt and jacket. "What's wrong with you?"

Marc stopped suddenly, blocking her way. "Would you object to me getting a puppy?"

"Do you mean that poor creature your friend Fiona brought over? Of course not. He would be a companion for Rufus with Jim and I both working full-time."

"Great. I'll go get him right now. Otherwise Fiona'll take him to the pound."

"Give me a minute to change and I'll drive you,"

Leone said. "There's a special on rump steak at the Pemberton market." Marc's eyebrows rose and she added, "Not for the dog!"

A short time later Leone was pulling onto the highway to Pemberton. "What's her address?"

Marc could have kicked himself—metaphorically speaking. He'd never asked her where she lived and of course she'd never volunteered such information. Then he remembered the notice—which he'd left sitting on top of his dresser in his hurry to be off.

"Let me think." Shutting his eyes, he visualized the sheet of paper. *Free to a good home: Jack Russell–cross puppy. Call Fiona 555-6283.* With the image of the numbers imprinted on the back of his eyelids, Marc felt in his pocket for his cell phone and dialed.

A young man answered and said Fiona was out in the barn and could he get her to call him back?

"Has she found a home for the puppy?" Marc demanded. "She hasn't taken it to the pound, has she?"

"No, the little fella's right here, snoozing on my lap. I think she's planning on taking him to the pound when she comes in." The young man added hopefully, "Why? Do you want him?"

"Yes. I'm on my way now. What's your address?"

Marc found pen and paper in the glove compartment and wrote down the address, repeating it aloud as he did so. Half an hour later they were pulling into the gravel driveway of an older-style home set on a large property outside town. Alpacas grazed in the field next to a red barn. Late roses bloomed along the footpath and red-and-gold dahlias were staked up in a garden bed under the windows.

But what drew Marc's attention was the wheelchair ramp that zigzagged from the path to the front door.

The absurd thought struck him that she'd been expecting him. Ridiculous. The ramp was weathered and worn, obviously in use for many years.

"At least you won't have a problem getting inside," Leone commented pragmatically. "Did you want me to come in? Because if not, I'll run down to the grocery store and pick up a few things for dinner."

"Go ahead. I'll be fine."

Leone got his wheelchair out of the car and tried to help him into it but Marc waved her off. The feeling of helplessness, of having to rely on others, was the part he hated the most. If he was forced to spend more than a few months in this contraption he'd be looking into a car with hand controls. But of course, it wouldn't come to that.

Leone stood back while he got himself settled and wheeled over to the footpath. "Shall I push you?"

"I'm *fine*." He softened his curt tone. "Thanks for the ride."

Leone got back into the car with a promise to return in twenty minutes. Marc started up the long ramp.

IN THE BARN, FIONA RAN the brush over Snowdrop's soft white wool and wondered what Angela Wilde was knitting with the animal's cria fleece. Something special, she hoped. She could ask Liz to find out…

What was her interest here, she asked herself sharply—Angela and the fleece, or Angela's connection to the Wilde family? Bill had told her he'd had to call Marc's cousin again to pick Marc up the afternoon she'd gone to UBC Marc hadn't been in the pub since. Had he finally found more worthwhile pursuits? For his sake, she hoped so.

She glanced at her watch and reluctantly put the brush away. No one had called about the dog. It was time to take him to the pound. With a heavy heart she walked back to the house, trailed by Bilbo and Baggins who'd waited faithfully at the barn door for her.

Jason greeted her at the door, cradling the dog. "A man called who wants to adopt the puppy. He should be here any minute."

"Wonderful!" The relief made her smile. "Who is he?"

"He didn't give his name but he sounded vaguely familiar," Jason said.

Just then, the puppy in his lap lifted his head, ears pricked. A second later they heard the sound of a car drive up.

Fiona handed Jason the dog brush so he could quickly groom the puppy. The animal didn't look quite so scrawny as when they'd first got him, but he still cowered whenever anyone put out a hand to pat him.

She hoped whoever was at the door wouldn't be put off by that but instead treated the dog with compassion and kindness.

There was a knock and she went through the living room to answer it. Opening the door set off a burst of heavy-metal rock music pitched at deafening volume. Fiona, who ordinarily used the back door, remembered too late Jason's latest "invention." Marc looked as startled at the sound as she was to see him.

"You!" Fiona exclaimed but the sound of her voice was drowned out by the ear-piercing twang of electronic guitar. "Come in," she yelled, motioning him over the threshold. She shut the door and blessed silence reigned. "Sorry about that. My brother is an electronics nut."

Marc's hands gripped his wheels. "I've decided to take the dog, after all."

Fiona crossed her arms over her chest. Secretly she was delighted but after the things he'd said she was going to make him work for this. "Are you sure you can take care of him?"

Marc glowered at her. "I can do a lot more in this chair than most people can on two legs."

"What will you do with the dog when you take off into the wild blue yonder?" she demanded, flinging an arm skyward.

"Not a problem," Marc assured her. "My aunt and uncle will be happy to keep him. If they fall through,

I've got two cousins. Between us we'll make sure he has a home."

Fiona tapped her foot, pretending to be debating the issue. "Why did you change your mind?"

"What difference does it make as long as the mutt has a home?"

"Admit it, you fell in love with him at first sight."

He glanced at his watch. "My aunt will be back in twenty minutes at which time I'm leaving, with or without the dog."

With a sigh, Fiona stepped aside and let him pass. "Go straight ahead. He's in the kitchen at the back with my brother."

Jason, his wheelchair parked beside the table, was still brushing the puppy. "Hi."

Marc came to an abrupt halt on the threshold of the kitchen and threw her an odd look.

"This is my brother, Jason," she said. "Jason, this is Marc Wilde."

"No wonder your voice sounded familiar on the telephone!" Jason exclaimed. "Wow! I can't believe you're actually in our kitchen. The last time I saw you on TV you were in Damascus with bombs going off...." Jason's voice trailed away as he realized what he was saying. "Gosh, Mr. Wilde, I'm sorry. About what happened, I mean."

"Forget it. Call me Marc." Marc wheeled closer to peer at the dog. "How's the pup?"

"He's coming along," Fiona said. "I took him to the vet for his shots and a microchip in his ear for identification." She paused. "The vet estimated he's about eight weeks old. He'll be the right age to be neutered in four months. You will do the right thing, won't you?"

"Don't worry—I'm not in the habit of leaving progeny scattered in my wake and neither will my dog."

He'd spoken absently and without even looking her way, yet Fiona felt heat creep into her cheeks. Good grief, anyone would think she was someone's maiden aunt. She moved to the other side of the island benchtop to get out the bag of dry puppy food. He's here for the dog, she reminded herself.

"You can take this to get you started," she said, setting the bag by the door. "Be sure to give him plenty of water."

"I've owned a dog before." Marc reached out for the puppy and Jason handed him over. Immediately the dog began trembling.

"He'll get used to you before long," Fiona assured him, worried Marc might change his mind even now.

Marc held the puppy and stroked it for a few minutes. The trembling increased. He put the dog on the floor where it huddled instead of running around and exploring. "Is he sick?"

"Just scared," Fiona said. "The vet checked him out thoroughly."

"Does he ever bark?" Marc asked.

Fiona glanced at Jason. "We've never heard him."

"Has he got a name?"

"I've held off calling him anything because I thought his new owner should name him."

Fiona stood between Marc and Jason and the three of them stared at the cowering pup. Hé really wasn't the most prepossessing animal.

"I'll call him Rowdy," Marc said at last. "Give him something to live up to."

Fiona couldn't help but smile. "I'm sure he will in time."

"Can you stay for dinner?" Jason blurted out. "I made minestrone soup. It'll give Rowdy time to get to know you before you take him away. And," he added shyly, "I'd love to hear about your experiences in the Middle East."

Marc looked surprised at the unexpected invitation. "Thanks, Jason—"

Fearing he was about to add a "but..." Fiona jumped in. "It's awfully short notice, Jase. I'm sure Marc has other things to do. Plus his aunt is coming back for him."

Marc glanced at her. "I could always call Leone on her cell phone and ask her to come later."

"Great!" Jason said. "I'll heat up some garlic bread."

"Fine," Fiona said wondering why she was reluctant for Marc to stay. Jason needed more male company, especially now that high school was over and his friends had gone off to college and new jobs. But not Marc. Instinctively she felt he would be a disturbing influence, infecting Jason with his discontent.

Marc's presence made the kitchen seem crowded and it wasn't just because his wheelchair took up extra space. Fiona moved nervously around the room, pulling out the table, setting an extra place, aware of Marc's gaze on her as he petted the dog.

"I gather you like Greece," he said, nodding at the posters.

"I've never been," Fiona admitted. "But I'd like to." She paused to gaze at one of the posters. "Something about the light and the blueness of the water and sky attracts me."

"You'll go someday."

She uttered a short laugh. "In my dreams."

Fiona carried the food to the table and they seated themselves. She bowed her head to say a few words of thanksgiving and then handed around bowls of Jason's steaming savory soup and hunks of buttery garlic bread sprinkled with fresh herbs from the pots she grew outside the back door.

In response to Jason's prodding, Marc told them tales of his travels through war-torn countries. She noticed he didn't embellish his own role or glorify war, concentrating instead on the bravery and fortitude of the local people who survived in near-impossible conditions. A different side to him shone through, one she admired.

"You've got a knack for bringing their stories to life," Fiona said. "Yasmina, the schoolteacher, seems as real as, well, me."

"People aren't that different the world over, not where it counts," Marc said with a shrug. "Jason, this soup is delicious."

Jason blushed to the roots of his hair. "Thanks."

"How old are you, seventeen, eighteen?"

"I turned eighteen last month."

"Then you've finished high school," Marc said. Jason nodded. "What are your plans for the future?"

"I want to go to university—" Jason began.

"Good plan," Marc said. "Education opens doors."

"—but Fiona won't let me," Jason finished.

Shocked her brother would say that in front of a stranger, Fiona froze as Marc turned to look in her direction.

CHAPTER FOUR

MARC'S GAZE FLICKERED from Jason to Fiona, trying to fathom the undercurrents of tension that had suddenly risen to the surface between brother and sister.

"That's not strictly true, Jase," Fiona said tightly. To Marc she added, "We're exploring his options."

Jason pulled apart the crust of his bread. "We've explored my options so long the fall term's begun and it's too late to enroll."

"Have you checked to see if you can put in a late application?" Marc suggested carefully.

"What's the use?" Jason muttered. "We can't afford for me to go to school."

"There are loans, bursaries, possibly even scholarships if Jason's marks are good enough," Marc said.

"His options include working for a year to save money for tuition," Fiona said.

"I've read the textbooks. I can do the work," Jason replied. "Why should I wait?"

Fiona cast a meaningful glance at her brother that said as clearly as words, *enough,* then turned to Marc. "Would you like some more soup?"

"No, thank you." Marc laid down his spoon beside his empty bowl.

An awkward silence descended over the dinner table.

Fiona rose and gathered up the empty dishes. "I'll get Rowdy's bed and then drive you home," she said to Marc. "I hate to rush you but I have studying to do. Jason, can you please disconnect that so-called music before we open the door?"

While Jason disappeared to another part of the house Fiona went to the laundry room and came back holding a cardboard box with one side cut down and packed with an old blanket. She put the box on Marc's lap and the puppy and his bag of food inside. "I'll go bring the car around."

Jason returned and wheeled as far as the front door with Marc. "Sorry things got a little uncomfortable."

"Don't worry about it." Marc hesitated, wishing he could say something more. Jason was a nice kid who deserved a break. But what could Marc do to help him? "Good luck with your studies." He made his way slowly down the ramp, careful not to tip Rowdy out of his box.

Fiona was waiting with the passenger door open and the trunk up. Marc transferred to her car and stroked the shivering dog while she loaded his chair.

"You shouldn't hold him back," Marc said when they were heading down the dark country road that led through Pemberton to the highway to Whistler.

She stared straight ahead, her hands gripping the wheel at the regulation ten and two o'clock positions. "I know how to take care of my brother."

"I'm sure you do. But if he's eager for a career why not do what you can to help him get one?"

"What goes on between Jason and me is none of your business."

"What if something happens to you? Who'll look after him if he doesn't have some way to provide for himself?"

She slowed to a halt at a four-way stop and swiveled in her seat to face him. "Do you think I haven't thought of that? I've got a plan. I've worked out our future. The problem is, Jason's young and wants everything right now."

"Fine. No need to get defensive."

"I'm not being defensive," she said, moving through the intersection. "You're interfering."

"I only said—"

"Don't!"

He held up his hands in silent surrender. She was right; it was none of his business. "How long has Jason been in a wheelchair?"

"Since he was eleven." Tension still gripped her voice; if anything it had increased. "His spinal cord was severed in the same car accident that killed our parents."

"I'm sorry," he said quietly. "Were you also in the car?"

"Yes." She hesitated. "I walked away with a broken arm."

"My mother was killed in a car accident when I was five," Marc told her.

"And your father?"

"He's been gone for fifteen years now."

She glanced sideways and in the dim light of the dashboard Marc caught an expression of understanding. "We have something in common," she said. "We're both orphans."

For all intents and purposes, that was true. "I was lucky. My aunt and uncle were like parents to me and Nate and Aidan, like brothers. How old were you when you lost your folks?"

"Eighteen. I'd just started university. I was home for the weekend when the accident happened. I never went back to school."

"How did you get your teaching degree then?"

"Correspondence courses while I worked at the pub. It took me six years." She sounded more resigned than bitter.

"It would be understandable if you were reluctant to let your brother get easily what you worked so hard to achieve." Marc chose his next words carefully.

"You're wrong," she interjected, shooting him an indecipherable look. "I don't begrudge Jason *anything*."

She denied it so quickly, so vehemently, Marc wondered if it were strictly true. "Still, caring for your brother under those circumstances would have been hard enough but with Jason also in a wheelchair… You're a mother to your brother and a savior to lost dogs." Marc regarded her thoughtfully. "Who takes care of Fiona?"

She flinched, just a tightening of her hands gripping the wheel but he knew he'd hit a nerve.

"I take care of myself, thank you very much," she said with a hint of the steel that must have supported her all these years.

She turned off the highway and onto the road that led to Tapley's Estate. Marc studied her in the street-light. Something else had surfaced just then, too, a wist-fulness, as if she wouldn't mind, just once, being taken care of herself.

A few minutes later Fiona pulled into Jim and Leone's driveway and parked the car. With proficiency born of practice she unloaded Marc's chair and held it while he transferred into it.

Rowdy's sniffing nose poked timidly above the lip of the cardboard box. She leaned over to stroke the puppy's head. "Bye sweetie," she crooned. "I'll miss you." To Marc she said, "Take good care of Rowdy. If you have any questions or problems just give me a call."

As she pulled out of the driveway, Marc wondered aloud, "Does it have to be about the dog?"

"Sit, Rowdy. Now, stay. Staaay…." Marc wheeled a few feet away then glanced over his shoulder. Rowdy was creeping hesitantly after him.

"No, no, no," Marc chided. With a combination of pushing on Rowdy's rump and pulling up on his lead Marc got him back into a sitting position. "Sit. Stay."

This time he wheeled backward down the driveway, keeping a stern eye on the dog. After a moment's hesitation, Rowdy started inching forward on his belly, ears flattened, wagging his tail in a submissive posture.

They were out in the front yard because Leone had complained about the dog's nails scratching her hardwood floors. But with all the distracting scents and sounds of the outdoors Rowdy was finding it hard to stay focused.

"Okay, boy, we'll try it once more."

He maneuvered Rowdy back into position. The dog sat for all of thirty seconds until a crow flew out of the spruce tree at the side of the house. Rowdy darted after it, barking loudly.

"So you've got a voice. Hurrah," Marc said wearily. "Come, Rowdy."

The dog ignored him. When the crow flapped his wings lazily and flew to a pine across the road, Rowdy charged after it, and was narrowly missed by an approaching car.

"Rowdy! Come!" Marc called, wheeling to the end of the driveway.

Rowdy looked over his shoulder at Marc as if to say, "are you kidding?" With more spunk than he'd shown thus far, he barked and continued to chase the bird. Marc called insistently, alternating between an angry and an encouraging tone. Nothing worked.

He was forced to follow the dog down the road, finally cornering Rowdy in a driveway where he was playfully barking at a beagle behind a gate.

Marc dragged Rowdy back to his own yard, scolding, "I can't run after you if you take off. What if you get hit by a car, or someone even more bad tempered than me dognaps you?"

Rowdy stretched his long body out on the grass and rested his muzzle on his paws, gazing up at Marc with wrinkled eyebrows as if he was as perplexed as Marc about how to solve the problem.

"I should never have agreed to take you," Marc told him. "It's all Fiona's fault for guilting me into it. No, don't look at me with those puppy-dog eyes. I can't train you properly and once I'm out of the chair I won't be around to look after you. I ought to take you to the pound right now."

Rowdy crawled forward on his belly and lovingly and thoroughly began laving Marc's bare foot with long flat swipes of his tongue. Marc's first instinct was to push him away but a second glance stopped him. Rowdy was concentrating his efforts on a scabbed over scrape he'd gotten when he'd bumped into a sharp corner after a shower and not felt it.

The dog was cleaning his wound with intense doggy devotion. It gave him the oddest feeling.

"Come on, then, mutt. We'll find an obedience class." Marc wheeled up the sheet of plywood Jim had put in place as a makeshift ramp and into the house. Rowdy trotted along on his short legs, apparently quite happy to obey when he agreed with the directive.

Marc spent half an hour on the phone trying to find a class but the one in Whistler was full and not accepting new members. Another class was starting in Squamish in two weeks but Marc didn't want to ask Leone or Jim to drive an hour each way.

"There's always the library," Marc told Rowdy then caught himself. He was talking to a dog.

"Did I hear you say you were going to the library?" Leone came into the room dressed to go out in black slacks and a dark green blazer with an autumn-colored silk scarf. It was Wednesday, her day off. "I can drop you there on my way to the hairdresser."

"Thanks." Marc put Rowdy in the fenced backyard with a bone and a squeaky toy, telling him, "I won't be long."

Built on the model of an alpine village, Whistler sparkled in the autumn sun beneath the glistening peaks of Whistler and Blackcomb Mountains. Tourists from all over the world strolled along the pedestrian-only lanes and squares, browsing the well-kept shops and restaurants. Sports enthusiasts, from mountain bikers in padded shorts and body armor to glacier skiers in long nylon pants and dark goggles rode or strode purposefully toward their individual pursuits, many heading for the chairlifts at the edge of town.

Leone pulled into the handicapped zone in the library parking lot. "How long do you think you'll be?"

"I'm not sure," Marc said. "I might go to the pub afterward. I'll get a taxi back." He could let Fiona know how the dog was doing. After a week's abstinence he had a thirst but it wasn't for bourbon.

Leone fingered the ends of her scarf, her expression troubled. "Marc, honey…"

"I know what you're going to say," he forestalled her before she could lecture him on his drinking. "But I'm a big boy. Don't worry about me."

"Jim and I *do* worry. You've never drunk too much before, not even when you first came of legal drinking age. Excess alcohol isn't good for your health and it might even affect your recovery."

"I know," Marc said, smoothing out the curling ends of the Band-Aids covering the blistered pads of his palms.

Leone noticed and heaved an exasperated sigh. "When are you going to do something about your hands? All it takes is a phone call to Nate and he'll bring you a pair of leather cycling gloves. I'll do it for you."

"Don't bother."

"Sooner or later, Marc, you'll have to accept your condition."

Marc's lips tightened. "I'll see you in a while. Thanks for the ride."

The library was bright and spacious, the hushed quiet punctuated by murmured voices at the checkout desk and in the reading corner. Marc found the reference number on the computerized catalog and cruised the nonfiction aisles till he found the books on dog training. He picked out several and took them up to the checkout desk.

"Your library card, please?" the librarian murmured. Brisk, white-haired and bespectacled, she opened the covers and stacked them one atop the other, ready for scanning.

Marc handed over Leone's card. The librarian glanced at it then at him. "You're not Leone Wilde."

"She's my aunt. I'm Marc Wilde...Mrs. Cameron," Marc added, taking note of her name tag. He made a slight gesture of apology. "I'd take out a card of my own but I'm not going to be in town long enough."

Naomi Cameron's mouth softened and she leaned forward over the counter. "Marc Wilde, of course. I've watched you on TV for years. I was very sorry when you made the news yourself." Then her blue eyes brightened behind her rimless glasses. "May I say, you have a wonderful speaking voice."

"Thank you," Marc replied warily, sensing from her tone that something else was coming. Sure enough.

"We have a program at the library on Thursday afternoons in which volunteers read from works of fiction," she told him. "Mainly seniors attend, those who have trouble with their eyesight, or just want an outing. It's very informal and social. We're always looking for people to help out if you have any spare time."

Marc pressed down on his arm rests, shifting in his seat. "As I said, I'm not going to be in town long."

"I see. Well, that's disappointing but I understand." She started to scan the bar codes into the computer. "If you change your mind, come and see me. Our volunteers enjoy the program as much as the listeners. It's very rewarding all around."

"I'm sure it is."

Do something for someone else instead of feeling sorry for yourself.

"Be quiet," he muttered to himself. Why did he keep hearing Fiona's voice at the most inconvenient times? Or was it only when he was acting like a jerk?

"Excuse me?" Naomi pushed the books back across the counter to him. "Were you speaking to me?"

"Just clearing my throat. I beg your pardon," Marc said, taking the books into his lap. "Thanks."

"Good luck training your dog."

Marc took out his cell phone and hit speed dial for the disabled taxi. Luck was with him; today the taxi pulled up within twenty minutes.

"Hey, Marc! Good to see you," the same affable driver greeted him. "Where you headed—the pub again?"

"Hi, uh…"

"Brent."

"Right. Brent. Yes, the pub again."

All the regulars were in their usual places when Marc pushed through the door. The old men were nursing their beer in the corner, the chronically unemployed were at the bar watching football on TV and the lady with the smeared red lipstick was drinking what was probably her fifth gin and tonic and trying to entice a couple of tourists into conversation.

Marc rolled over to his usual table, chagrined to realize he *had* a usual table. Being a regular barfly was pretty pathetic when he came to think of it. He scanned the room again. Only Fiona was missing. He felt an unexpectedly strong stab of disappointment. Of course she didn't spend all her time here. She could be teaching or at the university library or at home—

"Hi, stranger." Fiona appeared from behind him in a blur of strawberry-blond hair and black skirt. She had a round tray tucked under her arm and one hip cocked at an angle as she took the weight off her foot. "How's Rowdy?"

"Undisciplined and disobedient." Marc held up one of his library books. "I'm aiming to change that."

"Good for you." Her smile was approving but fleeting. "What'll you have? The usual—bourbon on the rocks?"

"Just coffee, thanks. Black, no sugar."

Surprise registered in a slight upward lift of her eyebrows. "Coming right up."

Marc watched her stride back to the bar, her slim hips swaying slightly and her thick mass of bright hair bouncing across her back with every step. It was a funny thing, when she smiled at him, the blackness receded.

When she returned she brought two cups of coffee. Passing one to him, she placed the tray on the next table and pulled out a chair. "Mind if I sit? I'm due a break."

Marc closed his book. "How've you been?"

"Okay," she said with a shrug. "Tell me about Rowdy. Is he eating well? Is he becoming less timid? I hope you're not growling at him."

"He has the appetite of a horse but he won't sit, won't stay, won't come," Marc complained lightheartedly. "The only time he's lively is when a bird is involved. I've tried to tell him they're flighty things and he's wasting his time but he doesn't listen."

Fiona smiled briefly. "Sounds as though he's doing fine. And you seem in better spirits, too."

"Today is a good day." Marc studied her face as she sipped from her cup, noting the faint line between her tawny eyebrows and her almost inaudible sigh. She seemed unusually subdued. Then she glanced up and he found himself gazing into clear eyes, gray-green and shiny, like a washed stone tumbled beneath a fast-flowing brook.

"What?" she said, frowning slightly under his scrutiny.

"Are you worried about something?"

"Kind of." Her slender fingers toyed with the heart-shaped amethyst suspended on a gold chain that hung around her neck. "I did a bad thing and it's bothering me."

Assorted incongruous possibilities flashed through Marc's mind—hit and run, cruelty to animals, shoplifting—none of them fit his image of Fiona. Intrigued, he asked, "What?"

She glanced away, then back at him, then leaned over the table. "I was in the parking lot at UBC, trolling for a space and getting anxious because I was supposed to meet my tutor at the library at a certain time. She only had forty-five minutes between classes and I had a lot of questions."

"You were in a hurry," Marc summarized.

Fiona nodded. "I saw a car pulling out of a slot ahead. I didn't think, I just went for it. Only as I pulled in did I notice a car waiting in the opposite lane, its indicator flashing." She sighed, shook her head. "It was there first."

"You stole a parking spot?" Marc said.

She covered her head with her hands. "It's one of those cardinal rules, isn't it? You don't steal parking spaces. What bothers me is that maybe I *did* see the car and subconsciously ignored it. What does that make me?"

"A very bad person." Marc shook his head solemnly.

Her eyes narrowed. "Are you making fun of me? I felt terrible all day. Even now I can't stop thinking about it."

"Did the driver come after you with a crowbar? Abuse you verbally?"

"Even worse," Fiona said, shaking her head. "She was an older woman, maybe fifty—"

"Don't tell my aunt that's old," Marc interjected. "She's forty-nine."

"Anyway, she rolled down her window as I got out of my car and said, 'that wasn't a very nice thing to do.'"

"Ooh, vicious. And this incident is still upsetting you?"

Fiona nodded. "I haven't told you everything. I saw her later…she was on crutches."

"Was it a handicapped spot you stole? Now that *would* be bad."

"No! I don't know why she didn't go for one of those. Maybe they were full or she didn't have a tag." Fiona fell silent, looking heartsick.

Marc reached for her hand and held it in both of his. "Look at me." She lifted her gaze. "You are not a bad person. A bad person would not have a guilty conscience about taking someone else's parking space."

"Yes, but I realized my mistake while I was still in the car with the motor running. I could have backed out and given her the spot."

"But you didn't, and that's what's bothering you."

She nodded. "I was late, I was frantic, and I just thought, stuff it. For once I'm going to be selfish."

"Maybe you need to learn to do that more often."

She eyed him askance. "But that's not me. And now I'm suffering for my actions."

"Listen. It was an honest mistake at first, right? You didn't register her presence when you pulled in otherwise you wouldn't have done it."

She nodded.

"You didn't know she was on crutches. If you had, you probably would have pulled out and given her the spot because you *are* a nice person."

Fiona thought about that a moment then nodded again.

Marc drew a breath. "Finally, do you think that woman is still thinking about what happened days ago?"

"No," she said slowly. "I guess you're right. Thanks. You've put it into perspective for me."

"The important thing is not to beat yourself up over things." He paused. "Since we're confessing… I didn't mean to imply the other night that you weren't doing your best with Jason. Anyone can see you two are very close."

"I overreacted. I'm a little sensitive about this subject. When my parents died everyone told me Jason needed 'proper care,' as if I couldn't provide it. My grandparents in northern Manitoba wanted him to live with them but he barely knew them and the facilities he needed weren't available. Being on our own *was* tough at first, for both of us, but we've managed."

"You've done a remarkable job getting him this far but now it's time to let go, let him find his own path."

Fiona gave him a withering look that said he'd lost the ground he'd just gained then drained her cup and rose. "I've got to get back to work. The place is starting to fill up with the lunch crowd."

"I'm not trying to interfere," Marc said. "It's just that my aunt, whom I love dearly, is mothering me to death with well-meaning kindness. It's driving me crazy."

Fiona gathered up his cup and stacked it with hers on the tray. "You think I'm driving Jason crazy?"

"No, of course not. But you should concentrate on yourself for a change."

"You don't know me, you don't know my brother, but you're giving me advice on how to live my life," she said, exasperated. "You, who can't even sort out your own problems. Do you want something else?"

"How about having dinner with me one night this week?" he said. "Jason, too, of course."

She shook her head. "You never give up, do you? I meant a drink or something."

"Going out for a drink would be fine, too," he replied, deliberately misunderstanding her.

"Thanks, but I'm afraid I can't."

"You've mainly seen me drunk and disorderly," Marc went on. "I can be quite charming once you get to know me."

Why he was being so persistent, he didn't know; no

romance was going to develop. She was far too nice for him. But she was engaging to be around, with a wit sharp enough to keep him on his toes—so to speak. And to be honest, he hated to think he'd completely lost his touch with women.

"I don't doubt it, but the answer is no."

Clearly she was as accomplished at turning down men as he was at flirting. "You're not even going to give me a reason?"

"I don't have to."

He sighed audibly. "You realize your callous rejection could drive me to drink?"

That won him a faint smile. "Good try. You're just trying to guilt me into going out with you."

"Will it work?" he asked in a reprise of their conversation from earlier in the week.

She laughed, an unexpectedly throaty chuckle, and the air around her seemed to sparkle. *"No."*

"Come on, I'm down in the dumps. I need inspiration, motivation."

"You've got a dog to train."

"That occupies an hour or two a day, max."

She started to walk away.

"Tell you what," he said. "If I do a good deed for someone, will you go out with me?"

"Are you even capable of doing something nice?" she asked skeptically.

If she only knew, doing a good deed was what had landed him in the wheelchair in the first place.

"Pollyanna," he said reproachfully. "I'm surprised at your sudden lack of faith in human nature. I did a good deed when I took Rowdy off your hands."

"That doesn't count," she said. "You've gained the most in getting him, whether you realize it or not."

"Fine, I'll do something else."

"It'll have to be something really good," she warned.

Marc held out his hand to shake on it. Hesitantly, she slipped her small hand into his open grasp. His fingers closed around hers as their eyes met. "Deal."

CHAPTER FIVE

MARC WHEELED SLOWLY down the sidewalk of Pemberton's main street, casting his eye around for someone for whom he could do a good turn. It *ought* to be a piece of cake but two days had passed and he'd encountered no one in need of whatever services he could render. The seniors reading program at the library he'd dismissed without a second thought as being time-consuming and ongoing.

He figured Fiona didn't seriously expect him to carry out his side of the bargain, thinking that by sending him off on such an errand she'd get him out of her hair.

He was just about to give up when an opportunity presented itself. An elderly woman juggling two large paper shopping bags came out of the grocery store. She glanced around anxiously as if expecting someone to appear and help her, then tottered over to the crosswalk and pushed the walk button with her elbow. In doing so she nearly lost her precarious grip on the bags.

Marc rolled forward. "Excuse me, ma'am. Would you like assistance? If you place your bags in my lap, I'll carry them across the street for you."

Suspicious gray eyes peered at him over the tops of the paper grocery bags. "What did you say?" she demanded. "I don't hear too good."

"Place your bags in my lap," Marc said loudly and distinctly.

"I'll do no such thing!" she retorted, clutching her bags more tightly. "Just because you're in a wheelchair doesn't entitle you to steal my groceries. I'm on a pension."

"I'm not trying to take your food," Marc said, but she sidestepped away from him, looking around in alarm. Frustrated, he moved with her, touching her arm to gain her attention so he could explain.

She jumped, losing her grip on the groceries. Eggs splatted on the sidewalk, oranges rolled into the gutter, a carton of milk hit the pavement and sprung a leak and tea bags burst from their box. She uttered an inarticulate cry, her mouth left gaping in shock at her scattered groceries. Marc cursed his clumsy approach and leaned over the side of his chair to pick up what he could.

"Don't touch my groceries!" she shrieked, hitting him on the shoulder with wild swings of her handbag. "Help! Thief!"

A teenage couple passing by responded first. The boy started to gather up the groceries while the girl helped the elderly lady to a nearby bench.

A middle-aged man in a baseball cap ran across the road when the light turned green and advanced on

Marc. "What do you think you're doing taking an old lady's groceries?"

"I was trying to *help* her," Marc explained testily.

"She's my mother-in-law. I was coming to pick her up." He scrutinized Marc through narrowed eyes. "Do you live around here?"

Marc was aware that his scruffy appearance didn't speak in his favor. At one time that wouldn't have mattered as he knew everyone who lived in the Whistler valley, and everyone knew him. Now he mostly encountered faces who were unfamiliar, and in the present instance—hostile.

Deflated, Marc pulled out his wallet, took out a couple of twenties and handed them to the man. "Give her this for the groceries. I promise you, I meant no harm."

With ill grace, the man accepted the money. "Next time, think twice before you accost little old ladies in the street."

Marc moved off down the street, muttering curses. Face it, he'd also lost his touch as a Good Samaritan.

MARC ROLLED INTO the pub the next day and chose his usual spot in the corner. When Fiona came over to take his order he said, "Bourbon and Coke. Make it a double."

Fiona ran a wet cloth over the table, casting sideways glances at him. "How's the good-deed campaign?"

"Forget it," Marc said. "That was a stupid idea."

"You can do something for me," she said. "Move closer to the bar. My feet are killing me."

"I don't want to be around people."

"Suit yourself." She pulled a pair of fingerless leather gloves out of her apron pocket and threw them onto the table.

"What's this?" he said, eyeing them suspiciously.

"A spare pair of Jason's gloves. I hate seeing you destroy your hands." She walked away.

Marc dropped his head in his admittedly mangled hand and massaged his temples. Why did he have to be such a jerk? Fiona didn't deserve his surly attitude. He reached for the gloves. They were worn but still serviceable, reinforced in the palm with a snap at the wrist and the fingers cut out to allow dexterity.

He glanced over at the bar. Fiona had her back to him, chatting to the bartender while she waited for her order. Marc drew on the left glove over his bandages and flexed his hand. It felt good. He put on the other glove and pushed to a table near the bar.

Fiona turned and saw him. She didn't quite smile but her face softened. Setting his bourbon on the table, she asked, "Do they fit?"

Marc nodded, adding gruffly, "Thanks." He noticed the bartender, a blunt featured man with sandy hair, was drying glasses at the far end of the bar and keeping a wary eye on him.

"So what happened when you tried to do a good deed?"

He took a big sip of his drink. "Nothing." No way was he going to recount his humiliation to her.

"Come on, it'll do you good to talk about it. My therapist always said, better out than in."

Chuckling, Marc said, "That's what Jim used to say when one of us boys burped at the dinner table, much to Leone's disgust." He studied Fiona a moment. "You were in therapy?"

She nodded. "After the accident. It helped but..." She fingered her amethyst. "Some things take a long time to get over."

He didn't pry, knowing very well some thoughts were too dark to express aloud, but he was curious. And then, without intending to, he found himself telling her about his encounter with the woman and the groceries. To his surprise he was able to laugh about it.

"Don't give up just because one thing went wrong," Fiona said.

"We'll see."

Fiona got out a large bag of pretzels to refill the bowls on the bar. She always moved with lithe grace but today Marc noticed a distinct spring in her step.

"You look pleased with yourself," he said.

She beamed as pretzels clattered into wooden bowls. "I got an A on my essay on reading disorders."

"Congratulations."

She put the pretzels away and began to fill stainless-steel dishes with lemon slices, olives and pickled onions.

Marc picked up his drink and wove around tables and chairs to the end of the bar near where she stood. He helped himself to a cocktail onion and popped the crunchy vinegary globe into his mouth.

"Hey!" Fiona objected. "You can't do that."

Marc took another onion and Fiona slapped at his fingers. With a wave of his hand, he made the onion disappear. Grinning at her startled expression, he leaned forward and appeared to pull it out of her ear. While she was still staring at him, he leisurely took and ate an olive.

"Where did you learn to do magic tricks?"

"Jim taught me when I was a teenager. I took it up again when I was in the rehab hospital to pass the time."

"That's it!" Fiona exclaimed. "My friend Liz is desperate to find entertainment for her six-year-old's birthday party. You could do a magic act."

"Oh, no." Marc held up one hand and with the other, pushed his chair away from the bar. "No way."

"Don't you like children?"

"Sure, some of my best friends are under twelve. But my magic is too rusty to perform in public and I know nothing about entertaining. I'd probably scare the kids."

"No, you wouldn't. You'd be great." Fiona's eyes started to shine as the idea took hold of her. "I know where we could borrow a clown costume—"

"A *clown*." This was getting worse and worse. "I don't think so. If I dressed up at all it would be in a top hat and tails."

"Okay," she said happily, taking his comment for agreement. "I'll call Liz and tell her the good news."

She reached for the phone sitting on the bar but before she could pick it up Marc slapped a hand over hers. "No."

She regarded him uncertainly. "Come on."

"No," he repeated more firmly. "You made me responsible for the fate of a dog but you're not going to reduce me to doing tricks for a child's birthday party."

"You might enjoy it," she said. "Did you think of that?"

"For the third and final time, *no*." He became aware of her hand trapped beneath his and loosened his grip.

She slid hers out and rubbed it with her other hand. "Fine, you win." Subdued and silent, she went on with her work.

Marc sat back and reached for his drink. He'd got his own way but he'd also wiped out her smile. If this was winning why did he feel like such a loser?

FIONA HELD HER HANDS over her ears as two dozen six-year-olds screamed with laughter. Marc, dressed in a top hat and tails with his face painted like a clown, was the grumpiest clown in history. At the moment he looked furious to have discovered a bouquet of silk flowers up his sleeve. The children laughed all the harder thinking his over-the-top bad humor was all part of the act. She didn't know what had made him change his mind—surely a date with her wasn't sufficient enticement—but she was glad he did.

The party was taking place in Liz's rumpus room. Marc held center stage at one end while the children sat cross-legged on the carpeted floor before him. Five or six mothers stood along the back. Balloons and crepe-paper streamers decorated the pine-paneled walls.

Marc lifted a hand to quell the excited laughter and cheering. "My next trick requires the help of my faithful assistant, Rowdy." He gestured to the Jack Russell who cowered beside his chair dressed in a tiny clown hat and a red ruff. "Rowdy insists on absolute silence when he performs," Marc growled at his audience.

Instantly the kids became so quiet that a pin dropped at the front would have been audible from where Fiona was standing.

"He's got them eating out of his hand," the blond athletic-looking woman next to Fiona whispered.

"And to think he didn't want to do this," Fiona confided in an undertone. "I'm Fiona, by the way. I've seen you around town but can't remember ever being introduced."

"I'm Val, Marc's physiotherapist." Val glanced at her appraisingly. "So *you're* Fiona."

"Ye-e-s. What's Marc been saying about me?"

Before Val could reply, ripples of children's laughter drew their attention back to the magic show. Rowdy was springing repeatedly into the air to snatch dog treats from Marc's fingers.

Next Marc produced a hoop and held the treat on the other side. "Jump, Rowdy."

Rowdy subsided onto his haunches at Marc's feet, his gaze shifting between Marc's face and the dog treat. Marc curved his mouth and eyes into an exaggerated frown and urged him once more. Rowdy, his ears plastered to his head, and his stubby tail wagging nervously, refused to budge.

"Ladies and gentlemen," Marc said. "My assistant appears to be suffering from stage fright. If you'll be patient, he's undoubtedly gathering his nerve as I speak."

Rowdy's barrel-shaped body twitched and Marc glanced swiftly sideways. Rowdy wagged his tail.

"We'll come back to that trick later." Marc deepened his husky baritone to order, "Lie down, Rowdy."

Rowdy leaped through the hoop.

The children laughed uproariously, some toppling over sideways in their mirth. Marc followed up this coup by pulling a lot of brightly colored scarves out of his breast pocket. Fiona glanced back to Val, curious to hear more about Marc.

"He just asked if I knew you," Val said, referring back to Fiona's earlier question. "He mentioned that you'd asked him to take care of the dog. I see you were successful."

"He grumbled about it but in the end he agreed. Under that hard cynical exterior I suspect he's a softy."

Marc again directed his remarks to Rowdy. The dog, head cocked and ears pricked, appeared to hang on every word.

Val watched her patient with concern. "A pet will be good for Marc if he lets himself care," she said. "He desperately needs an anchor, something to hang on to when his anger and depression get too much for him."

"He's been through a terrible experience," Fiona agreed. "At least he'll recover the use of his legs."

Val glanced at her sharply. "Did he tell you that?"

Alarm quickened Fiona's blood. "Yes. Isn't it true?"

"His medical reports indicate he had excellent post-trauma treatment, which increases the odds of recovery. His injury is classified as borderline incomplete meaning he has the potential for some sensation and muscle control. But you wouldn't find a doctor on the planet who would guarantee Marc will walk again."

A hollow sick feeling in her stomach made Fiona wrap her arms around her waist. She, of all people, who'd cared for a paraplegic for years, should have known how nebulous the prognosis of any spinal-cord injury was. She realized then how much she'd *wanted* to believe Marc. Suddenly she was angry at him, not so much for fooling her—she could understand a man's need to appear strong—but for fooling himself.

Or *was* he fooling himself? After all, he'd talked about suicide. She'd convinced herself he was joking but maybe she should have taken him more seriously.

"He's not being realistic, at least not to me," she said to Val. "You mentioned he was depressed. Do you think he's capable of harming himself?"

Val shook her head but the gesture was one of uncertainty rather than negation. "I'm no psychiatrist. He's got tremendous willpower but he's going through huge changes in terms of self-image and loss of control. Hanging on to the fiction that he'll walk again might be the only thing that's keeping him sane."

"If only there was something I could do," Fiona murmured, forgetting her vow not to get involved.

"He's getting all the specialist care he requires," Val said. "What he needs most right now are friends who provide cheerful diversions from the reality of his everyday life. And possibly his future."

"I can do that," Fiona said, more to herself than to Val. "I've done it with Jason for years."

"Be careful how you couch your interest," Val said. "I'm sure you wouldn't deliberately mislead him, but it's easy for a man in his position to mistake friendship for something else. He may not seem vulnerable, but he is."

"I take your point," Fiona said. "I'll be careful not to get *too* close."

The children crowded around Marc at the end of his magic show even though he was still scowling through his clown makeup. One little girl hugged him and at first Fiona was afraid he would snap at her. For a split second his expression softened and his arms moved jerkily, as if he would hug her back but wasn't sure how to. Then Liz called everyone over for birthday cake and with a roar of approval the children stampeded across the room to tables set up with brightly colored plastic cups and plates. When Fiona looked again, Marc's scowl was back in place.

"That was more exhausting than an all-day rock climb," he said, coming over to her.

"You were tremendous," she enthused. "I think you missed your calling. Instead of a journalist you should have been a children's entertainer."

Grimacing, he said, "I'd sooner slit my wrists."

Coming so soon after her conversation with Val, Fiona started at his choice of words.

Marc glanced at her oddly. "I'm joking, for God's sake. I'm just glad it's over."

"The kids enjoyed your act. Children don't fake that kind of enthusiasm."

"I've fulfilled my end of the bargain and done a good deed." He slipped a hand inside his sleeve and whipped out the bunch of silk flowers which he presented to her. "Now will you go out with me?"

Ridiculously flustered she made a pretense of sniffing the flowers. "Did I say I would? Doesn't sound like me."

"You said it, and I'm holding you to it."

Marc's vulnerable emotions aside, she couldn't let

herself get romantically involved with him. In her experience, once men realized Jason would always be her first priority they quickly lost interest in a long-term relationship. But now, looking into Marc's blue eyes she felt as though she was doing loop-the-loops in a small airplane.

"Would you like some cake?" she asked.

"Don't change the subject. You can't put me off forever."

"Okay, I'll go out with you," she said. "But it's not a *romantic* date. We're just friends, right?"

His high cheekbones flared with color, as if she'd slapped him in the face.

Liz came over with an extralarge slice of chocolate cream-filled cake and a huge dollop of vanilla ice cream. "Thanks are so inadequate," she said, handing Marc the plate. "I'd like to pay you for today."

Marc held up his hand. "That wasn't part of the deal."

"No, really," Liz insisted. "I would have had to pay any other entertainer. If you like, you can use the money to buy a new ruff for your dog. I noticed it tore a little when the kids were petting him."

"It's only a scrap of muslin my aunt threaded onto elastic. Don't even mention it."

"You could use the money to hire a dog trainer," Fiona suggested.

"Very funny. Help me out here," Marc appealed to her.

"I think you should accept the money. You worked for it, and you deserve it."

"That's settled. I'll go get my wallet," Liz said above Marc's protests. She ran up stairs.

"Why didn't you stop her?" Marc demanded. "Couldn't you see I feel uncomfortable taking money?"

"You've got to be practical," Fiona told him. "You're not working and you could use an alternate source of income if—" She broke off, reluctant to come right out and say, *if you never walk again*. That would be like kicking the man when he was down. "If for whatever reason you don't go back to being a globe-trotting reporter."

When his mouth settled into a thin straight line she knew he'd interpreted her comment correctly.

Liz returned with a handful of twenties and tried to give them to Marc.

"No," Marc said, looking furious.

Liz tucked the money deep into the sport bag hanging off the back of his chair and gave Marc a grateful smile. "You *have* to accept it, if only to clear my conscience. Don't be surprised if you get a rash of moms calling you up to entertain at their children's birthday parties."

"Heaven forbid," Marc murmured. He turned to Fiona. "I'll call you about that date."

Liz glanced from Marc to Fiona with interest. "Are you two going out? Don't forget this Saturday is girls' night, Fi."

"Oh, Liz, I forgot to tell you, I can't. Jason's friend Dave was coming home for the weekend but he bailed at the last minute. Jason's pretty down about it so I promised I'd hang out with him."

"He's a big boy, Fi. He's got to get used to disappointments."

"But he's had so many," Fiona said. "It's not fair."

Liz lowered her voice. "You baby him. When are you going to get a life?"

Fiona glanced toward Marc, conscious he was probably thinking the same thing. Other people didn't understand what it was like to be responsible for a paraplegic brother and not be able to do a thing to make him well. As for her getting a life, she'd been out of action so long she didn't know how to have a "good" time. Staying home and watching videos or playing Scrabble with Jason was easier than meeting men. Men who would eventually make demands on her time and emotions she couldn't fulfill.

"I'm sorry, Liz. I really can't. We'll do it another day. Okay?"

"I'll let you off the hook this time," Liz said reluctantly. "But someday soon we're going out and you're going to have *fun*."

Marc turned to her with a dry smile. "Whether you like it or not, Pollyanna."

CHAPTER SIX

"ROWDY, SIT." MARC POINTED to the ground next to his wheelchair. Rowdy slowly lowered his shivering rump to the wet grass with a pained expression.

"*Stay.*" Marc backed his chair away an inch at a time. Rowdy held his position, his gaze shifting back and forth between Marc's eyes and the pocket where he kept the dog treats. Marc was elated. This was the longest Rowdy had sat so far. Perhaps this time he would stay until Marc gave the signal to come.

The sliding door to the kitchen opened and Leone came out, bringing with her the scent of cinnamon and nutmeg. She wore a bib-front apron over her slacks for indulging in her favorite pastime, baking. Rowdy ran toward her, wriggling and cowering and wagging his stubby tail.

"Who's a good doggy-woggy?" Leone crooned, stooping to scratch him behind his ears. "*You* are. Yes, you are."

Marc sighed.

Leone straightened. "Nate and Angela are here."

"I'll be right in." He called Rowdy back, thinking to end the training session with some small task to reinforce obedience. Too late. Rufus bounded through the open door and immediately the two dogs were off, circling and leaping, taking no notice of the humans watching.

"It's wonderful they have each other to play with," Leone said happily. "Coming, Marc?"

Inside, Nate and his wife, Angela, were helping themselves to a piece of the carrot cake Leone had just taken out of the oven. The sounds of the football game on TV came from the living room and Marc knew Jim was ensconced in his recliner for the afternoon. Leone bustled about the kitchen putting on the kettle.

"Don't bother with coffee, Mom," Nate was saying. "We're not staying long." Dark haired and broad shouldered, he was dressed in mountain-bike gear; reinforced padded shorts and a loose T-shirt. Angela was blond and sassy in designer jeans and a black-leather bomber jacket.

"Hey, buddy, how's dog class going?" Nate said as Marc shut the sliding door behind him. Nate had one arm draped around Angela's shoulder. After being estranged for ten years they'd recently gotten back together and to Marc's love-starved eyes they behaved like a pair of turtle doves.

"He's a smart dog but easily distracted." Marc helped himself to a piece of cake. "Going for a ride?"

"It's another competition, after he told me he quit racing," Angela complained good-naturedly.

"Just the weekly loonie race," Nate corrected her. "Hardly the World Cup."

Marc knew he was referring to the local practice of participants putting a couple of bucks into the winner's pot—the name coming from the loon on the Canadian dollar coin.

"*Loony* race, more like," Angela said. "You have to be crazy to do what you do on those bikes."

"We stopped by to see if you wanted to come and watch," Nate said.

"I don't know." Marc tended to avoid sporting events since his accident. "Where is it? I probably can't get there in my chair."

"We're going up to Mosquito Lake near Pemberton," Nate told him. "The finish line crosses a logging road so your chair won't be a problem."

"Please come," Angela urged. "I *really* need someone to talk to during the long wait before Nate whizzes by in a blur of dust."

"Well, okay," Marc agreed grudgingly. He'd been cooped up in the house all day and could use some fresh air.

"Excellent," Nate said. "Now that's settled, we have something to tell you all."

Leone paused in spooning coffee into the plunger pot and looked up hopefully. "I'm going to be a grandmother?"

Angela smiled. "Sorry, not yet. We're renewing our wedding vows."

Suddenly everyone was talking at once. Nate was telling his mother the ceremony was to be held in two weeks' time, Leone was exclaiming her congratulations and Jim had wandered into the kitchen during halftime demanding to know what all the commotion was about.

"Nate and Angela are renewing their vows," Leone told her husband in between hugging her son and daughter-in-law. "Isn't it wonderful? They haven't given us much time to plan, though." She took Angela aside. "Where are you having it? Have you got a dress? A guest list? Do you want me to make the food?"

While Leone and Angela went over details and Jim got himself a beer from the fridge and went back to the game, Marc turned to Nate. "Do you have room for one more today, possibly two?"

"Sure," Nate said. "Who are you thinking of?"

"Fiona, the barmaid at the pub, and her brother. He's a paraplegic—" Marc stopped himself before he said "too." Being temporarily crippled didn't make *him* paraplegic.

"A woman, eh?" Nate grinned. "Now you're sounding more like the Marc I used to know."

"Forget it," Marc said. "She's not my type and I'm sure not hers."

"And that's why you want to take her out. Makes

sense to me." Nate turned to his wife. "Come on, Ange. We'd better go or I'll miss the start of the race."

"Take some cake with you." Leone cut more pieces and packed them into a plastic container. "I'll make a thermos of coffee."

"Mom," Nate protested. "We'll only be gone a couple of hours. We're not going to starve out there."

"Speak for yourself," Angela said. "Thanks, Leone. I'd love it."

"Are you sure you're not…you know?" Leone cast a meaningful glance at Angela's flat stomach.

"Don't worry, you'll be the first to know—after Nate, of course." Angela embraced her mother-in-law. "I'll call you tomorrow and we can talk more about the ceremony."

"I'll begin baking right away," Leone said. "I'll do my curry puffs—everyone likes those. Maybe some crab cakes…."

They left her planning the menu and headed north to Pemberton where Marc directed them to the road outside town where Fiona and Jason lived.

"Oh, she's *that* Fiona!" Angela exclaimed when she saw the alpacas grazing in the field beside the house. "I'm knitting with wool from those animals."

When Nate pulled into the driveway the timid creatures' heads came up with a jerk and they darted away in a tight group. Slowing, they became curious and made their way over to the fence. Their long necks waved back and forth, up and down as they studied the newcomers.

"She's not expecting me." Marc suddenly wished he'd called ahead. "She probably can't come on short notice."

"I'll run in and ask her," Angela said, hopping out. "You don't mind, do you? It'll save time."

"Remember to ask for Jason, too," Marc said.

"You don't have time to look at the alpacas," Nate called out the window, correctly divining his wife's hidden agenda.

Thwarted, Angela veered back toward the house, casting a reproachful glance over her shoulder at Nate as she went up the steps beside the wheelchair ramp. Marc saw the door open and Fiona push back her bright mass of hair as she turned her gaze toward the Jeep. She looked surprised. Would she feel put on the spot?

Then the door shut and Angela ran back to the vehicle. Marc fully expected her to convey Fiona's apologies. Instead, she said, "They're coming," and went around to open the back for Jason's wheelchair.

Fiona got into the back seat first and sat beside Marc. Then Jason pulled himself in while Nate folded his chair and stowed it. With Fiona sitting next to him Marc was barely aware of the bustle of activity. He hadn't anticipated this close contact, the jostling and scrunching over. He'd never felt more handicapped than when he had to lift his legs and move them to give her more space. He wished she'd seen him when he was whole. No one had stronger legs, more upright carriage, more power in his stride.

"I should have called first," he said to break the awkward silence in the back seat as Nate turned the vehicle around and headed back to the highway. In the front seat Nate and Angela were discussing directions to the trail and a good vantage point for them to watch from.

"It's fine," Fiona said. "I like doing things on the spur of the moment."

"No you don't, Fi," Jason immediately objected. "You plan everything ahead as if it was a military operation."

"Thanks, Jase." Her throaty laughter sounded nervous. Turning to Marc, she said, "This is our date, right?"

"I was thinking more along the lines of dinner and a movie."

"But you asked me to come with you and I accepted. This is a date." She nodded, as though satisfied their excursion fulfilled all the appropriate criteria.

"A date, huh?" Smiling, Nate met Marc's gaze in the rearview mirror. "That's interesting, seeing as you're not her type."

"Who said you're not my type?" Fiona demanded.

"Am I?" Marc asked.

"No, I just wondered who said so."

"I did."

"How do you know what my type is? You barely know me." She pretended to be miffed. At least he *hoped* she was pretending. They'd ventured into new territory; bantering.

"Do you *want* me to be your type?" he asked, smiling. "Because you haven't given any indication of that so far."

"She doesn't have a type," Jason interjected. "She never goes out with anybody."

"It's not too late to take you home," Fiona said, elbowing her brother.

"Ow! But it's true."

Marc glanced at Fiona just as she turned to look at him. Their eyes met and they exchanged a small silent smile before she glanced away. This shouldn't be happening, Marc thought, his heart pounding. Sure he'd pestered her for a date but it was more out of a desire to prove he could than anything else. He was in no physical shape to start a relationship, nor did he have the emotional stability to maintain one.

Nate turned off the highway onto a gravel road and drove to the assembly point for the cyclists competing in the race. While the others waited in the car he got his bike off the roof rack then spread the map on the hood of the Jeep to show Angela.

"The finish line is here under the power lines, where the trail and the logging road intersect." Nate's words could be heard through the open window. "With level ground and good visibility it's a perfect spot to observe the last big downhill of the race." He started to don his bike helmet.

"Hang on." Angela wound her arms around his neck and kissed him, long and passionately.

"She hates it when he races," Marc said dryly.

"I can tell." Fiona seemed embarrassed at the intimate display because she tugged on her skirt which only drew Marc's attention to her bare legs.

"Look, Fi," Jason said. "There's a guy with a hand-cycle. Cool!"

Marc followed Jason's gaze. With mixed feelings he watched a young man with powerful chest and arm muscles transfer from his wheelchair to a low-slung three-wheeled bike pedaled by hand controls.

"Being in a chair doesn't mean you have to give up sport," Fiona said quietly, guessing his thoughts.

Possibly, but it would never be the same.

They watched the start of the race from the Jeep. The men set off first, a couple of hundred contestants bunched up across the wide dirt double track. By the time they were out of sight a quarter mile away around a bend in the road they were already stringing out. Nate's bright red helmet and red-and-white T-shirt were clearly visible near the front of the pack.

They waited until the women took off before Angela started the car and drove back down the winding road to the location Nate had shown her. She parked on the wide gravel shoulder at the base of a long hill where red flags were staked out to mark the finish line. "We'd better get ourselves set up quickly so we can get a good spot."

The day was partly overcast with small white clouds scudding low across the blue sky and gathering on the surrounding mountains, obscuring the peaks. Marc was glad he'd worn his warm jacket and turned the collar up against the wind.

A double row of power lines marched up the hill and beneath them a dirt track snaked through bracken and fireweed, curving up and away into the distance. Fiona suggested they move to the other side of the gravel road so Jason and Marc's vision wouldn't be obscured by other spectators. Years of living with a paraplegic had clearly made her sensitive to Jason's needs.

But for Marc, getting set up was embarrassing. He should have been out there competing instead of having two women fuss over positioning his wheelchair as if he were from a convalescent home and they were his volunteer carers taking him on an outing.

"I'm *fine*," he said testily when Fiona asked him for the third time whether he wasn't slanting forward on the gravel verge. He was, and he knew it would become uncomfortable after a while but he was damned if he wanted her maneuvering him around anymore.

"Just asking." She backed away, hands up.

"Hey, sorry. Come back here." He reached into the

bag slung off the back of his wheelchair for a plastic container. "Have a piece of my aunt's carrot cake." Fiona took a piece and Marc offered the cake around. "Jason? Angela?"

Fiona peeled the cream-cheese icing off the slice of cake. Marc thought she was worried about calories, but no, she was eating it first. As she dropped it into her mouth she cast him a glance and her innocent expression was laced with guilty pleasure. Marc laughed aloud.

"What?" Angela said, her mouth full of cake.

"Nothing." His gaze met Fiona's again. Her cheeks were suffused with pink. "Have we got enough cups for coffee?"

"Of course," Angela said, going to the Jeep for the thermos and plastic mugs. "You know Leone—she always packs for the multitudes."

"How long before the cyclists get here?" Jason asked, accepting a mug of coffee.

"Another ten or fifteen minutes," Angela said, glancing at her watch. She poured coffee for Fiona. "I'd love to hear about your alpacas. Liz told me she sourced her wool locally. I'm knitting a sweater using white cria wool. It's from one of yours, right?"

Fiona nodded. "From Snowdrop. She's a darling, just a baby, really. Cria wool is the first clipping," Fiona explained to Marc. "It's softer and finer than later clippings." She turned back to Angela, adding, "Come by and see them sometime, if you want."

"I'd love to! Do you knit?"

The women started talking knitting. Marc exchanged a manly roll of the eyes with Jason. At least he thought he had until Jason said, "I knit, too."

"I beg your pardon?" Marc asked, even though their chairs were parked not two feet away from each other.

"Our grandparents were from Scotland where it's common for men to knit," Jason explained. "My grandmother taught us but my grandfather was better at it. Well, that's what *he* says. I do socks and slippers, mostly."

"An electrical engineer who knits. Interesting." And a useful sedate hobby for a wheelchair user. Every atom in Marc's being rebelled against the image.

Jason accepted another piece of cake. "Must be rough being confined after being a top athlete," he said matter-of-factly, nodding at Marc's wheelchair. "There are special skis and snowboards for paraplegics. Or maybe you'll get a handcycle."

"I'll be snowboarding on my own two feet again, don't you worry." Marc nodded to himself in affirmation.

"Of course," Jason said politely.

"Don't you believe me, either?" Marc heard an edge to his voice but he couldn't have changed his tone if he wanted to.

"If anyone can, *you* will." Jason paused then stated simply and without emotion, "My spinal cord was completely severed. I'll never walk again."

Marc didn't know what to say, or how to speak past the blockage in his throat even if he could think of something more than a platitude. The kid had guts, more guts than Marc had, to face his future with such calm acceptance.

As if guessing what Marc was thinking, Jason shrugged. "It's not like I have any other choice."

"They're coming!" Fiona shouted suddenly.

Over the crest of the hill, around the bend, came the cyclists. The first ten or so were spread out in a long line, followed by another dozen.

"Is Nate in front? Can you see his helmet?" Angela demanded.

"I *think* it's him but he's not the only one with a red helmet." Marc strained forward, eyes squinting. "We should have brought Jim's binoculars."

Beside him, Fiona was on the balls of her feet, her hands clenched into fists. "There's something about a race that gets my blood going."

"Your killer instincts are coming out, Fi," Jason said laconically, but his unwavering gaze was also fixed on the approaching cyclists.

Halfway down the hill the double track narrowed to single track forcing the cyclists to jockey for position. From a distance the trail looked fairly smooth but clearly it wasn't. One by one the cyclists caught air flying over a large rock embedded in the trail, most landing successfully, some slewing sideways into the bushes.

"Ow, that must have hurt." Unaware she was doing so, Fiona dug her fingers into Marc's shoulder.

"No kidding." Marc glanced pointedly at her hand.

"Sorry!" She smiled sheepishly and massaged the hurt out of his shoulder. "That better?"

"A little to the right…" Marc suggested. It really wasn't fair to take advantage when she was distracted….

Fiona did as he asked. "Do you think he'll win?"

"Nate's the best," Marc said simply. "He's older than a lot of these kids but he's still the best."

Her hands paused their massage and clutched tightly again. "They're almost here. That *is* Nate in front."

Angela shrieked. "Oh, no! The guy behind is gaining."

Now the cyclists were so close the strain on their faces was visible and Marc could hear the sound of the tires singing. Nate, who'd been in front by two bicycle lengths had fallen to one, then a half. He glanced over his shoulder, saw the other cyclist and his jaw set in grim determination. Rising off the pedals he bore down, thigh muscles standing out as he put on a last spurt of effort.

Come on, Marc urged Nate silently, his own hands tightly gripping the arms of his chair. But as Nate roared past in what was a clear victory, Marc's pride in his cousin was tainted by a surge of jealousy so strong it brought a bad taste to his mouth. He wanted to participate, not sit on the sidelines.

"I'll be back." Angela ran off to find Nate.

"That was wonderful!" Fiona said, her face alive with excitement. "Thanks for bringing us, Marc. Wasn't it great, Jason?"

"Awesome!" Jason was still grinning widely.

"I told you Nate would win." Marc forced himself to smile though he felt the blackness creeping over him. He'd kept it at bay for several days, a hug from a little girl at the birthday party had briefly banished it, but now it was back, blurring his mind with darkness.

"Are you okay?" Fiona asked, a frown appearing as she studied his face.

"Sure. I'm fine." Could she see what he was feeling?

Nate approached, walking his bike, one arm linked around Angela's waist, and all attention flowed to the victor.

"Congratulations," Fiona said.

"Awesome race," Jason agreed.

"Thanks but it was nothing, honestly. Luckily it's just for fun. And a share of the pot."

"Fun or not, you like to win." Marc's voice came out oddly tight. Nate looked at him in surprise and Marc was ashamed at sounding mean-spirited. Sure, his emotions were all mixed up but he wouldn't allow himself to have bad thoughts about Nate.

"Good going, buddy," he said, reaching out to grip Nate's hand. "I mean it. You're the greatest."

Nate's face cleared. "No, *you're* the greatest." He

turned to Fiona and Jason. "You should see the trophies Marc's collected. Puts me to shame."

"I've read about your competitions. I'd love to see the trophies," Jason said excitedly. "Can we do that now?"

"I don't think Nate meant that suggestion literally, Jase." Fiona was watching Marc's face.

"Why not?" Angela said, exchanging a glance with her husband. "Instead of going to the après race get-together let's go back to Marc's house. I've never seen all his sporting trophies, either."

Great. Nate and Angela thought they were lifting his spirits by celebrating his achievements. Think again, gang. He hated the thought of everyone exclaiming over his *past* glory, admiring the man he used to be. "They're not so interesting."

"Don't be modest," Nate said. "You won the Canada Cup, the World Cup, the Commonwealth Games gold medal…the list is endless. I'll never know why you gave it all up to go chasing war stories."

"Come on, Marc," Angela said. "You've got to let us see them. If only to reduce Nate's ego to human proportions."

"Leone won't be expecting a crowd," Marc protested.

"Mom loves entertaining," Nate scoffed.

"Maybe tonight's not a good time for her," Fiona said.

"She'll be delighted," Nate insisted. "Right, Ange?"

"Guaranteed," Angela agreed.

"Come on, Fi," Jason begged. "Please."

"It's up to Marc," Fiona said quietly.

He met her eyes. *She* knew what he was feeling. Somehow that made it worse. And at the same time, bearable.

With a shrug and a fatalistic smile, he gave in. "What the hell. Let's go."

CHAPTER SEVEN

FIONA HUNG BACK as the others crowded into Marc's bedroom, gravitating toward the bookshelves packed with snowboarding and skiing trophies with the odd rock-climbing medal thrown in. She wished they hadn't invaded his private space but at the same time she was curious to learn more about the man.

Nate showed off the various awards since Marc was reluctant to do so, picking up each in turn and telling where and when Marc had won, accompanied by colorful anecdotes about a broken leg, a wild victory party, a particularly grueling competition.

"These are so cool," Jason said, turning a gold medal over his hands.

Angela touched his World Cup. "You should display them in a glass cabinet in the living room."

Marc had backed his chair against the wall at the end of his neatly made bed. "It's not that big a deal."

While the others examined the trophies, Fiona glanced around at the posters on the walls. Interspersed with shots of hotdogging snowboarders and glittering snowfields were photographic portraits of people of Middle Eastern, Asian and African extraction. Women, children, old men, young men with rifles, some in tribal dress, some in ragged Western clothes. Whatever the nationality, the focus was on their expressive faces; smiling, scowling, proud or desperate, their humanity shone through. Fiona could have looked at them for hours, especially the pictures of the children. Despite hardship and poverty their eyes shone with innocence and, unbelievably, hope.

Leone poked her head in the open door. "I'll bet you folks haven't had dinner. Would anyone like lasagna?"

"That sounds great," said Nate.

"I'll give you a hand," Angela offered.

"Thanks, but we couldn't impose on you," Fiona said.

"It's not an imposition," Leone insisted. "I always make as much as if I'm feeding three active teenage boys. Even though they've been on their own for years I can't get used to cooking for just Jim and I."

"Still…"

"Come on, Fi," Jason urged. "Why not?"

She might as well give in with good grace. This was the date that would fulfill her part of their silly bargain. She had to admit she was enjoying herself. Being part of Marc's warm family gathering felt good. At least she'd insisted on stopping off and picking up her car so Nate wouldn't have to drive them all the way back to Pemberton. "All right. Thank you."

"Wonderful," Leone said. "Dinner will be ready in twenty minutes. Come and have a drink first."

Again Fiona waited until the others had filed from the room, this time to talk to Marc alone. Gesturing to the photo portraits, she asked, "Who took these?"

"I did, to accompany interviews I did with the local people. It was kind of a sideline, when I wasn't reporting on the main events of battle. Civilians were being killed and we knew so little about them. It seemed wrong to me."

"You should write up those interviews. I bet I'm not the only person who'd love to read them."

"I've still got my notes around somewhere. I'll dig them out." He rolled his chair toward the door. "Do you want a drink?"

"In a minute." She glanced around for a chair, saw none, and after a moment's hesitation, sat on his bed. "I'm sorry we all trooped in here. You're not comfortable with this kind of attention."

"Who would be?"

"Lots of people. Nate for one. I don't know him well but it's easy to see you were right, he does like to win. There's nothing wrong with that but you're different."

"Winning's not important to me," Marc agreed. "It's the *doing* I like." He nodded at the trophies. "So you're not dazzled by gilt trinkets?"

"I'm impressed by your achievements and I don't think you should dismiss them so lightly. But I'm more interested in what you're doing now."

"Surviving."

The single word, so bleak and revealing, showed her more than anything that beneath his cynical banter he was hurting, maybe even depressed as Val had suggested. Impulsively, she reached out and squeezed his hand.

His fingers lay inert beneath hers. "I don't want your pity."

"You don't have it. You have my compassion."

He turned her hand over and stroked the palm with his fingertips. Fiona felt warmth spread through her at his caress. She knew she should remove her hand but it had been so long since she'd been touched like this. Marc glanced up and met her eyes with his impossibly blue and penetrating gaze. Heat flared in her cheeks. She tugged her hand away and got off his bed—what had she been thinking? "We should join the others."

"Was Jason telling the truth when he said you don't go out?" Marc asked, ignoring her suggestion. "It doesn't seem right, a beautiful woman like you being alone."

"I'm alone by choice," she said. "I don't have time for a social life. But I don't mind. I'm busy working and studying and taking care of Jason. The other will come."

"Meanwhile you get a little older every day. How old are you, Fiona?"

Bristling, she walked across the room. Among the

neatly arranged items on the dresser was a small bronze skiing trophy that looked older than the rest. "Not that it's any of your business, but I'm twenty-six. I'm hardly on the shelf."

"No, but you should live and love while you're young." He moved out from the wall. "You never know when something could happen to change your life."

"Too late for that," she said, unable to keep a tinge of bitter regret from her voice. "The accident that killed my parents and paralyzed Jason changed my life." She turned to him. "Who are you to offer advice to people on how to live their life? You can't even face up to the possibility you may never get out of that wheelchair."

His face lost color, his mouth became set and grim. "What are you talking about?"

She took a step toward him. "Why did you tell me you were guaranteed a full recovery when it's not at all certain?"

He held his ground, glaring up at her. "You've been talking to Val."

"At the birthday party." Fiona reached for the bronze trophy and shook it at him. "Trophies are wonderful but they're only a part of who you are. Your life isn't over just because you're in a wheelchair."

His frowning gaze on the trophy in her hands, he said, "Doctors never stick their necks out and guarantee anything. I'm telling you I'm going to walk again because *I'm* going to make it happen."

He spoke so fiercely she realized he truly believed what he was saying. Her heart was torn for him; he would need that conviction in his struggle but oh, how much deeper would be the abyss if he failed.

"I can see you don't have the same confidence in me," he said stiffly. "That's all right. Time will tell."

"Maybe you will walk again," she said, "but in the meantime don't *you* wait to start living."

Into the silence came the sound of Rowdy barking outside and Jason's laughing voice saying, "Fetch." And a second later, "Come on, boy, bring it back. Rowdy, come!"

Marc smiled and shook his head. "Obedience isn't Rowdy's strong point."

Fiona remembered the bronze skier in her hands and really looked at it for the first time. The name engraved on the brass plate said Roland Wilde 1979. "Whose is this?"

Marc wheeled over, took the trophy and replaced it carefully on the dresser. "My father's. He was the greatest skier of his generation. He gave me this trophy as a going-away present when I was five. He keeps the rest in New York."

"Keeps," Fiona repeated. "I thought you said he died."

"I said he's been *gone*. After my mother died he left me with Leone and Jim so he could pursue his skiing career."

"He's not still skiing now, surely."

"Not for years. He remarried when I was thirteen and wanted me to live with him and his new wife. By then my life was here and I didn't want to go. We fought about it, and he left. I haven't spoken to him in a very long time."

"Doesn't he visit or call?"

"He talks to Jim and Leone," Marc replied. "I have nothing to say to him."

"He's still your father." Fiona, who would give anything to have a living parent, couldn't understand how Marc could dismiss Roland so easily.

Marc's expression, already tense, turned grim. "He's a stranger to me."

"Why *did* you give up snowboarding at what must have been the peak of your career?" she asked.

Marc met her gaze steadily. "I didn't want to be like him."

And yet he kept his father's skiing trophy positioned just so between a photo of him and his cousins as teenagers and his leather-encased press pass.

"Marc, Fiona," Leone called. "Dinner's ready."

Marc's face slackened with relief. "Let's go."

FRIDAY EVENING FIONA carried a sack of mixed grain out to the barn for the alpacas and tried to mentally organize her weekend work schedule at the pub around two essays due on Monday. It wasn't easy with Jason pestering her.

"When are we going to see Marc again, do you think?" her brother asked, following her to the barn.

Some days she regretted that she'd had a concrete path paved from the house to the barn so Jason could tend to the animals when she wasn't home. "I don't know, Jase. But I wouldn't get too excited about being friends with him, okay? The guy has problems."

She would have to work a double shift since they were nearing the end of the month and the electricity bill was due. Next up would be the gas bill.

"He's just bummed about being stuck in a chair. I understand that. I could help him. Why don't you call him and ask him over for dinner again?"

Fiona slit open the burlap bag, scooped out some grain with an old yogurt container and poured it into the feed trough. "Because I don't want to," she said tightly.

"He likes you, Fi, I could tell. Don't you like him?"

Sometimes her brother could be so obtuse. It was *because* she liked Marc that she didn't want to see him again, but forget about a guy ever understanding that. Taking out another scoop, Fiona held her irritation in check. "Sure, I like him. I'm just not attracted to him. I wouldn't want him to get the wrong idea."

If she wrote an outline on her break at the pub she could flesh it out Sunday morning, leaving Sunday evening to write the second essay.

"Well, he could be *my* friend, couldn't he?" Jason asked. "*I* could invite him over."

"He's a lot older than you, Jase. He's got grown-up

things to do." Getting sloshed in the pub, for one. Though to be fair, he hadn't done that for over a week.

"I bet he'd be interested in my electronics stuff. He was asking me all about it at dinner the other night."

"He was being polite." *She would talk to her bank manager about consolidating her debts—*

"I don't think so. He said he used to rock climb with a guy who's a professor of electrical engineering."

"Don't you understand?" she rounded on him, exasperated. "Marc doesn't want a *gimp* as a friend. You'd be a constant reminder that *he's* paralyzed, too. Having you around would be like looking in a mirror and seeing his worst nightmare."

Stricken, Jason rolled backward. "I never thought of it that way," he said in a subdued voice. "He seemed so nice to me that day we watched Nate race."

"He's not cruel or anything." Not like *her*. The hurt in her brother's eyes cut her to the bone. She threw down the grain scoop and put her arms around his neck. "I'm sorry, Jase. Forgive me. That was a horrible, *awful* thing to say. I don't know what comes over me sometimes."

"Is something bothering you, Fi? You seem tense lately." Jason patted her back, looking alarmed when she drew back and there were tears in her eyes.

"No, I'm fine," she said, blinking, then let out a huge sigh. "Actually, I'm kind of stressed. I've got two essays due on Monday, a double shift at the pub tonight and all the bills seem to come at once."

"Don't we have enough money?"

"Sure, we'll be fine. Don't you worry about it."

Jason shook his head. "You treat me like a child, Fi. If we have financial problems I should know."

"What do you propose to do about it?" she said, getting exasperated again. "I keep suggesting you get a job but you won't apply."

"It's not that I don't want to work. I just don't want to work for Jeff, in Pemberton." His voice rose a notch and two spots of color stood in his cheeks. "How many times do I have to tell you that before you understand?"

Fiona planted her hands on her hips. "You don't have a lot of options."

"You're *narrowing* them for me."

"Okay, you want to know about our finances?" She picked up the grain scoop and furiously started shoveling grain into the barrel. "We'll go over our accounts together. Then you'll see what I'm talking about."

"Hello?" a woman called from outside causing Fiona to fall into abrupt silence. Her voice was familiar but not immediately identifiable. "Anybody home?"

Who was it, and had she heard them arguing? Fiona looked at Jason who shrugged, equally mystified. She walked to the barn door and looked out.

Angela Wilde waved at her from behind the gate. "I hope you don't mind me dropping over. I've been dying to get a closer look at your alpacas."

"Come on in," Fiona said, a little embarrassed. "I was just feeding them."

But if Angela had heard anything her sunny smile gave no indication as she opened the gate and came up the path in a sleek charcoal-gray pantsuit and designer shoes. "I should have gone home and changed, I know, but I was coming from work in Vancouver and I knew if I stopped I'd never get moving again."

"Don't worry, alpacas are pretty clean beasts," Fiona said. "Unlike horses and cows they don't even relieve themselves in the barn."

"How considerate of them." Angela stopped on the threshold as three delicate camel-like heads swiveled sideways on long necks to pin her with curious gazes. "Oh! Aren't they gorgeous! Hi, Jason," Angela added belatedly. "How are you?"

"Good. I had a great time watching Nate race the other day. Thanks for taking us."

"It was fun, wasn't it? Before I forget..." She dug in her purse. "Marc thought you might be interested in a handcycle so Nate checked into it for you." She handed him a folded piece of paper with models and prices. "He's not touting for business but if you decide you want one he could order it through his store and get you a better deal. He's trying to talk Marc into getting one."

"Cool! Thanks." Jason glanced up at Fiona as if to say, *see*.

Angela reached into her purse again and pulled out a small square envelope, which she gave to Fiona. "Nate and I would love you and Jason to come to our renewal-of-vows ceremony. No presents, no flowers, just a big party. It's next Saturday. Sorry about the short notice."

"Thanks. I don't know what to say…"

"Please just say you'll come. I'd like to get to know you better and if you're there, Marc won't skulk around like the Grim Reaper's stalking him."

Fiona smiled uncertainly. "Marc and I aren't—"

"Oh, I know you're not a couple," Angela cut in hastily. "But he likes you and you're good for him. Please come."

"Okay. Thanks for the invitation."

"Now, tell me all about these adorable creatures. What are their names?"

"They have registered breeder's names but I call them Ebony, Snowdrop and Papa John." Fiona didn't need any more encouragement to talk about her favorite pets. Jason, having heard it all before, excused himself to go start dinner.

Half an hour later, Fiona walked Angela back to her blue Subaru. "I'll see you in a couple of weeks."

"If not before," Angela replied. "Don't forget, I have first dibs on Ebony's next clip."

"I won't forget. I'll let Liz know, too, so she doesn't promise it to anyone else."

Three hours later, Fiona was weaving through

crowded tables with a full tray of glasses of draft beer. The Vancouver Lions were playing the Calgary Stampeders on the big-screen TV in the corner and both pool tables had customers lined up to play. Every time the door to the partitioned-off smoking section opened it let out a billow of gray smoke. Saturday afternoons started out slow then gradually built into a rip-roaring night on the town.

Fiona delivered beer, gathered empties and kept an eye on the door. Liz had promised to come by with her new boyfriend, Frederik, a skier from Switzerland who worked on Whistler Mountain. Liz had split with her husband three years earlier and Fiona hoped Liz would find happiness with Frederik.

"'Nother round over here, darlin'," Reg Turnbull, a Saturday-night regular, yelled over the noise of the jukebox, the TV and a hundred voices talking at once. Reg was a trucker with an enormous beer gut, a bushy black beard and a bad habit of grabbing her.

"Coming right up." Fiona gathered up the empty glasses and placed them on her tray before making her way back to the bar. "A dozen draft, a Moosehead and a dry cider, please, Bill," she said to the bartender who filled glasses as fast as she could bring him the empties.

Fiona shifted her weight onto one leg to rest the other one, recaptured her escaping hair in a purple scrunchie and twisted to glance at the door. A table had come free near the bar and she was hoping Liz would show up soon and claim it. The door opened. Marc wheeled through. Her hands froze on her hair. Marc didn't usually come in the evening, seeming to prefer the quiet of the afternoons.

His gaze homed in on her, catching her with her arms raised, her cheeks flushed and perspiration sticking her white blouse to her midriff. He raised a hand and she nodded in greeting.

"Your order's ready, Fiona," Bill said, placing a bottle of cider and an empty glass on her tray along with the glasses of foamy draft beer.

"Oh, uh, thanks." She balanced the heavy tray on her upraised arm and was about to move away when she noticed Marc scanning the room for a table. She caught his eye again and waved him over to the bar. "Hold this table for my friend in the wheelchair, would you, Bill?"

"He's your *friend* now, is he?" Bill said, eyebrows raised. "I thought you didn't like drunks."

"He's not a drunk, he's…troubled." She set off for Reg and his trucker pals where she started unloading glasses of beer. Just as Marc edged past, Reg reached out and grabbed her breast. She shot upright, glaring at the burly man, one arm clamped protectively over her chest.

Before she could tell him off, Marc had jammed his wheelchair between her and Reg and had a handful of Reg's flannel shirt in his fist. "Hands off!"

"Hey now," Reg chortled. "The crippled guy thinks

he can take me on." He stood up, half dragging Marc, who clung with the tenacity of a bulldog, out of his chair. Reg pushed his sleeves up his beefy forearms as if making ready to fight.

"Stop it, Reg!" Fiona cried sharply. The trucker had a mean streak and a reputation for brawling. Last year he'd broken a man's arm for accidentally tripping him on the way to the washroom. She had no doubt he was capable of beating up a disabled man. "Marc, *let go!*"

Abruptly Marc released his grip on Reg's shirt and fell back into his chair, glaring at Reg.

Fiona pushed Reg in the chest hard enough to make him stagger backward. "You're a brute. Don't you ever touch me again." She turned on Marc. "As for you! If you start a fight, you're out of here."

Shaking, she collected money from the truckers and stalked off. By the time she took more orders and returned to the bar Marc was at the table she'd saved for him, sipping a beer. She gave Bill her order and sank into a chair across from Marc. "Stay away from that guy. He would kill you as soon as look at you."

"He manhandled you," Marc said. "I won't let him."

"I can take care of myself," she said. "Or call the bouncer if Reg gets out of control."

Marc's face was stiff with fury, whether at her for refusing his help, or himself for being unable to take on Reg, she wasn't sure. She wanted to let him know she was grateful for his concern and the fact he couldn't beat someone up didn't matter to her. He'd taken trouble with his appearance tonight. Freshly shaven, new haircut, dark green suede jacket over black denim, he looked sharp.

Abandoning her resolution not to get too close, she leaned over and kissed him swiftly on the mouth. "You're crazy and brave and a bloody idiot." Then she fled, while his eyes were still wide with questions.

She kept busy after that, cruising the floor, refilling the cooler for Bill, chatting to customers. When Liz and Frederik came in, Fiona pointed out the table where Marc sat nursing his second beer.

"You don't mind sharing, do you?" Fiona said to Liz. "I won't get to talk to you at all if you're on the far side of the room."

"Are you kidding?" Liz eyed Marc with interest. "I've been dying for a chance to hear some of his war stories."

Around eleven o'clock Fiona took a short break. Getting herself a big glass of iced water she squeezed into a chair between Frederik and Marc. "Well," she said to Marc, "have Liz and Frederik exhausted you with all their questions?"

Frederik's shaved head and once-broken nose made him look a little scary until he turned on his engaging smile. "His eyewitness accounts are fascinating."

"I've relived every major skirmish in the past two years in the Middle East." Marc was scowling but by now Fiona had learned to detect variations in his bad temper and she figured at least fifty percent of it was put on, as now.

"He was just telling us about a little boy who was injured the same night he was." Liz turned back to Marc. "What happened to him?"

"I never did find out," Marc said. "He left in the ambulance before me. Anyway, enough war talk." He turned to Frederik. "I understand you work with my cousin, Aidan."

"He's a great guy but very private, *ja?*" Frederik said. "The girls, they are all over him but he doesn't care. He spends all his time on the mountain or with his daughter."

"His wife died on Whistler six years ago," Marc explained. "He never got over it."

Fiona knew the story. Aidan's wife, Charmaine, had died tragically two months after their daughter, Emily, was born, falling from the mountain during a blizzard. Aidan had managed to save his baby daughter but not Charmaine. Cruel speculation had dogged Aidan about the manner of his wife's death. Fiona, who didn't know Aidan, had never been convinced he had any part in causing it but some folk in the valley still believed he was guilty.

"I heard the rumors about that," Frederik said. "I don't believe them."

"Are you staying in Whistler long?" Fiona asked,

knowing this was a burning question in Liz's mind but that she didn't want to ask Frederik for fear of pressuring him.

"I want very much to get a job on the ski patrol. Whistler is a skier's paradise but there are attractions even greater than the mountains." He glanced at Liz, who dimpled and slid her hand into his under the table. He joked to Marc, "Maybe you put in a good word for me with your cousin."

"I'll see what I can do," Marc promised.

"While you're at it, use your powers of persuasion to help me convince Fiona to go on a girls' night out," Liz said.

"I don't know about that," Fiona said. "Jason—"

"Come on, Fi," Liz complained. "Not Jason again."

"If Jason's at a loose end I'd be glad to spend some time with him," Marc said.

"But—" Fiona sputtered.

"Jason needs guy friends to hang out with, right?" Marc's tone challenged her to deny it.

Reluctantly, she nodded.

"Then it's settled." Marc glanced at his watch. "Time has passed quickly for once. The taxi I ordered should be outside. Nice to meet you, Liz, Frederik." He met Fiona's eyes, briefly touched her hand. "See you later."

Fiona watched him weave his way through the pub to the exit.

"He's a really nice guy," Liz said.

Fiona nodded. That, not his attitude, was turning out to be the problem.

CHAPTER EIGHT

ALTHOUGH IT WAS NEARLY noon, Marc lay in bed, brooding on fate and wondering for the millionth time what *had* happened to the little Syrian boy. He hadn't mentioned to Liz and Frederik that he'd gone back to help the injured boy minutes before the bomb exploded. If he hadn't heard his cry for help, if he'd ignored it, Marc wouldn't be lying here unable to move his legs.

If he could go back and do things differently, would he? No, he honestly could say he would not. Knowing that didn't make his present situation any easier to handle.

He found himself thinking, too, about Fiona. How tired she looked near the end of a shift. Sometimes she must have to get up and teach the next day. Yet she never complained, was always cheerful. She wasn't the kind of woman he'd been attracted to before his accident; he would have thought her too small-town. But that was because he wouldn't have bothered getting to know her. Now that circumstances allowed him to do that, he wasn't in any shape to attract her.

Ah, who cared anyway?

A cold moist nose nuzzled his hand hanging over the side of the bed.

"What the—?" He pushed at the dog's muzzle. "Go away, Rowdy." The darn dog was always there, wanting affection or trying to give it. He'd attached himself to Marc with the devotion and expectations of a faithful servant.

Rowdy licked his hand then stood with his paws on the bed, ears pricked, hoping to be invited up.

"Forget it," Marc growled. "Go away."

Rowdy subsided to the floor with his nose on his paws, waiting and watching for Marc's next move. Marc looked away; he couldn't even satisfy a dog's emotional needs.

There was a time when he'd given of himself freely—affection, money, time, whatever another needed—his pockets were deep, his heart was large and time meant nothing, unless he had a plane to catch.

Now he felt empty, as though he had nothing anyone would want or need. Worse, he didn't care. All he craved was to be left alone.

There was a knock at the door. "Marc, are you awake?" Leone called.

He groaned silently. "Yes?"

The door opened and his aunt entered, going straight to the window to open the curtains. "It's so dark in here. I don't know how you can stand it."

Marc put an arm over his eyes, shutting out the sudden light. "I like it."

"Well, you'd better get up. You're due at the library in less than an hour." She bustled around the room, picking up his dirty socks and underwear.

"Stop, Leone, I'll do that." He dragged himself to a half-sitting position propped up on his elbows. "What's this about the library?"

Leone paused, her arms full of dirty clothes. "I found just the thing for you with your wonderful voice. It'll give you something to do besides go to the pub, and get you out of the house besides."

"Oh, no, you didn't…" he began.

"I volunteered you to read to the seniors. I was renewing your library books and got chatting with Naomi—she's the librarian, you know."

"I know. She already asked me and I refused." His aunt meant well but this was too much. The worst of it was, he couldn't get mad at her.

Leone's green eyes widened. "So that's why she was surprised and asked me if I was sure you'd want to. I assured her you would."

"Sorry, I won't." He slid back into the pillows and shut his eyes.

The next thing he knew, the covers were being dragged from his bed, leaving his naked body exposed to his aunt's furious gaze.

"What are you doing?" he demanded, trying to cover himself with his hands.

"Oh, don't bother. I've bathed you as a little boy and

as a man. You get up out of that bed and get down to the library. There's no earthly reason you can't help out at least for today. Naomi is desperate—her regular reader can't make it and there's no time to let people know."

"Oh, all right. But just this once, and only because you gave your word."

Forty minutes later Leone was dropping him off at the library. "Give me a call on my cell phone when you want a ride home."

"Okay." He paused. "Thanks, Leone, for driving me around and for everything. I know I'm a pain in the butt sometimes, but I appreciate all you do for me."

Leone smiled and gave him a hug. "Marc, darling, you're one of my boys." She hesitated, her hand resting on his shoulder, and added gently, "Your father called again, asking about you. Why don't you phone him? He's worried and he'd sure like to hear from you."

"Maybe," Marc said, with no intention of following through. "See you later."

He rolled through the automatic doors and toward Naomi Cameron at the central desk. When she saw him she broke into a wide smile. "Marc! Thank you so much for coming. When your aunt offered your services I was so grateful. Our seniors are looking forward to meeting you. Come right over."

Marc followed her to a section of the room where a group of older people were seated in chairs arranged in a semicircle facing a lectern. Most were women but there were a handful of men.

"This is Marc Wilde, the TV reporter," Naomi gushed to the assembled group. "He's going to read."

The chorus of oohs and aahs that greeted this announcement reminded Marc why he'd shied away from volunteering in the first place. He wasn't after hero worship and he wasn't somebody these people should look up to. He'd simply done his job while satisfying a thirst for adventure.

"Please," he said when they broke into spontaneous applause. "That's really not necessary."

From the corner of his eye he caught sight of glowing hair and a pair of trim legs. Fiona. He turned to see her heading to the study carrels, her arms loaded down with books. She paused when she saw him, her gaze taking in the hardcover book Naomi had placed in his hands and the rows of seniors waiting expectantly. A brilliant smile lit her face before she ducked into a carrel.

"I'll leave you to it," Naomi said and hurried away before he could change his mind.

Buoyed by his glimpse of Fiona, Marc wheeled to face the rows of expectant faces. "Good morning."

Excited murmurs erupted among the female members of his audience.

"Doesn't he have a wonderful voice?"

"What *blue* eyes."

Marc pressed his hands down on the arms of his

chair, shifting uncomfortably. He glanced at the cover of the tome in his lap. "What are we reading?"

"We started a new book last week," said a sprightly white-haired lady in the first row with a Scottish accent. "*Outlander,* by Diana Gabaldon."

Marc recognized the title as one his aunt had read. She'd remarked more than once on the frequent and explicit love scenes. He was supposed to read this aloud, in public? What had he gotten himself into? "Isn't it a romance?"

"It's a bit of everything—romance, history, time travel," the Scottish woman informed him. "The hero is a lusty highlander." With a knowing glance she nudged her neighbor, a small quiet woman, who giggled then pressed her lips together.

"It's a wonderful story," another woman said enthusiastically from the back row. "I've read it twice."

"In that case, maybe you'd like to hear a different book?" Marc suggested, looking to the few men in the audience for support.

"Oh, no," everyone chorused.

Resigned, Marc opened the book and started reading from where the previous volunteer had left off. Just his luck; he started with a love scene, loaded with graphic and emotive descriptions of the hero and heroine's sexual encounter. His deep clear voice seemed to boom in the quiet room. In the pauses between words he could hear the scratch of Fiona's pen on paper in the study cubicle. Knowing she was listening to him increased his discomfort tenfold. Within seconds he felt his cheeks begin to grow warm. He paused and glanced up.

"Carry on," the Scottish lady urged. "You're just getting to the really good bit."

A stifled giggle came from behind the wall of the study cubicle. Groaning inwardly Marc cleared his throat and soldiered on. Finally Naomi was at his side, waiting for him to finish a paragraph. "You'll have to leave it there," she said. "I let you go on longer than usual because everyone seemed to be having such a good time. Will you be back next week?"

"No, I—" Marc began.

"Please come back," said the quiet woman in the front row. It was the first time she'd spoken and her cheeks went pink with self-consciousness. "It's such a pleasure to listen to you read."

Hearing that made him feel good inside in ways he wouldn't have expected. Still Marc hesitated about committing himself. "I'll read until you can find someone else," he said to Naomi. "I'm only in town temporarily, remember?"

"Of course." She turned to the seniors. "Let's thank Mr. Wilde for a wonderful session." And they all broke into applause again.

"Thank you," Marc murmured, wishing they wouldn't. He glanced covertly at his watch; it was past one o'clock but Fiona's brown-and-cream sweater was still hanging off the back of her chair. Maybe she'd be ready for a break and have coffee with him.

But he wasn't allowed to get away that easily. The Scottish woman stayed behind to thank him personally for reading and an upright gentleman with thick white hair and a hawklike nose reminisced about his World War II experiences. Another half hour passed before Marc could politely bid him farewell.

He wheeled over to Fiona's carrel. She was gone. More disappointed than he cared to admit, he made his way to the exit. He was fishing in his pocket for his cell phone when he heard his name called. Fiona was sitting on a bench waiting for him.

"You're still here," he said, trying not to show how pleased he was.

Her red-gold cloud of hair glinted in the sun and her eyes were protected behind tortoiseshell sunglasses. "I wanted to say how impressed I was that you volunteered your time to the seniors."

"Leone's responsible for this good deed, I'm afraid." He nodded at the books stacked beside her. "Do you always study in the library?"

"Sometimes," she said. "Jason likes to play his music loud when he's working on his electronics, as he is today, and I hate always putting a damper on him. Besides, there are fewer distractions here." She chuckled. "Usually."

Marc shook his head. "That book was a bit risqué for

reading aloud, but you know seniors and their dirty minds."

Fiona laughed aloud. "They loved it. You were great. Leone may have set you up for it but you carried through. You didn't have to."

Marc arched one eyebrow. "You don't know Leone."

Fiona put her purse over her shoulder and gathered her stack of books in her arms. "Want to get a coffee?"

Virtue is supposed to be its own reward, but Marc would choose Fiona's company any day. "There's an outdoor café in the Village Square that serves carrot cake almost as good as my aunt's."

Marc lifted his face to the sky as they strolled through the pedestrian walkways on this gorgeous autumn day. The maples in planters had turned yellow and orange, and the sun was cool and bright in a cloudless sky. The scents of charcoal grill and fresh coffee drifted tantalizingly on the crisp air.

The fall was prime time for mountain biking and their path was crossed more than a few times by bikers heading for the Valley Trail or up to the end of the village where the ski lift would carry them to the multitude of trails in the bike park.

"Thanks for that information on handcycles," Fiona said. "I'm going to save up for one for Jason for Christmas. Are you getting one?"

"What's the point?" Marc asked. "I'll no sooner get it than I won't need it anymore."

"Right." Her forehead puckered with concern. "Oh, Marc, have you thought at all about what you'll do if you don't walk again?"

Marc watched a couple of young guys clump by in ski boots carrying snowboards under their arms, undoubtedly heading up the lift to Blackcomb glacier. He had to shut his eyes, quelling a surge of longing and resentment. Even in paradise, with a princess at his side, the blackness was never far away. He thought of his vials of pills, hidden at the back of his middle drawer. "I've got contingency plans."

She paused to rest her hand on his shoulder and her smile blossomed. "I'm really glad to hear that."

Her smile was a wonder of nature, like a perfect rose or a beautiful sunset, Marc thought, thankful he wasn't dead yet. "Nate's bike race wasn't much of a date," he said. "Can we try again?"

"You *did* do a good deed for Jilly's birthday," she admitted. "Angela and Nate's vow-renewal ceremony is this weekend—"

"We can't count that." Marc didn't want to waste a date sharing her for the evening with a hundred others.

"Okay, but my girls' night with Liz is the following Saturday."

"Which I'll be spending with Jason."

"Right. How about the week after that?"

It seemed a long way off but at least he had a goal and something to look forward to. "Great."

NATE AND ANGELA renewed their commitment to each other and their marriage in a moving church ceremony. Their vows, which they'd written themselves, recounted how they'd married young then spent ten years apart before finally admitting they still loved each other.

Afterward they invited everyone to the church hall for the reception. Nate, sharply dressed in a dark gray suit, greeted their guests. Angela, standing next to him, was radiant in a short ivory linen dress.

"You look marvelous," Fiona said, greeting Angela with a kiss on both cheeks. "And Nate looks as proud as a peacock."

Angela glanced around. "Where's Jason?"

"He sends his apologies. His best friend is in town unexpectedly and, well, you know teenagers."

"I understand." Angela's French polished nails brushed Fiona's elegant lacy wrap of fine gray wool. "Is that alpaca? It's gorgeous."

"This is cria wool that Liz spun and knit for me." Soft and warm, the wrap made a welcome layer over her lavender-colored sleeveless dress on this cooler than expected last day of September. Fiona glanced at the backlog of guests trying to enter the hall. "I'd better let you go."

"Talk to you later," Angela said. "Look for your name card when it's time to eat. You're next to the head table."

Fiona moved along to congratulate Nate, then

paused to say a few words to Jim and Leone. Over Jim's shoulder she could see Marc a few yards away looking very handsome in a dark brown suit and tie. He kept glancing her way as if he was impatient to talk to her.

Part of her wanted to go right over but she felt oddly nervous, too. Their relationship had changed subtly since they had coffee together in the Village. She was seeing him not as a bar patron or even a friend; she was seeing him as a man. Agreeing to a date, a *real* date, had sparked the transformation.

Was she ready for this? Was he?

Anticipation and trepidation fizzed in her veins like the champagne she plucked off the tray of a passing waiter.

Jim spoke, regaining her attention, to introduce her to Angela's sister, Janice, and Janice's husband, Bob.

"Our son, Ricky, is here somewhere," Janice said, glancing around in vain. "Angela was in Whistler to baby-sit him while we were on holiday when she got back together with Nate."

"Janice takes full credit for their reunion," said Bob, a lanky man with brown hair and lightly pockmarked skin. "Even though she wasn't even here at the time."

"I knew when I asked her to take care of Ricky she'd be bound to run into Nate," Janice said indignantly. "I set them up and let nature take its course."

"Yes, dear," Bob said, with a smile. "Nate and Angela themselves had nothing to do with it."

Fiona laughed. "I'll let you two sort it out. Nice meeting you both."

She drifted away from the reception line and glanced around for Marc but she'd lost sight of him. She moved through the crowded hall, chatting in passing to the guests she knew, mostly parents of the children in classes she occasionally taught. A waiter circulated with a tray of hot hors d'oeuvres. Fiona took a bite of a curry puff and heard a distinctive voice from behind her.

"Leone made all the appetizers," Marc said, taking two and a paper napkin. "She wanted to tackle dinner, as well, but Nate and Angela convinced her that with over a hundred guests they had to hire a catering firm."

"She's really something," Fiona said. "My mom wasn't much of a cook but she loved to sew." She smiled, remembering little things—a favorite home-made dress, her mother's red-gold head bent over the humming machine.

"You must miss her, and your dad," Marc said quietly.

"Yes." She blinked away the beginnings of tears. "Weddings always make me emotional. It's seeing families so happy together." She paused. "Was your father invited?"

Marc glanced away. "He couldn't make it. His daughter just had a baby."

"That's wonderful," Fiona exclaimed. "You'll be an uncle. Was it a boy or a girl? What's it called?"

"A boy." He shook his head as he added, "They named him Marcus."

"Oh, Marc! You have to contact your father now."

"I don't *have* to do anything," he replied stubbornly. "It's also Roland's middle name, after his father."

Someone tapped on a microphone and the sound of static and feedback drew everyone's focus to the small raised dais near the head table at the front of the room.

"Could everyone please find their places?" Jim said into the microphone. "Dinner will be served shortly."

"I suppose you're with the head table," Fiona said preparing to part. "I'll talk to you later."

He gave her an odd smile. "Sure."

She made her way to the table nearest the dais and began hunting for a place card with her name. Marc, she noticed, had followed her. "Aren't you sitting with your family?"

"There's no ramp up to the dais so Angela placed me at this table." He wheeled his chair into the gap between two chairs and glanced at the cards on either side of his. "Here you are, right next to me."

No ramp, huh? Fiona was certain Nate and Aidan would lift Marc bodily to sit with the family—unless Marc himself had asked to be seated with her.

Kerry Martin, an attractive divorcée whose son Fiona sometimes taught sat on the other side of Marc. "Hi, Fiona. Nice to see you again. Tim always loves it when he gets you as a substitute."

"How *is* Tim?" Fiona asked.

Before Kerry could reply, they were distracted by the arrival of Rachel, who managed Nate's Vancouver bike store, and her boyfriend, Dean. Denise, editorial director at the women's magazine where Angela worked in marketing, took the remaining empty seat.

"You lucked out tonight, buddy," Dean said to Marc, with a knowing nod at the three women ranged around him.

Fiona nudged Marc. "Lucky—that's your middle name, remember?"

He smiled at her. "Yeah, sometimes I do get lucky."

Ribald laughter greeted his comment which sparked a succession of double entendres, each more groanworthy than the last. Fiona watched Marc banter and flirt, his blue eyes twinkling with good humor. He amused Rachel and Dean and charmed Kerry and Denise—herself, as well, to be honest. Tonight Marc seemed a much different man to the drunk who'd done a face plant in the pub. If this was what he was like before his accident she wouldn't have stood a chance at resisting him. Then again, he probably wouldn't have noticed a sheltered schoolteacher. In a sense, his being in a wheelchair had brought them together.

After dinner Nate rose and thanked everyone for coming and promised there would be no speeches. He gazed adoringly down at his wife. "Let me simply say how happy I am that Angela has come home. This time

I won't let her run away—" he grinned "—no matter how crazy she makes me."

Laughter rippled through the hall. Spoons set wine-glasses ringing until Angela stood up and the couple obliged with a prolonged kiss.

Watching them, Fiona rejoiced in their happiness but also felt a strong stab of envy for a love so deep and strong it could survive even ten years separation. Maybe soon Angela would become pregnant and their love would expand to include a baby. Fiona wanted to teach and to travel but she also wanted a family of her own. Marc was right. While she was struggling to create a better future for her and Jason, life was passing her by.

During dinner, a band had set up in the far corner. As the strains of a waltz began, Nate and Angela moved onto the dance floor. They glided around the room, their gazes locked.

"They look wonderful together," Fiona said.

"Yeah," Marc muttered.

Fiona glanced at him, surprised at his unenthusiastic response. His mood had taken an abrupt nosedive. He wasn't even watching Nate and Angela; he was shredding a paper napkin with his fork.

"What's wrong?" she asked.

"Nothing." He managed a smile but it was forced.

The band switched to a livelier tune and Fiona's foot started tapping. A man at the next table met her eye hopefully but her gaze turned to Marc. "Would you—?"

"No." He tossed down his fork and moved back from the table. "I'm going to mingle."

Fiona felt as though she'd been slapped in the face. Then she realized he probably felt self-conscious about being on the dance floor in a wheelchair.

Someone touched her shoulder. The man from the next table. "Would you like to dance?"

"Thanks, I would." Just because Marc wouldn't dance didn't mean she had to stay on the sidelines.

After that, Fiona was rarely off the dance floor yet always she was conscious of Marc watching her even as he chatted to his family and friends. Every now and then their eyes would connect but he would look away.

It was midnight before she decided that if he wasn't going to get over himself, she would have to make him. He was at another table, temporarily alone when she walked up to him and held out her hand. "Let's dance."

Marc's mouth twisted up in a grimace. "You must be mistaking me for someone with legs in working order."

"Come on, silly." She grabbed his hands in both of hers and pulled him onto the dance floor.

"Now what?" he demanded, an angry flush climbing his cheeks as she moved to the music in front of him. He sat in his wheelchair, stolid and still.

Fiona was half regretting her impulsive decision but

she couldn't let him slink off the dance floor now. Everyone was watching and he'd end up more embarrassed than he already was. "You've got arms. Use them."

"Good idea." He jerked his chair around and started to push away.

"Marc, don't."

He stopped, his back to her. Even then she thought he would roll off the dance floor and leave her there. Abruptly he wrenched his chair and clumsily attempted to move in time to the music.

"That's it," she encouraged him.

Gradually Marc's actions became more coordinated and his scowl gave way to a smile. Just when he seemed to be enjoying himself, the music sped up and became difficult for him to move to. Determined not to let him leave, Fiona grabbed the handles at the back of his chair and turned in a tight circle, swinging him around.

Marc threw his head back and smiled up at her. "You're making me dizzy."

"Me, too." She stopped spinning and wobbled lightheadedly on her high heels. The wheelchair bumped into her thigh and she toppled sideways.

His arms went around her, pulling her into his lap. "Gotcha."

Fiona put her hands on Marc's shoulders and struggled to right herself. He clamped an arm around her waist, holding her close. "I thought you wanted to dance?"

"Yes, but—" She glanced around. The band had segued to a slow romantic number. Couples had moved closer, the lights had dimmed. "This is…" *Intimate*.

"Nice," he supplied. "This is *nice*." He took her hand and held it up and out, speaking against her temple in a voice that vibrated through her slight frame to hum in her breastbone. "Close your eyes. Make believe we're really dancing."

Hesitantly she rested her cheek against his, holding herself rigid to reduce the amount of contact. Before long the seductive warmth of his body caused her to slowly melt.

"It's okay, Fiona." He moved his hand over her back in slow circles. "The world won't come to a halt because you take a moment to relax."

She *was* tense. How long had it been since she'd been held by a man? Too long, as Liz was constantly telling her and as she knew herself in her heart of hearts. Willing her body to soften, she looped her arms around him and sank into his chest with her face pressed into the warm angle of his neck. With each breath she inhaled a little of him, with each heartbeat she melded closer. She was hungry for a man's touch, yes, but not just any man. *Marc's* arms were where she wanted to be.

She didn't notice they'd stopped moving until Marc turned his head and she was looking directly into dark pupils ringed with cobalt. She didn't realize she'd stopped breathing until he touched his lips to hers, releasing a sigh that came from deep within.

With that featherlight kiss, lights, flowers and colorful dresses disappeared in the darkness behind her closed eyelids. Then he deepened the kiss and music, conversation and laughter faded until all she could hear was the thrumming of her heart. Tenderness and passion fused into a single sensation that she'd been missing all her life.

Marc drew back and searched her eyes. "That wasn't so hard, was it?"

"It was…nice," she teased. Resting a hand on his perspiration-dampened shirt, she was conscious of a new familiarity between them, as real and tangible as Marc's rock-hard chest and beating heart. Val's warning flashed through her mind but she pushed it away. How could something that felt so right, go wrong?

The music stopped for the DJ to take a break. The lights came on. Couples started leaving the dance floor, glancing at them in passing and smiling.

"Let me go," she whispered, suddenly aware of how conspicuous they were. She blushed to recall how she'd kissed him in front of all these people. In front of his family.

"Why are you in such a hurry to get away from me?"

"I must be crushing you." Any excuse would do.

"A little thing like you? I don't think so, besides…" His smile faded. His arms loosened their hold. "I can't feel a thing below my waist."

She could have kicked herself for inadvertently drawing attention to his handicap. Knowing how sensitive a guy's ego could be she wanted to reassure him that in her eyes at least he was all man.

"What is it?" he growled.

Staring into his set face she realized the last thing he wanted was to have to be reassured. What he wanted was not to be handicapped. She couldn't give him that but she could say what was in her heart.

"Your kiss—" her voice softened dreamily. "—was the best I've ever had."

His slow sexy smile goosed her heart rate. "You weren't so bad yourself."

CHAPTER NINE

"I'VE GOT MY CELL PHONE with me so if you or Jason need anything just call," Fiona finished after explaining where she was going and how long she'd be.

Marc attempted to listen but his mind was buzzing at Fiona's astonishing transformation. Gone was the prim schoolteacher and in her place was a sex pot. She'd piled her hair on top of her head and wore a strapless dress in a dark purple fabric that deepened the slate-green of her eyes. Across her shoulders and chest she'd applied iridescent body powder, which sparkled and glistened like new snow. As if he were on the sweetest downhill run of his life, Marc's gaze descended the sloping curve of her neck to her bare shoulders before switching back, up and over her collarbone only to change course again to skim the mound of first one breast then the other.

"Marc? Did you hear what I just said?" Fiona asked.

He started guiltily. "Pardon?"

"I said, I'll come by on my way home to pick up Jason. Will eleven o'clock be too late?"

"Stay out as long as you want," he replied, just to torture himself. Between her teaching and her school work he'd hardly seen her all week. But he'd been thinking about her, imagining what it would be like to do more than kiss. Now that she stood before him, doubts and questions crowded his mind.

Who was she dressing up for? She didn't have a boyfriend. Was she hoping to find one tonight? She didn't seem like the type to pick up guys in bars, but who knew? How could she kiss him the way she had and then go looking for someone else? Had he sparked her desire and now she wanted a real man to satisfy her?

"What are you two going to do?" she asked.

Straight-faced, Marc said, "I bought a case of Wild Turkey and hired a couple of strippers."

She smiled. "You're a very bad liar."

"My aunt and uncle are at a golf-club dinner and dance," Marc explained. "Jason and I'll order pizza and watch some DVDs." Turning to the teenager he added, "Sound okay to you?"

"Fine," Jason said happily. "Anything's good, really."

Marc invited Jason to check out the DVDs on the living-room coffee table while he saw Fiona out.

"Don't worry," Marc said when she hovered on the step, looking over his shoulder to where Jason was out of sight in the living room. "We're big boys. We can take care of ourselves."

"I'm sorry. I've been responsible for Jason so long I just can't help being protective."

"Overprotective. We're two guys in wheelchairs. How much trouble can we get into?"

"Of course. I'm being silly."

"You, on the other hand," he said, dropping his voice to a husky murmur, "need to be careful when you go on the town looking like every man's wildest dream."

"Do you really think so?" She unconsciously shifted her hips in a manner which to Marc, seeing it at eye level, seemed highly provocative.

"Enough to make me wish there was no such thing as a girls' night out," he growled.

Her cheeks bloomed pink. "Stop it." Standing straight, she said, "Thank you for asking Jason over. He's been looking forward to tonight all week."

"It's nothing. I've looked forward to it, too."

"Nevertheless, you're very sweet." She hesitated then leaned over and touched her lips lightly to his.

Her faint floral scent suffused his nostrils and he lifted a hand to her cheek. His fingertips slid away as she stepped back a pace, her cheeks a deeper pink.

"I…I'll see you later," she said, looking everywhere but at him.

"Don't go all shy on me, Fiona." He smiled, trying to hold her gaze by sheer force of will.

She laughed nervously and glanced at her watch.

"Liz is going to send out a posse if I'm not at her house within ten minutes."

Marc watched her run down the steps. A burning hunger hollowed his gut like he hadn't felt since before the explosion had hurled him against the brick wall. Fiona's delicate sensuality created vivid images in his mind of physical love that had him craving her in a way that fantasy alone couldn't satisfy.

One glance at his lifeless legs and the blackness blotted out any idea of himself and Fiona together, bringing him crashing back to reality. Memory and imagination were his only playmates in bed now.

With a frustrated groan he spun his wheelchair around and moved toward the kitchen. As he passed the living room he paused to call to Jason, "I'm going to order the pizza. Want a beer?"

Jason's head swiveled around, eyebrows riding high beneath the shock of reddish hair. "Cool!"

Marc brought out a six-pack and tossed one to Jason. "Got a movie picked out?"

Jason handed him the latest action-thriller release to insert into the DVD player and popped the tab on the can of Labatt's Blue. "Fiona wouldn't like me drinking. I'm underage."

Marc put the DVD in the player and moved back to his place. "She keeps a pretty close eye on you, doesn't she?"

"We take care of each other," Jason said defensively.

"I'm all she's got, and vice versa, if you don't count our grandparents. And you can't, because they live thousands of miles away in northern Manitoba."

Marc pressed the play button on the DVD and settled back to watch. But again his mind was elsewhere, roving over the nightspots of Whistler trying to figure out where Fiona and Liz would have gone. If he couldn't have her, he didn't want anyone else to. He was jealous, no two ways about it.

The pizza took over an hour to arrive, slow even by Whistler standards where the high tourist population meant restaurants and takeouts were chronically overloaded. By then they'd polished off two beers each and were well into their third.

Jason drained the last of his Labatt's. "Got any more?"

"You want to learn to pace yourself," Marc warned. "Especially if you're not used to drinking." Even he could feel the effects of the alcohol.

"You can't eat pizza without beer," Jason said, as if he had beer and pizza every Saturday night.

Marc debated with himself, feeling a slight qualm about leading the young man astray. Ah, what the hell. Let the kid live a little. It wasn't as though either of them was driving anywhere. He brought out another six-pack.

Jason held the fresh can of beer at an angle and popped the tab. Foam spilled over the edge of the can and onto his pants. Giggling, he mopped it up with a paper napkin. Marc winced. Jason was tipsier than he thought.

The movie built to a dramatic finale, culminating in a chase that destroyed enough cars to fill a dealership parking lot. In the reflection of the TV screen Jason's eyes shone brighter with each explosive collision.

"Do you ever think about getting your license?" Marc asked when the movie was over and he'd switched the DVD player off.

"I wish. But Fiona's workin' hard jus' to keep a roof over our heads," he said, slurring his words slightly. "Another car, 'specially one fitted with hand controls'd cost too much."

"A man needs his independence." Marc set his beer can on the table with an unexpected bang. He was a bit tipsy himself. "Get a job. Buy the car yourself."

"I dunno. Don't think Fi would want me drivin'."

"*I'll* help you." Marc picked up his beer again and tilted the can at Jason. "But you gotta promise you'll never drink and drive."

Jason nodded solemnly and held up a hand as if swearing an oath. "I promise." He sipped his beer, belched and confided, "I kinda had a problem riding in cars for a coupla years after the accident but I'm okay now."

"I know what you mean," Marc said. "For months I couldn't go *near* a brick wall." Jason regarded him blankly. "Sorry," Marc said. "Lousy joke."

"Oh, I get it." Jason laughed belatedly. "I don't mind when *you* make wheelchair jokes because you're in the same position."

"I've walked a mile in your shoes," Marc agreed.

Jason groaned. "Quit while you're ahead."

"At least with the bomb explosion I didn't know what hit me until it was too late. Did you see the logging truck coming at you?" Jason didn't say anything. "Sorry," Marc said again. "Don't mean to bring up bad memories."

"It's okay. My psychologist told me it was good to talk through my feelings. You know, get out all the grief and anger."

"Anger? Toward the logging-truck driver or your dad?"

"Why my dad?" Jason asked, frowning.

"Because he was driving and you ended up a paraplegic." Anger toward his own father made him grip his half-empty can enough to dent it. Accidents happen. That's what everyone said but some accidents were preventable. His mother might be alive today if his dad had been more concerned with his family and less with making the World Championships.

Intent on his own thoughts he didn't notice Jason hadn't replied until he glanced up. The young man's face was unusually pale. "Jason? What is it?"

"Dad wasn't driving that night. Fiona was."

"Fiona!" Marc shook his head and stared. The information would not compute.

"We were coming back from Squamish after visiting family friends. Dad had a few drinks with dinner and didn't want to drive. Mom was tired. So they let Fiona drive." Jason's hands clenched into fists on his thighs. "She'd just got her license six months earlier. She wasn't used to driving at night."

Marc's heart swelled in sympathy and horror. Fiona'd been driving the car that killed her parents, paralyzed her brother and she'd walked away with barely a scratch. His shoulders sagged just thinking of the huge burden of guilt she must carry.

"It wasn't her fault," Jason added quickly. "The RCMP highway patrol said so at the time, and the accident investigation confirmed it. Don't tell her I told you, okay? She feels so bad about it, I know she'd hate for you to know."

"I won't, I promise."

Jason unclenched his hands and watched the blood flow back into the skin of his palms. "That's why when she gets anal about taking care of me I understand and try not to mind too much."

Marc digested that in silence. "But if you were more independent maybe she wouldn't feel so guilty."

"I suppose that might be true," Jason said slowly, obviously not having thought of that before.

"Of course it's true. You shouldn't let what happened eight years ago stop either of you from going after what you want out of life."

"I want a career in electronics engineering. She wants everything—to travel, teach, marriage, children."

"You can bet she's not going to go off and leave you. *You've* got to be the one to make the change," Marc said. "You've been marking time ever since high school finished, trying to figure out when your life will begin. It's time to take action. Seize independence instead of waiting for it to be given to you."

Jason sat up straighter, leaned forward. "How?"

"Enroll in university. Don't wait for spring, do it now." The beer made him expansive, prone to wild gestures. "Buy a car. Roll, don't crawl to the nearest driver-instruction center for disabled drivers. Find a job, any job, so you can afford to get your own apartment."

Jason, who'd been listening wide-eyed to Marc's impassioned speech, abruptly became uncertain. "My own apartment?"

"Why not?" Marc demanded. "How can you cultivate a love life with your sister sleeping in the next room?"

Jason blushed. "I don't have a love life."

"Exactly my point!" Marc declared. "And how can your sister have a love life if she's playing nursemaid?"

"She always says she doesn't mind…."

Marc eyed him. "Do you really believe that?"

"I guess not. So I'd be doing her a favor by getting out of her hair," he added thoughtfully.

"You'd be growing up."

More than anything else, that captured Jason's attention. His chest puffed out. "I'm eighteen. I'm almost a man."

The doorbell rang.

"Who could that be?" Marc glanced at his watch as he went to answer the door. "It's only ten-thirty."

Fiona stood on the doorstep, looking rather glum for someone who was supposed to be on a fun night out.

"What happened?" Marc rolled backward so she could enter.

"What *didn't* happen, is more to the point," she said, stepping inside. "First Liz's car broke down, then her daughter got sick and Liz had to go home. I would have hung out with her but *she* started feeling ill, as well." Fiona felt the glands under her jaw. "I hope I'm not coming down with something."

She paused on the threshold of the living room. Her jaw went slack as she took in the pizza box on the floor and the coffee table strewn with empty tins. Her shocked gaze came to a halt on Jason. "What have you been up to?" Before he could answer, she turned on Marc. "What are you doing giving my brother beer? He's barely eighteen."

"A not unusual age for young men to experiment with moderate amounts of alcohol under the supervision of an adult in a safe environment," Marc said with what he thought was impressive dignity. Then he spoiled the effect by hiccuping.

Jason giggled.

Fiona emitted a small scream of rage. "You call yourself an adult!"

Jason quelled his glee and succeeded in emulating Marc's lofty tones. "Fi, I've decided I'm not waiting any longer before I start university. I'm going to learn to drive and find an apartment in Vancouver. It's time I was more independent."

"Learn to drive? Apartment?" Fiona turned on Marc. "You've filled his head with fantasies. These things all cost money…money we don't have."

"Oh yeah," Jason added. "I'm gonna get a job, too."

"I tried to persuade you to ask Jeff at Electronics Shop for a job but you won't even consider it." Fiona's gaze returned to the coffee table, counting cans. "If you drank half, that's a lot of liquid," she said to Jason. "Have you used your catheter lately?"

"For cripe's sake, Fiona." Jason turned beet-red.

"Well, *have* you?" she insisted on knowing.

"No." Glaring at her, he turned to Marc. "Where's your bathroom?"

"Down the hall, to your left." When Jason had rolled out of the room Marc said to Fiona, "You're keeping him a child. It's time he spread his wings."

"This is none of your business," she declared heatedly. "I asked you not to interfere!"

"When you're too close to a situation you lose perspective. I can be more objective. Remember the parking-lot incident?"

"That was completely different!" Fiona raised her eyes to the heavens as if asking for help or at least forbearance. "You are *so* infuriating. You think you have all the answers. Well, you don't."

Jason returned, looking subdued.

"Are you okay, Jase?" Fiona reached out to feel his forehead.

Jason moved his head away. "I'm *fine*."

She gripped her hands together. "Ready to go?"

Jason nodded. "Thanks for everything, Marc. I had a great time."

"No problem, buddy. I had a good time, too. Remember what I said about giving you a hand with things." Marc turned to Fiona. "I'll call you."

"Don't bother," she said, still furious. "I wouldn't go out with you now." She stalked to the front door. Jason followed her out.

All the noise had woken Rowdy. He trotted into the room, his nails clicking on the hardwood, to sit by Marc's chair and lick his hand. For once Marc let him.

"I blew it, Rowdy." Marc scratched behind the dog's ears. "She wanted an excuse not to go out with me and I handed her one on a plate."

Marc made his own trip to the bathroom, shutting his mind off to the mechanics of what he had to do there. Although he had some control over bladder and bowel, he used a catheter at night to make sure he got through until morning accident free. When he'd finished, he returned to the living room and began clearing away the empty tins.

Fiona's disapproval affected him more than he would have liked, leaving him morose and irritable. Whatever hopes he'd been harboring were crushed like the pizza box between his hands.

Why should he care so much what she thought of him, anyway, he thought as he stuffed the cardboard into the recycling bin. In a few weeks, months at the most, he'd be out of here.

CHAPTER TEN

Fiona opened the front door Monday afternoon after teaching all day in Squamish. Tired and hungry she wasn't prepared for the *1812 Overture* to blast forth. Over the sound of artillery and blaring trumpets, she bellowed, "Jason!"

Slamming the door she listened in the ensuing silence for his answering call. Nothing. There was no aroma of cooking dinner, either. Was he even home?

She threw her purse down and went to the kitchen. Jason was seated at the table, talking on the phone in a persuasive voice. "First term has only been going a month. I'm sure I could catch up."

"Jason!" Fiona deduced he was talking to someone at the university and her stomach twisted. Her brother hadn't just been full of beer and bravado. He was really trying to get into university. And it was all Marc's fault.

Jason saw her and put a finger to his lips. "Are you sure?" he asked. A moment later the reply caused his shoulders to slump.

Thank goodness, Fiona thought, relieved. Time to talk some sense to him.

"Could you send me an application form anyway?" Jason said and gave his address.

"You knew that would happen," Fiona said gently when he'd hung up a few minutes later. She could afford to be conciliatory now that she knew he couldn't get in. "Why set yourself up for disappointment?"

"You never know until you try," Jason replied angrily. "Isn't that what you always say? If you hadn't insisted you could take care of me all those years ago I would have been shipped off to Manitoba. If you hadn't been determined to get your education while working you'd be nothing but a barmaid."

"Waiting tables is good honest work," she said. "It kept us eating for years until I got my degree. It still keeps us out of debt when I don't get many teaching jobs."

"The point is," Jason went on, building steam, "you never placed limits on yourself because something looked too hard. Yet you want to limit me." He rolled across the room to the cooking area. "I can't even have a few drinks with a friend without you humiliating me."

"I was worried about you," she explained wearily for the umpteenth time.

"That's no excuse for treating me like a little kid," he said, his voice tight with fury. He rummaged in a cupboard and brought out a pot which he slammed onto the stove. "You're my sister, not my mother. Legally, I'm an adult now."

"Until you start *acting* like an adult, what I say, goes."

"You're trying to control me and I'm sick of it," he yelled. "I wouldn't even be in this chair if it wasn't for you."

Fiona felt the blood drain from her face and a trembling start in her hands. Jason had never thrown that at her before. She stared at him. Her baby brother had grown into someone she didn't recognize.

"I'll regret that forever," she said quietly. "I can't change what happened. All I can do is try my best to make the rest of your life as good as it can be."

"Then listen to me," he demanded. "Try to see my point of view."

Numbly, Fiona walked to the back door, wanting only to be with her alpacas, whose nonjudgmental presence soothed and calmed her.

"Fiona," Jason began again. "I'm serious about this. Things have got to change."

"You're right," she said, pausing on the threshold. "You can begin by disconnecting that annoying music from the front door." Deaf to his further curses and entreaties, she walked out to the barn.

In the quiet warmth of the stall she laid her head on Papa John's soft shoulder and cried. The rift with Jason churned up all the grief and guilt she'd carried for eight years. Yes, she'd failed Jason. She'd been trying ever since to make up for it. Why couldn't Jason see she was only trying to do right by him?

MARC ATTACHED Rowdy's leash to the frame of his wheelchair and proceeded down the driveway. The dog lunged forward, straining at the leather strap until Marc found himself half wishing for the cowering pup Fiona had brought him.

The dog had doubled his weight, grown several inches and had more energy than a hyperactive toddler. Marc, in his off-the-shelf wheelchair, couldn't keep up. Jim had tried to talk him into a custom-built chair, or at least a better quality one but Marc had seen a move like that as an admission he would be using it indefinitely.

That wasn't the way it was going to be. He had pins and needles in his legs more frequently now, his bladder and bowel control was getting better, not worse. Heck, he wanted to recover so badly it just had to happen.

In the meantime, what to do about Rowdy? The dog needed regular exercise and lots of it. By the time Marc had wheeled around the block a few times he was bored stiff and Rowdy was just getting warmed up.

That night in Dusty's Pub, five minutes down the road from Whistler in Creekside, he mentioned his problem to Nate and Aidan. If nothing else, it was a way to stop his cousins from razzing him about Fiona. Even telling them about the debacle with Jason hadn't been enough to stem their glee that Marc had finally fallen hard for a woman.

"It must be love for Marc to put on a public show," Nate said to Aidan.

"Cupid's arrow straight to the heart." Aidan mimed being shot in the chest.

Marc sighed. "Knock it off, guys. Fiona's crossed me off her list of eligible bachelors. Nate, what can you tell me about handcycles? I need a better way to get around than this clunky old wheelchair."

"So you've seen the light on that subject, too. There's hope for you yet." Nate proceeded to advise him on different makes and models, culminating in Marc asking him to place an order.

Once that was decided, however, his cousins reverted to giving advice on Marc's love life.

"She'll get over her snit," Nate assured him. "Just lay on the old Wilde charm and she'll be eating out of your hand again in no time."

"She's become depressingly immune to my charm." Marc leaned an elbow on the table and sipped his drink gloomily.

"It's that attitude of yours," Aidan counseled. "You've got to lighten up."

Nate's gaze shifted over Marc's shoulder. "Guess who just walked in the door?"

Marc glanced toward the entry. Fiona and Liz. Fiona'd done something different with her hair; turned it into long loose ringlets. The two women paused near the door, looking around for an empty table.

Nate stood up and waved them over.

"What are you doing?" Marc said, alarmed at the potential for public humiliation when Fiona rejected Nate's invitation and sat elsewhere as she was sure to do. "I thought we were here to get Aidan hooked up with someone."

"What?" Aidan demanded, turning on Nate. "I told you guys I'll find my own woman when I'm ready."

"Great going, Marc." Nate made calming motions with his hands. "Settle down, you two. We can kill two birds with one stone. Marc can patch things up with Fiona, and Aidan can get to know her spunky friend."

"Liz has a boyfriend," Marc said. "Some Swiss dude."

"Frederik Hoffner," Aidan said. "He works on the mountain with me and I'm not going to poach his girlfriend. Besides, I've met Liz before and while she's very nice, she isn't my type."

"According to you, no one's your type," Marc retorted.

"They're coming over," Nate informed them.

Sure enough the women were headed their way with Liz tugging determinedly on Fiona's arm. "She's being dragged here against her will," Marc said. "I'm getting a taxi home."

Aidan clamped a hand on the arm of his chair, anchoring him to the spot. "If I have to suffer through this, so do you."

"Two gorgeous babes are joining us and you two are complaining?" Nate eyed them incredulously. "Aidan, you haven't had a date in six months and you, Marc, are obviously head over heels for Fiona. What the hell's wrong with you guys?"

Head over heels? Marc thought. Was he?

Liz arrived at their table with Fiona in tow. "Hi, guys," Liz said brightly. "Got room for us?"

"Please, sit down." Nate shifted his chair over to make space for Liz between himself and Aidan, leaving Fiona to reluctantly take the seat beside Marc. Nate rubbed his hands together. "What'll you ladies have to drink?"

"Vodka tonic for me," Liz said as the waiter glided over in response to Nate's upraised hand.

"Fiona?" Nate asked.

"I'll just have a mineral water." She sat upright and stiff, in sharp contrast to the soft red-gold ringlets that trembled around her shoulders when she moved. Marc had the urge to hook his finger through one of those spiral curls and gently pull it straight just so he could watch it spring back.

"Oh, come on, Fi," Liz protested. "This is supposed to make up for having to cut short our girls' night. Live a little."

Fiona opened her mouth but Marc spoke first. "If she wants mineral water, that's what she should have."

She looked at him directly for the first time and said coldly, "I've changed my mind." Turning to the bar-maid, she added, "White wine, please."

A chilly silence descended on the table. Marc mentally cursed Nate and racked his brain for something to fill the deafening quiet. Then he and Fiona spoke at once, but not to each other.

Marc asked Liz, "How is your daughter?"

"Are you and Angela going on a honeymoon?" Fiona said to Nate.

Liz and Nate started to speak together, looked at each other, laughed and fell silent again, each waiting for the other to talk. Nate gestured to Liz to go first.

"Jilly had an ear infection but we caught it early and she'll be fine. Thanks for asking." Liz nodded to Nate with a conspiratorial wink. "Over to you."

"Ange and I are waiting until the cycling season has wound down then we're going to Hawaii for a couple of weeks," Nate explained.

"Lovely," Fiona said.

"I work with your friend Frederik," Aidan said to Liz, picking up the conversational ball.

Liz brightened at a topic obviously dear to her heart. "He loves it here so much and he really wants to stay. Is there any chance his contract will be extended to the winter season?"

"It very well could," Aidan said. "Our winter program has been expanded this year and we need extra people." He and Liz launched into a discussion about the coming ski season.

The waiter brought their drinks. Nate took his glass and rose. "I see my bike mechanic, Kevin, at the pool table. I think I'll challenge him to a game."

Which left Marc isolated beside the stubbornly silent Fiona. He cleared his throat, gaining her attention, and gestured vaguely in a circular motion. "You, uh, did something to your hair. It's very pretty."

"I curled it." She hesitated then softening, added, "I wind strands of wet hair around my finger and pin them to my head. When they're dry I take out the pins. *Et voilà*."

Encouraged, he asked, "How's Jason? Did he survive the other night?"

She fixed Marc with an accusing stare. "He threw up all night and had a nasty hangover the next morning. He spent the whole day on the couch with an ice pack on his head."

Marc chuckled. "Sorry, but it's part of the ritual coming of age. How else is he going to learn his limit?"

"By being warned when he's drinking too much instead of being encouraged to have more and more. *I* came of age without ever making myself sick."

His smile fading, Marc gazed at her coolly. "How do you know I didn't try to warn him?"

A shadow of doubt clouded her eyes momentarily but was quickly repressed. "Whether you did or not is beside the point. You still gave him the beer. He doesn't need a drinking problem on top of everything else. I don't think he should hang out with you anymore. You're not a good influence."

Marc glanced at Liz and Aidan but they were engrossed in conversation. The noise level in the pub ensured Marc and Fiona's conversation was private. "I don't think it's the drinking that worries you."

"What else would it be?"

"Oh, I don't know, maybe the idea of Jason getting a job, an apartment, a car. Why does the thought of him becoming more independent terrify you so much? I'd have thought you would welcome less responsibility and more time to live your own life."

"I don't have a problem with caring for Jason," she said stiffly.

"Nobody's questioning your commitment to your brother's welfare but his needs have changed and you've got to recognize that and adapt. He's chafing at being confined to the Whistler area. This is one of the most beautiful places in the world but it's like a prison when you have no other options."

"Are you sure you're not projecting your own feelings onto him?" Fiona said pointedly. "Jase has never said anything about feeling confined. We're very close. He would tell me."

"Not necessarily," Marc said. "He doesn't want you to feel any more guilty than—" He broke off in time but the implication hung in the air. *Than you already do.*

Fiona leaned forward and responded in a low, sharp voice, "I've sacrificed my youth to care for Jason. I have *nothing* to feel guilty about. *Nothing.*"

Methinks thou doth protest too much. "Jason doesn't want you to martyr yourself," Marc said, also in an undertone but milder. "All he wants is a life."

"I know Jason better than you do," she said, bristling despite Marc's efforts to be conciliatory. "He's shy, doesn't mix well. He wouldn't be happy all alone in a strange city trying to make his way among thirty thousand other students."

"You may know him but I have a better understanding of where his head's at," Marc argued. "Unless you let him grow up and make his own decisions he'll take the matter into his own hands, with or without your permission. Why not help him and stay friends?"

"You're telling me that everything I've strived so hard for the past eight years has been pointless," Fiona said, her voice rising in pitch. "You're telling me I'm a bad sister."

"No—"

"Well, I'm *not.*" She emphasized her words with a thump of her fist that made the liquid shiver in her wineglass.

Liz glanced over. "Everything okay, Fi?"

Fiona smiled tightly. "Fine."

Liz turned back to Aidan and Fiona carried on. "When I find steady work as a teacher I'll earn enough money to pay for Jason's education while supporting us both. It's a *good* plan."

"It's *your* plan," Marc countered. "It's a safe plan. Jason won't have to risk entering the real world for a good long time and you won't have to face being alone."

She was struck silent. Under the low lights of the pub her face seemed pale. Marc hadn't actually thought about Fiona's motivation beyond the obvious—she was being overprotective of her little brother. But now he wondered if he hadn't inadvertently struck a sensitive nerve.

"You don't understand," she said. "How could you? You've only been in a wheelchair a couple of months and rightly or wrongly, you expect to resume a normal life eventually. Jason *never* will. Jason *needs* me."

"Of course he needs you," Marc agreed. "You're his sister and he loves you. But he also has to be allowed to grow up. And you—" He hesitated, knowing she wouldn't like to hear what he had to say, then plunged in. "You need someone to make love to you and mean it."

"You've got a nerve," she gasped, her throat and cheeks suffused with deep pink. But she didn't deny it.

Liz darted another anxious glance across the table. "Are you sure you're okay, Fi?"

"I'd like to go soon," she said in a strangled voice. "But go ahead and finish your drink."

Liz picked up her glass and was drawn back into conversation with Aidan.

"I don't mean to offend you," Marc said. "And I wasn't necessarily offering my services, such as they are. But I had a good time the night of the wedding and I'd like us to try again."

"I don't know." Fiona rubbed her temples wearily. "I'm not good company these days. I have too much to do at home, school and work. Too much responsibility."

My point exactly, Marc thought.

She threw him a swift sideways glance. "I know what you're thinking and you're wrong."

"You promised me a real date," he reminded her.

"You must have a hide like a rhino," she said, shaking her head.

"Deep down I know you really want to go out with me."

She laughed. "And an ego the size of an elephant."

"Shall we say Saturday?"

"Sorry. This Saturday is fix-it day at my house. I've got plugged gutters, a broken doorknob and a bunch of other stuff I've been putting off for ages. Anyway, regardless of whether I'm free or not, I'm still annoyed over Jason and don't want to spend time with you."

"Don't spare my feelings, tell me what you really think."

"You want to know what I really think?" She put down her glass and turned in her seat to face him directly. "You kiss well but I wonder if you have staying power. In the weeks I've known you, all I've been hearing is how much you want to get away from Whistler and how quickly you'll leave once you regain the use of your legs. You talk about 'making love' but you don't really know what that means. I'm just a brief interlude to you, an Indian-summer dalliance. My brother is of passing interest because he's in a wheelchair. But when you're long gone *I'll* still be here for him and *he'll* be here for me."

Marc jerked his head back feeling as though he'd taken a sock to the jaw that rendered him speechless. He wanted to shout that he wasn't that shallow, that careless with other people's feelings. But there was a grain of truth in what she said and it kept him silent while she drained her glass and gathered up her purse.

"Liz, are you ready?" Fiona said, rising. Liz nodded. Fiona's polite gaze took in both Marc and Aidan equally. "Thank you for the drink."

Marc watched her walk away, head high, rejecting the admiring glances and good-natured advances from the men she passed. Just as she'd rejected his advances.

She was like Sleeping Beauty, cloistered in her castle and protected by invisible thorns while the world passed her by. If he did one good deed during his stay in Whistler, Marc vowed it would be to free Fiona from her self-imposed prison.

FIONA STOOD ON the top rung of the ladder leaning against her house and scooped out handfuls of soggy dead leaves from the clogged gutters. Her thick leather gloves were soaked through and her blue-plaid flannel shirt was streaked with mud and slime. It was a dirty job but someone had to do it and unfortunately that someone was her.

Pushing aside a strand of hair with the back of her wrist, she paused in her labors, leaning against the ladder for a moment's rest. The sun was shining, the sky was blue, her alpacas were grazing peacefully in the field below. All *should* have been right with her world. Instead she felt weighed down by a vague unease.

It wasn't the hard work that was getting her down, she thought, trying to analyze her feelings. Oh, she grumbled sometimes and felt stressed too often but she thrived on being busy; it kept her from thinking—and feeling—too much. Was it something to do with Jason? She tentatively probed that avenue in her mind as she might a sore tooth. Yes. It hurt a little. After the night he'd gotten drunk she'd scolded him as if he were a child. Sure he'd done a dumb thing but he'd experienced no lasting harm. Judging by his miserable experience the morning after she doubted he'd be in a hurry to drink too much again.

Worse was the barrier her reaction to his misdemeanor had raised between them. Since then he'd been more determined than ever to go his own way, regardless of her feelings.

She continued to probe her conscience. Could her emotional discomfort have something to do with Marc? A twinge of pain like a nerve being jabbed made her attack the gutters with renewed vigor, distancing herself from uncomfortable thoughts. Leaves flying, she cleaned as far as she could stretch, only drawing back when the ladder wobbled ominously.

As she descended to the ground her emotions dropped with each step down the ladder. She'd been too harsh on Marc. *Staying power.* She groaned at the memory of that particular gaff. This to a man who had stuck to his post reporting the news from war zones while all around him people were fleeing for their lives.

Face it, he'd put her on the defensive with some of his remarks and she'd lashed out with the first verbal weapon she could think of.

With a little grunt she picked up the ladder and carried it around the corner of the house. Dead leaves littered the ground at her feet. She'd rake those up later but while she had the ladder out she should change the burned-out lightbulb above the garage door. After that she needed to tighten the loose hinge on the barn gate. The hinge brought a tiny frown to her forehead. Anything to do with hammer and nail left her with swollen thumbs and ten bent nails for every one that went in straight.

However, thinking about chores was easier than contemplating Marc. She owed him an apology. Heck, she owed him a date. But…

He was in a wheelchair.

There, she'd admitted it, if only to herself. His handicap *did* matter, just not in the way he might think. His blunt talk about her needing someone to make love to her had triggered long-repressed yearnings. Even though he'd claimed not to be offering his services she couldn't help but think of him in this context. She'd done enough reading to know paraplegics could have satisfying sex lives and she had no doubt Marc could satisfy a woman.

But the fact remained, as he'd said, once he was out of the wheelchair he was "outta here." She could count on one hand those people who were her true friends, who she'd be close to in a year, in a decade, at the end of her days. When she fell in love she knew it would be for life. Could anyone blame her for guarding her heart so closely?

She was halfway up the ladder on the second side of the house when a four-wheel-drive SUV she didn't recognize turned into her driveway with an extension ladder strapped to the roof rack. Then she caught a glint of sunlight on curving metal in the back. A wheel.

Marc? Her heart, traitor to logic and the need for emotional equilibrium, beat faster.

Aidan emerged first, his dark brown hair tossed by

the wind, followed by a little girl with blond curls and blue corduroy pants who ran over to the fence, drawn by the alpacas. Aidan had gotten Marc's chair from the car by the time Fiona recovered herself enough to climb down from the ladder to greet them.

"Hi," she called out. Shading her eyes from the sun she walked over to the car. "What brings you out this way?"

"We've come to work," Marc told her, hauling a tool belt from the back of the vehicle. "Just tell us what to do. Aidan will tackle the high stuff but anything at waist height that needs repairing or building, I'll take care of it for you."

I'll take care of it for you. The simple phrase touched off insidious longings, becoming in her mind, *I'll take care of you.* All her life *she'd* been the one to do the protecting.

"We both worked for my uncle building log homes before we followed our own career paths," Marc went on when she didn't speak. "There's not much we don't know about construction and we're pretty good amateur plumbers and electricians."

A guy who could fix things. Build things. A man who could ease the burden of her life. Or not ease it so much as share it. The fantasy was as seductive as a fresh box of chocolates.

He was looking at her strangely, head tilted against the sun, waiting for a response.

The fantasy was false; she couldn't afford to fall for it. Modulating her tone to a level of confidence she didn't necessarily feel, she said, "That's very kind of you but I've got it all under control."

He glanced at the ladder propped against the house and at her filthy shirt. A smidgen of uncertainty brought his eyebrows together.

"Honestly," she insisted. "There's *nothing* I can't handle by myself."

Suddenly his expression cleared and he started issuing orders. "Aidan, you can help Fiona finish those gutters." He gestured to the tool belt spread across his lap—pliers, tin snips, screwdrivers, hammer. "What do you want me to do?"

She opened her mouth to protest again.

He held a hand up. "Don't bother. I'm onto you. Just point me in the direction of a problem."

With a helpless shrug that hid a surge of gratitude, she nodded toward the barn. "The hinge on the gate is loose. No matter how often I tighten it, it ends up worse than before. If you can fix that I'd be eternally grateful."

"Your wish is my command."

His smile softened the lines around his mouth and eyes. He still looked tough and hardened but more in the manner of the strength and grit of a pioneer than the cynical battle-hardened soldier.

And he looked damn sexy in that tool belt.

CHAPTER ELEVEN

"I CAN'T TELL YOU how grateful I am to you both," Fiona said to Marc and Aidan, several hours later as they sat on the back porch eating Jason's barbecued hamburgers. "Instead of taking all weekend to get through the chores we've finished in an afternoon."

Jason offered the men a beer and handed Fiona her flavored mineral water. The he took a beer for himself with a mild yet defiant glance in her direction.

She bit her tongue, determined to give him credit for not repeating his mistakes. "Thanks, Jase."

"You shouldn't have any more trouble with that gate," Marc said. "Whoever installed it didn't use a cross brace and the weight dragged on the hinge, bending the metal. The other problem was someone used nails instead of screws, which don't hold, as well."

"The previous owner built the gate but I'm responsible for the nails. I'm a Jill-of-all-trades and mistress of none."

"You do okay." He grinned. "For a girl."

She threw a potato chip at his head. "I do better than okay."

Emily wandered around the backyard gathering stones and leaves which she placed in an old leather pouch slung around her neck for some game of make-believe. Rowdy followed her, his alert gaze on the half-eaten hamburger in her hand, politely waiting for a crumb or a chunk of meat to fall.

"She's lovely," Fiona said to Aidan. "You've done a wonderful job of raising her." After getting to know him a little, she believed the rumors surrounding his wife's death even less. A more gentle man she'd never met and yet there was that Wilde strength under the surface, like the hard granite mountain beneath the mantle of soft snow.

Aidan's doting gaze followed his daughter's apparently random path from hydrangea bush to woodpile to mound of fallen yellow maple leaves. "She just started school and already she's reading at a grade-two level."

Emily tucked a hydrangea petal into her pouch, noticed her hamburger was still in her hand and generously fed it to Rowdy who gulped it down in two bites.

Fiona laughed. "Kids are so cute."

She and Aidan talked more about Emily and school but her attention was diverted when she heard Marc say to Jason, "I copied some information off the Internet for you about engineering at UBC. I also noticed that the old friend I was telling you about is now head of the department. I'll give him a call."

"Cool," Jason said.

Fiona felt her cheeks grow warm and it wasn't from the last of the afternoon sun beating down on the back deck. What part of the phrase "don't interfere" didn't Marc understand? Did he think her such an ogre that she didn't want her brother to get an education? Or was it his opinion that studying by correspondence was inferior to attending classes?

"I'm sure that'll come in useful *someday*," she said.

"I've got something for you, too." Marc wheeled down the ramp onto the concrete path that led around the house and returned a few minutes later with a battered leather briefcase. He removed two folders of stapled pages; one he handed to Jason, the other to Fiona.

"What's this?" she asked, leafing through single-spaced typewritten pages.

"My interviews of the people in the photos I took overseas," Marc said. "They're nothing much—just my observations, personal anecdotes, and so on but you were interested."

For someone so infuriating, he was difficult to stay mad at for long. "Thanks," she said and set the folder on the table behind her. "Would you like another drink? Maybe another hamburger?" she asked Aidan.

"No, thanks. We should be going." Aidan rose and called to Emily.

"If there's anything else you need just give us a call," Marc said. "That includes you, Jason."

Fiona walked them to the car. When Marc was settled in the passenger seat he reached for Fiona's hand. "I'm not against you, I'm for you."

"Will you promise not to corrupt my brother with subversive ideas?"

A glint appeared in Marc's eyes. "I won't get him drunk again."

"That's not what I mean and you know it."

The vehicle's powerful engine rumbled to life. Fiona stepped back, her fingers stretching out the contact with Marc's till it broke and she raised her hand in a farewell wave.

That evening she curled up in front of the TV with a bowl of popcorn to watch an old movie Jason had taped for her. For once a romantic comedy of a bygone era failed to hold her attention. Images of Marc, his biceps flexing in a snug-fitting T-shirt as he wielded a hammer, were fresh in her mind. She recalled the warmth and strength of his arms when he held her on the dance floor and her eyes closed as she relived their kiss.

Longing, sharp and strong, swept through her. She wanted to love and be loved, to experience the real thing instead of always living vicariously. Marc, maddening, sexy and strong, had stoked those dormant feelings to life. The question was, what was she going to do about them?

"HERE YOU GO, DUDE, your brand-new Freedom Ryder." Nate wheeled the gleaming blue-and-gold handcycle out of his bike store in Whistler Village and down the steps to the square where Marc waited. "She's a beauty."

Marc ran a critical eye over the rig. The back wheels slanted in at the top and the pedals and crankshaft were placed higher than the front wheel so they could be operated by hand. A padded seat and back were slung low to the ground between the front and rear wheels.

"Is it fast?" Of all the things he loved about snowboarding, speed topped the list.

"Oh, yeah. People race them. You've got twenty-one speeds and the frame comes apart so you can stash it in the trunk of a car. You can even go off-road with this baby."

"That'll be great for taking Rowdy for walks." Marc transferred himself down and across as Nate braced the bike. His legs were stretched out horizontal to the ground and supported by foot rests. "Feels stable."

"That's because of the low center of gravity," Nate said. "You steer by leaning with your body."

Marc turned the pedals and the bike moved across the wide paved square. He leaned to the right and the bike turned. The more he leaned, the tighter it turned. With a bit more experimentation he mastered shifting gears and applying the brakes.

Finally he returned to where Nate was waiting patiently for the verdict. "Well?"

"Pretty cool," he acknowledged grudgingly. "Have you got a helmet?"

"Sure thing. I'll store your chair while you take the bike for a proper test-drive." Nate ran back into the store.

Marc watched his cousin take the steps two at a time and forced away his envy and resentment. *Negative feelings accomplish nothing.* Some days it was easier to believe than others.

Nate returned with the helmet and a new pair of gloves. "Which direction are you headed? Just so I know."

"I'll take a run out to the Meadow Park Sports Centre on the Valley Trail." Marc strapped on the red-and-black helmet and pulled on the gloves. "I've got a hydrotherapy appointment there in a half hour. If I can save Leone a trip or myself a taxi ride on a regular basis this bike'll be worth the purchase price."

"I'll see you when you get back. Or do you want me to drop off your chair at home when I leave work?"

"Yeah, do that. Thanks." Marc gave him the thumbs-up. "Catch you later."

Marc cycled through the Village and across Highway 99 to Tapley's Road. The breeze blew across his face as he descended the curving street into the Valley Trail and his spirits rose. *Not bad.* The movement and the sensation of riding the handcycle was a lot like skiing.

The day was sunny with just enough of a cool bite

to make him glad of the warmth that working the pedals brought. The Valley Trail, a narrow paved path for cyclists and pedestrians in summer and a cross-country ski trail in winter, ran for miles through the valley, past lakes and golf courses. The path Marc rode paralleled the River of Golden Dreams, a slow-moving stream meandering through low bushes and grassy banks full of birds and wildlife. He saw a couple in a canoe paddling lazily downstream. The thought occurred to him that canoeing, even kayaking, were still open to him.

The trail went right past the Meadow Park Sports Centre before crossing the highway again to circumnavigate Lost Lake. As Marc left the trail and rode through the parking lot toward the Sports Centre he realized he hadn't anticipated the logistics of leaving the bike to go inside. One way or another, he was going to make an entrance. The automatic doors parted and he rode straight in.

"Hey! You can't—*Marc*, is that you?" Chrissy, the tall redhead behind the reception desk, sputtered.

"Can't stop now," he called as he breezed by. "I'm late for hydrotherapy."

"But, but…" At a loss, she petered out completely and sat down, shaking her head.

"You can't ride a bike inside the center," Val scolded as he transferred off the bike and stripped down to the swimsuit underneath his track pants.

Marc lowered himself into the steaming pool and

shifted into position near a water jet. "I thought you'd be glad I'm exercising."

"I am. The bike will help build your upper-body musculature and enhance your balance. Not that you're lacking in strength or balance. You've been working out at home, haven't you?"

"Every day." He shut his eyes and let his muscles relax, enjoying the sensation of weightlessness.

"Don't get comfortable, pal. You're here to work, not kick back." Val, in a black one-piece Speedo, motioned him over to the stainless-steel rails at the other end of the hydrotherapy pool. "Get that leg up on the bar…that's right. Now stretch."

Dutifully, Marc ran through the exercises. He was in the middle of stretching his hamstrings when he thought he felt a muscle twitch deep in his thigh. He paused in midstretch, motionless and alert. No sooner did he try to focus on the feeling than it disappeared.

"What is it?" Val's cheeks were flushed with steam and exertion.

"Nothing," he muttered. His arm had been lying atop his thigh. Maybe he'd imagined that sensations experienced in his forearm were located in his thigh. It wouldn't be the first time his body had played tricks on his mind.

"Don't get discouraged," she said. "You're doing really well. Your muscle tone and range of movement is excellent."

Marc nodded. She might be pleased with his

progress but these things meant nothing unless his legs could actually move under their own steam.

"So what's next after the handcycle?" Val said as he toweled off at the end of the session. "A car with hand controls?"

"I won't be in a wheelchair long enough to make that worthwhile." Silence followed his pronouncement. Marc lifted his shoulders. "I know you can't confirm that, but as long as the doctors say it's a possibility, no matter how remote, I'm determined to make it happen."

"You're so damn stubborn you just might pull it off." Then she wagged a finger at him. "Don't quote me on that."

Marc grinned. A firm maybe was good enough for him.

FIONA TURNED IN to Marc's driveway and cut the engine. She grabbed the package lying on the passenger seat, slid out of the car and headed up the walk. Odd, Marc's wheelchair was parked at the base of the ramp but he was nowhere in sight.

Leone opened the door to her knock. "Hello, dear. Marc's ridden to the Sports Centre on the handcycle Nate ordered for him."

"Would you tell him I came by?" Fiona held up the paper bag. "I wanted to give him this as a thank-you for the other day."

"Come in and have a cup of tea," Leone urged. "He shouldn't be too long."

Fiona followed Leone to the kitchen at the back of the house where warm yeasty aromas were rising from the bread maker. Rowdy and Rufus came trotting forth at the sound of their footsteps. Fiona paused to pat them, laughing with delight when Rowdy sprang repeatedly into the air. "Talk about energy! This guy's thriving."

"That dog lives to run. Hopefully Marc will be able to take Rowdy for walks when he's riding his hand-cycle. It'll do Marc good to get out more, too, instead of moping about in his room or the pub." Leone put the kettle on to boil and dropped a couple of tea bags into a pot. "I hope you like green tea."

"That'd be great, thanks." Fiona slid onto a bar stool and gazed around at the well-appointed kitchen. Copper pans hung above the stove and colorful bottles of raspberry vinegar and chili oil lined up along the black granite benchtop. She hesitated, not sure how clued in Leone was to her nephew. "How is Marc doing with his physiotherapy? Have his chances of walking again improved any?"

Leone sighed. "Marc believes he can accomplish anything if he wants it badly enough. The trouble is, no amount of wanting will make nerves function once they're destroyed. On the other hand, he has so much drive I know he'll achieve his maximum potential."

She paused to make the tea. "I overheard him talking to his producer in New York the other day, sounding the man out about going back to work. Of course Marc may have to start with a desk job."

"Somehow I can't see him being satisfied with that," Fiona said.

"Probably not. Still, he's a lot more chipper these days." Leone smiled. "I think you might have something to do with that."

Fiona felt her face grow warm. "I don't know. We've had our differences."

"He respects your opinion. And the way you've cared for your brother all these years." Leone got china cups out of the cupboard and poured out the tea.

Fiona laughed. "That's not the impression he gives me."

Leone hesitated, as if choosing her words carefully. "He can be judgmental at times but that doesn't mean he doesn't also admire you. He has high standards, none so high as those he applies to himself."

Fiona knew *she* could be too sensitive, too defensive at times. "He's lucky he's got you and your husband for support. Especially since his father won't get involved."

Leone drew back, head on the side, and looked at her strangely. "What exactly did Marc tell you about his dad?"

"That he more or less abandoned Marc after Marc's mother died so he could pursue a professional skiing career." Fiona noted Leone's frown and pushed on.

"Marc said they're completely estranged. I gather his father hasn't spoken to Marc since his accident."

By now Leone's frown had deepened to two sharp creases between her eyebrows. "There's some truth in all that, but it's not the whole story by any means. Roland is a good man who had one tremendous talent— skiing. It was his passion as well as his livelihood. When Marc's mother died, Marc was just about to start school. Rather than drag him around the world on the pro-skiing circuit Roland left him with Jim and I, to be raised with our two boys. It seemed the best solution at the time and Marc was very happy here. Roland visited and called Marc regularly. As Marc became more and more entrenched in our lives here, Roland grew reluctant to take him away.

"Even so, when Marc was thirteen, about to start high school, Roland made the attempt. He'd remarried the previous year and relocated to New York to be close to his new job as a sports broadcaster with one of the major TV networks."

"What happened?"

"Marc refused to go. Well, you know how stubborn he can be." Leone shook her head and raised her cup to her lips. "He was at a difficult age and didn't take kindly to being uprooted by a virtual stranger to go live with a family he didn't know. Roland tried to insist. The disagreement escalated into a huge fight until neither was speaking to the other. I was never told the whole story and neither Marc nor Roland would reveal any details. After that Roland went away and Marc shut his father out completely. Roland still calls to get news of Marc, but he doesn't ask to talk to Marc directly. The more time that goes by, the harder it is for Marc to make the first move."

"That's terrible," Fiona said, aghast. "Especially now when he needs his father more than ever."

"I know. We've all told him that." Leone paused. "Maybe if *you* talked to him."

Fiona's eyebrows rose. "Why would he listen to me if he wouldn't listen to his family?"

"Precisely because you're *not* family and can be objective." Leone sighed and pushed a hand through her auburn hair. "I just wish he'd listen to *someone*. I think it's eating him up inside."

"What's eating who up inside?" came Marc's voice from the hall. Rowdy trotted out to meet him.

Marc entered, cheeks flushed and hair damp with perspiration, looking exhilarated. "The handcycle is awesome!" he said, apparently having already forgotten his question. "You wouldn't believe how great it is to get up some speed. Like flying. Like skiing. I haven't felt this good in months. Come and see, both of you." He leaned over to ruffle his dog's fur. "Rowdy, have I got a treat for you."

Fiona and Leone followed him outside to where the shiny new handcycle was parked. He wheeled his chair beside the bike to pull himself across. Both women started forward, ready to help.

"I can manage," he grunted. With Rowdy leaping excitedly around him, Marc positioned himself in the padded seat, hoisted his legs into the stirrups and released the brake. "Watch this."

He turned around and cycled onto the road. By the time Fiona and Leone had walked to the end of the driveway Marc was two blocks away, slaloming down the middle of the quiet residential street. With a tight turn that elicited a gasp from Leone he raced back, Rowdy chasing alongside. Twenty yards away he started to brake and came to a smooth halt beside them.

"Nice!" Fiona exclaimed. "I wish I could afford one for Jason right away. Is it hard to learn to ride?"

"Not a bit. Maybe you can get one secondhand. Or wait a few months and you'll be able to buy mine. Want to try?"

"Really? Okay. I'll go get your chair."

She brought his chair over and when he'd transferred himself back—more difficult because the chair was higher than the handcycle—she lowered herself onto the seat.

"It feels so low," she said, turning the pedals with her hands. "And strange to have my feet immobilized."

"You never quite get used to that," Marc said wryly. "Go on, take it for a spin."

She pedaled slowly down the street with Marc beside her in his wheelchair. When they came to the end of the block, she paused. "What do I do now?"

"Lean left to turn," Marc said. "We'll go around the neighborhood."

Fiona safely navigated the corner and pedaled down the road between towering hemlock, spruce and fir. Nestled among the trees were log and timber homes, landscaped with large granite boulders and small patches of emerald-green grass.

"What were you and Leone talking about when I came in?" Marc said.

"Pardon?" Fiona asked, distracted by a car backing out of a driveway two houses ahead. "How do I stop this thing?"

He showed her the brake. "Don't worry. He's waiting for us."

And Marc was waiting for her answer to his question. Fiona didn't speak until they were past the idling car. She gave the driver a wave and glanced sideways up at Marc, her glance reproachful. "Your father."

Marc averted his gaze. "What about my father?"

"How come you told me he'd abandoned you when all along it's been you who've refused to speak to him?"

CHAPTER TWELVE

SO MANY CONFLICTING EMOTIONS surrounded his father. Marc thought about trying to explain those feelings to Fiona, but how could he make her understand when he couldn't even bring himself to talk about his dad with Nate and Aidan?

"You jumped to conclusions," he said. "I told you he tried to force me into a stepfamily I hated—"

"Whom you'd never met!"

"—far away from the place I loved."

"You could have come back for summer vacation. Or Christmas," she amended, remembering his passion for snowboarding. "I can understand you being reluctant to leave everyone here but there are ways of dividing your time. Why did you let me think your father never called?"

"All I said was, we haven't spoken in years."

"Which is just as much your fault as his from what Leone told me."

Exasperation made Marc push his chair faster. "You don't want me interfering in your life so stay out of mine. This is my problem. I'll deal with it."

"That's the trouble—you're not dealing with it. I'd give *anything* to have a parent," she said, her grip tight on the hand pedals. "You've got one and what do you do? You shut him out. It's crazy. It's wrong. I don't care what your differences are, you can't let them fester."

"Leone put you up to this, didn't she?" Marc said angrily.

"She's concerned about you." Fiona leaned in to take the corner onto Easy Street, her forehead puckered with concentration. When she straightened up she said, "I don't understand why you haven't called your dad since your accident to let him know you're okay."

"I'm *not* okay. I'm in a goddamn wheelchair."

"You're alive, aren't you?"

Marc felt his chest tighten, so much it was hard to speak. "If I didn't call my dad when I was whole I have no right to call him now that I'm a paraplegic."

Fiona fumbled with the pedals, momentarily losing her grip. "You're wrong! That's exactly when you should call him. I'll bet you anything he'd be thrilled if you asked him for help. You're his child. That means something."

"He has other children, a grown-up son and daughter by his second wife." The thought of his father's other family made him burn with jealousy even now.

"But you're his only offspring by your mother."

At the mention of his mother, Marc's resentment grew until he couldn't contain his feelings. "That doesn't mean much. It's his fault my mother died."

"What! I thought your mother died in a car accident when your dad was away on a ski tour."

"Oh, I don't mean he literally killed her, but as good as. The brakes on her car failed as she was coming down a steep hill into Horseshoe Bay," Marc said. "She went through a stop sign and crashed into a dump truck, dying on impact." He paused. "She was six months pregnant with my baby sister."

Her voice filled with horror, Fiona exclaimed, "I'm so sorry. But how is that your father's fault? He wasn't even there."

"Roland went off to Europe knowing the brakes needed to be replaced. He forgot."

"Oh, Marc. It was an accident. How did you even know about the brakes?"

"He told me after the funeral, admitted it was all his fault. I think he barely knew what he was saying, probably never thought a five-year-old would remember." Grimly, he added, "I happen to have an extremely good memory."

"And you reminded him when you were older, didn't you?" she accused. "That's what you fought about when you were thirteen and he wanted to take you to New York."

Marc felt the pain as fresh and jagged as if it were yesterday. It tore at the barriers he'd erected over the years and his shameful confession spilled out. "I accused him of letting my mother and my unborn sister die so he could marry another woman."

"Oh, Marc," Fiona said. "Did he even know your stepmother back then?"

"Yes. She was a skier, too. However, I have no idea if they were involved before my mother's death."

"Then you should give him the benefit of the doubt. A thirteen-year-old's logic isn't the best, especially when he's hurting," Fiona said. "You're not going to be able to forgive yourself until you call him."

Marc stared at her. "*He's* the one who needs forgiveness."

"So why haven't you? He didn't get the brakes fixed so he felt guilty and blamed himself. That's no reason you should. Things like worn brakes don't happen overnight. Your mom probably knew about them, too. She could have put the car in the shop."

The pavement moving beneath him blurred and Marc felt a prickling run over his shoulders and neck. Strange, he'd never even thought of that. He coasted to a stop. Fiona took a moment to find and apply the handcycle brake by which time she was several yards ahead.

Marc eased himself forward. "What do *I* need to forgive myself for?"

"For keeping your father estranged all these years."

"I told him I didn't want him in my life and to stay the hell out. Even if I forgave myself, why should he?"

Fiona gripped his hand. "He will, I'm positive. All he wants is to hear the sound of your voice."

If only he could believe that. For a moment her optimism infused him with hope, then he shook his head. "Too late. The damage is irreversible."

"Isn't that what the doctors said about your spine?" she demanded.

Suddenly Marc laughed. "You know just which buttons make me work, don't you, Pollyanna? Well, not this time."

They turned back onto Balsam Way and a few minutes later pulled into the driveway.

"Coming in?" Marc asked.

"Just to pick up my purse. I've got to work tonight."

Fiona got her purse from the kitchen and handed him the paper bag. "This is for you."

"It's not my birthday." He hefted the package. A book by weight and feel.

"Just a little thank-you for helping the other day."

"It's not necessary but thanks." He reached into the bag for the book and read out the title. *The Care and Training of Jack Russell Terriers.* "I hope they've got tips on obedience training. I cannot get that dog to come when he's called."

"Jack Russells are notorious for that."

"Now you tell me." He laid the book on the counter and reached for her hand. "Sit down."

Hesitating at first, she gave in and slowly lowered herself onto his lap. He wrapped his arms around her waist as if he was holding a butterfly; clasp her too tightly and he'd crush her, too loosely and she'd fly away.

"You look tired," he said, massaging her lower back. She closed her eyes and let her head drop back. He watched the pulse beat at the base of her neck. That slender column of pale skin looked so vulnerable. "Do you really have to work at the pub during the school year? You should take it easier."

Immediately her head came up. "I'm okay."

Marc made a tsking sound. "Fiona, Fiona. How am I going to rescue you from yourself if you won't cooperate? Can you at least take a weekend off?"

"I guess so. Why?"

"You still owe me a date."

"Oh, that." As if stalling she straightened his shirt collar where it had been sticking up, her fingers brushing his skin with the softness of tiny wings.

Marc held his breath; alive to the tantalizing sensations created by her touch. His torso had become ultrasensitive following the loss of feeling below his waist. He found himself wondering what her skin would feel like next to his.

"Yes, that," he said. "I've been very patient but it's time I called in my accounts. What do you say to going away with me this weekend?"

"Away?" Her hand dropped from his shoulder.

"We don't have to go out of town. There're plenty of hotels right here in Whistler."

"That's not the point. Don't you think sharing accommodation is rushing things?"

He brought her hand back to his mouth and touched his lips to the inside of her wrist. The faintest of tremors ran through her. "We don't have to be intimate. You don't even have to stay overnight. I'd just like to have someplace quiet we can be alone. I love my aunt and uncle but sometimes I feel as though I'm living in a fishbowl."

She was silent, thinking. "I won't promise to stay overnight but I'll do my best to get this Saturday off."

"That's all I ask." His hand slid up her arm to curl around the back of her neck.

She lowered her mouth to his in a kiss that was sweet, chaste and all too brief. Then she slipped off his lap and backed away, fingers raised in farewell. "I'll see myself out."

Marc stroked his tongue along his mouth, tasting her lip gloss. Honey and vanilla. "Till Saturday."

SATURDAY MORNING, Fiona stopped at Electronics Shop on her way home from grocery shopping. Jeff was hunched over the innards of a personal computer at the back of the store. He grunted once to acknowledge her presence and carried on with what he was doing. Sweat beaded on his forehead as his sausagelike fingers worked a computer card into a narrow slot.

Jason could have performed the same operation in a quarter of the time, Fiona thought impatiently. Finally

Jeff clicked the card into place and sat back with a wheezy exhalation.

"I've come to pick up those electrodes Jason ordered," she told Jeff. "Did they come in yet?"

"Just this morning." Jeff rose and made his ponderous way over to the cash desk where he rummaged through a box of plastic Ziploc bags stapled to order forms. He pulled out one with Jason's name on it. "Here we go."

"Thanks." Fiona took out her wallet and handed him her overworked credit card. "Have you ever thought about hiring Jason? He's a whiz with computers and can manage almost anything to do with electronics."

"I know what Jason can do," Jeff said. "If he wants a job he should ask me himself."

"He's shy about things like that."

Jeff drummed his stubby fingers lightly on the counter while he waited for the credit card to ring through. "Has he got a car?"

"He doesn't drive." She wanted to add, *he could learn,* but something stopped the words in her throat. Her heart balked at the idea of her baby brother behind the wheel of a car. Was this constant anxiety about a child's safety what all parents felt or was she overprotective, as Marc said? "Please, just give him an interview."

Jeff handed her the receipt to sign. "All right. Tell him to be here next Monday at 10:00 a.m."

"Thank you." Fiona dashed off her signature and picked up her purchase. "He'll see you then."

"FIONA'S OUT GETTING GROCERIES," Jason said when Marc showed up unannounced Saturday morning.

"That's okay, I'm seeing her later today. I mainly wanted to talk to you." Marc glanced over his shoulder at Aidan, who'd brought him here. His cousin and Emily were walking over to the alpacas, Rowdy bounding along at their side through the long grass.

"To me?" Jason said.

"Yes, but before I forget…thanks for the use of these." He withdrew the gloves Fiona had lent him from the sling beneath his chair and handed them to Jason. "Do you still want to go to university?"

"Well, yes, but—"

"I told my friend Paul how keen you are to study electronics and he's agreed to meet with you. I told him that with your aptitude and background knowledge you'd have no problem catching up if you were allowed to enroll late."

Jason's mouth dropped open. "Oh, wow, I can't believe it. This is the best thing ever."

"We'll drive down Tuesday morning with Nate and Angela and stay overnight at their apartment. We'll see Paul that afternoon and if all goes well, we'll spend part of the next day finding you a place to live, hopefully on campus."

"Wait till I tell Dave. And Fiona." Jason stopped short, as if realizing his sister wouldn't be quite as happy as he was at the opportunity.

"If you like, I'll discuss it with her today at lunch," Marc said.

"No…" Jason replied. "No, it'd be better if I did. I'll choose the right time, when she's in a good mood."

"If that's what you want. Just don't leave it too late." Rightly or wrongly, Marc was happy to go along with Jason's wishes, if only to avoid unnecessary conflict between him and Fiona right before their big date.

"I'd better go," he said. "Aidan's dropping me off at Lost Lake and I'm taking Rowdy for a run with the handcycle before I meet Fiona."

"Fiona told me about your handcycle," Jason said eagerly. "Have you got it here? Can I see it?"

"You can take it for a test-drive."

Marc gave Jason a demonstration of the bike's capabilities then handed it over to Jason to try.

Jason rode up and down the quiet road in front of their house. "That is so fun," he enthused. "I want one."

Marc met his gaze and winked. "If you want something badly enough, all you have to do is go after it."

FIONA WENT STRAIGHT HOME and ran up the stairs to burst through the front door. She was greeted by the rippling melody of cathedral bells and Jason's grinning face.

"How do you like that sound?" he said over the chimes. "Better than guns and bugles, eh?"

"Much." She moved farther into the room, turning slowly in the center of speakers mounted in each corner. The music was so loud it made the walls reverberate. "Bit of an overkill, isn't it?"

"Pardon?" he shouted.

"I said—" she yelled back.

Jason rolled to the door and shut it. The bells stopped abruptly.

Fiona's shoulders relaxed. "Whew! Maybe if you turn the volume down a tad."

"I guess I can do that." Whistling he wheeled back to his room.

Fiona followed. Seeing the old pair of leather cycling gloves on Jason's dresser made her start. "Was Marc here?"

Jason threw her a quick glance and waited until he'd made an adjustment on the control console before saying, "Just for a few minutes. Why?"

She quelled a stab of disappointment at missing him. "Was he looking for me?"

Jason's cheeks colored. "No, he came to show me his new handcycle."

"Oh." That was understandable. So why was Jason acting so strangely? "Well, he forgot his gloves."

"He returned those because he got new ones. Aidan drove him out, then he was going straight back to

Whistler to take Rowdy for a run. He said he was seeing you later."

"That's right. We're starting with lunch in the Village." Marc had refused to tell her any more than that but she had an idea he'd planned something big. She hadn't yet made up her mind whether to stay at the hotel but she would go prepared for anything.

Fiona leaned against the dresser and surveyed her brother's immaculate room. He'd learned early he had to keep the floor clean so he could move around in his chair. "Are you still spending the night at Dave's?"

"Yes, why?"

"I just wanted to know in case I'm away overnight."

Jason's eyebrows rose. "Oh. Okay."

Had she heard a note of concern in his voice? "I'll call and leave the phone number of where I am."

Jason eyed her a trifle impatiently. "I'm sure I'll survive for one night."

"Of course you will. Let me put away the groceries and I'll take you over. Oh, I got the electrodes you wanted." She produced the package from her purse.

"Thanks, Fi." He reached for the bag and tore it open. "Now I can finish making my robotic dog."

"Oh, guess what? Jeff wants you to come in for a job interview on Monday. Isn't that great?"

"Huh?" Jason's attention was focused on his new components.

"Jason! You have an interview for a job at Electronics Shop. Aren't you a little bit glad?"

Jason said nothing as he concentrated on inserting one of the electrodes into a complicated system of wires and resistors attached to a Meccano framework that vaguely resembled a canine form.

Fiona watched, frustrated by his total lack of enthusiasm. When he was wrapped up in his electronics, he was in another world.

"10:00 a.m. Monday. Don't forget."

"Will do," Jason said absently without looking up.

Fiona rolled her eyes and walked out of the room. She'd have to remind him again on the day.

MARC SET OFF CYCLING from Lost Lake on the Valley Trail with Rowdy on a long retractable lead. This was their first long "walk" and he was anxious to see how Rowdy would handle it. At first the dog surged ahead or lunged sideways into the grass after some elusive scent until Marc reeled him in. Eventually Rowdy learned he was better off galloping alongside and settled into a rhythm. The dog never seemed to tire. They'd gone about a mile when Marc decided he would have to slow down or Rowdy would run till he literally dropped.

"Whoa, boy." He came to a halt in Meadow Park next to the river. To his left bushes crowded the river bank, obscuring the view of the water. To his right, a grassy lawn slanted up to a picnic area and playing fields. He let Rowdy run the length of the leash to explore among the bushes while he went over his plans for his date with Fiona. He wanted to give her the best time he could, to lavish attention on her, to make her feel like the extraspecial woman she was.

Rowdy's loud urgent bark wrenched Marc out of his daydream. The dog gave a sharp pull on the leash, yanking it out of Marc's hands. Out of sight behind the bushes, the dog continued to bark. Marc cursed. Rowdy never came, especially if there was another dog around. Marc called anyway. Rowdy had a big dog brain in a little dog body; he went after anything.

"Rowdy! Come here, boy."

Rowdy trotted out of the bushes, his ears pricked. He looked at Marc as if to say, "come and get me if you want me," then ran back out of sight. Marc cursed again and pedaled off the path after him. A loud crashing of broken twigs made his heart sink. Where was the owner of the other mutt? Rowdy would be just a mouthful to a rottweiler or a Doberman.

Then he heard a deep low growl that made every hair on his body stand up. That was no rottweiler. Pedaling past a bush he saw Rowdy, his ruff erect from his neck to his tail, snarling at a black bear.

Bear sightings weren't uncommon down by the river, especially in autumn when berries were ripe. If Marc had been alone he would have quietly backed up, keeping an eye on the bear until he was far enough away to make a speedier exit. But he wasn't alone and he couldn't leave his dog.

"Rowdy. Come here, boy." He spoke low and urgently.

Rowdy ignored him and kept on barking.

"Rowdy, come!" Marc said in more commanding tones. The dog glanced over his shoulder then returned his attention to the bear. The bear lifted his head and sniffed the wind.

Marc felt a cold sweat break out on his forehead. The bear wasn't more than five yards away. Luckily Marc was downwind. If the breeze shifted or the bear changed position… He pedaled backward a few feet, hoping Rowdy would follow. Nope. He whistled. Rowdy continued to bark at the bear, jumping around like a windup toy.

"You stupid dog," he muttered. Then louder, *"Rowdy!"*

The damn dog didn't come. The bear, head lowered again, took a step toward Rowdy. Marc wiped the sweat out of his eyes. Adrenaline surged through him, his heart pounding in his ears. Rowdy snapped at the bear's nose. The bear lifted his huge paw, claws extended.

Marc's muscles bunched, ready to fight, prepared for flight. "ROWDY! COME!"

At the last second the dog responded to his command but it was too late. The bear took a swipe at his retreating body and clipped him on his side. With a yelp of pain, Rowdy leaped into Marc's lap. Blood streamed from gashes down his side. The bear bounded forward, planted his paws and lifted his nose to the wind again. For one heart-stopping moment he swayed on the spot, then he turned and crashed away into the bushes.

Marc tried to pedal, obeying his instinct to get away as fast as he could. Something was blocking the wheels. He looked down. His legs had come out of the stirrups and were sprawled on the ground at awkward angles. He stared uncomprehendingly. Had he lifted them out? No, he wouldn't do that, useless things that they were. Had they been jolted loose and fallen? No, he'd barely moved the handcycle.

There was only one possible explanation—they'd moved on their own while he'd been in an extremity of fear.

He tried to move them again. Nothing. He strained muscles he couldn't feel, labored to exercise nerves that wouldn't function. Tears came to his eyes with the effort to raise his feet a few inches off the ground.

The next thing he knew Rowdy was licking the salty moisture from his cheeks. The poor dog was bleeding profusely and still trying to comfort him.

Marc pulled off his sweatshirt and wrapped it as tightly as he dared around the dog. "Hang on, boy. You're going to be fine. You're going to be okay."

CHAPTER THIRTEEN

"NEVER LET IT BE SAID I don't know how to give a girl a good time." Marc held Fiona's hand as they sat in the vet's waiting room while Rowdy was being stitched up.

Fiona laughed despite the knot of anxiety in her stomach. "Next time you ask me out I'll know to dress down."

She'd been sitting in her living room, watching the clock and fretting because Marc was late when he'd called on his cell phone, breathless and nearly incomprehensible.

"Rowdy's been mauled," he'd choked out. "I'm on the handcycle and Leone isn't home. Can you pick us up?"

She'd had the foresight to grab Jason's extra wheelchair before jumping into the car and heading out on Highway 99. Now, two hours later, they were waiting for Rowdy to be given the all clear. The vet had assured them Rowdy would survive but Fiona knew she wouldn't rest easy until she saw the Jack Russell wag his stubby tail.

"Your dress is ruined." Marc touched the dark stain that spread across the gray-green fabric when she'd cradled Rowdy in her arms while Marc transferred to the car.

Fiona shrugged off the loss. "It doesn't matter. All that matters is that Rowdy is all right."

"He will be. He's got guts." Marc squeezed her hand. "He came to me in the end. It took a bear to scare him into it, but he finally obeyed." Marc hesitated. "A strange thing happened—"

"What?" Fiona asked. Something in Marc's eyes, his tone of voice, held her attention.

"Nothing." He rubbed his thigh with his free hand and dried blood flaked off his sweatpants. "It's probably nothing."

A door opened and gray-haired Dr. Bannister emerged, tucking a pair of folded glasses into the breast pocket of his white coat. "Rowdy's sleeping now. He'll be fine."

"Thank God," Marc said fervently.

Fiona rose. "Can we see him?"

"Come through to the operating theater."

Fiona stifled a gasp at the sight of Rowdy stretched out, eyes closed, his entire side shaved beneath three rows of stitches.

But it was Marc who was suffering now. His eyes swam as he gently stroked the top of his dog's head. "I almost lost him."

"He'll be all right," Dr. Bannister said. "He won't be chasing bears for a while, though. I'll keep him overnight for observation. Check back tomorrow. We open at noon on Sundays."

Fiona drove Marc home so he could change then they went back to her house so she could do the same. Marc wheeled inside behind her. The house was silent for once.

"Where's Jason?" Marc asked.

"He's at his friend Dave's house overnight."

"So you won't have any explaining to do if you don't come home tonight." Marc followed her down the hall.

"My private life is my own business. Whether Jason's here or not has no bearing on whether I choose to stay out all night." Fiona smiled and shut her bedroom door on him.

That wasn't strictly true, she thought as she stripped off her soiled dress and searched for a clean outfit. Part of the reason she'd never had a boyfriend stay at the house overnight was for fear of what Jason would think, or feel. But he was older now and she shouldn't have to censor her behavior. The thought was liberating and scary in equal measures.

She still hadn't made up her mind about tonight but she believed Marc when he said they could be together without being intimate. She packed a toothbrush and change of underwear into a zippered pocket of her oversize handbag—just in case.

"I'm ready," she announced, coming into the living room. Marc was positioned at the window, watching the alpacas play king-of-the-hill on Machu Picchu. Snowdrop lost her balance and slid down the side of the dirt mound.

Marc turned away, chuckling, then went silent when he saw Fiona. "Hello!"

"Too dressy?" Fiona glanced down at the black clingy sheath with the three-quarter-length sleeves and a plunging neckline. She hadn't planned to wear it, not wishing to give Marc the wrong impression. But then, she hadn't planned to clasp a bleeding dog to her bosom, either.

"You'll hear no objections from me."

She brought out her car keys. "Let's go then."

Marc shook his head. "I ordered a taxi. You're having a night off *all* responsibilities."

She could get used to that. Correction—she *couldn't* get used to that, as in she couldn't afford to relax that much—but she would enjoy it for one night. "Thank you. No objections from me, either."

Brent came to pick them up. Smiling and friendly as always, for once he didn't gab to his passengers the entire trip, just winked at Marc in the rearview mirror and drove.

Fiona admired the glow of the late-afternoon sun through the yellow-and-orange maple leaves and felt a pleasant buzz of anticipation. "Where are we going on your mystery tour?"

"I'd planned lunch and a movie but now we don't have time. So I thought we could grab a bite to eat then stroll around the Village galleries and the boutiques."

"Window-shop?" she said, delighted. "I never get to window-shop."

Fiona shoved aside the slightly guilty feeling that she should be working or studying and ordered herself to relax and enjoy the rest of the day. It wasn't hard in Marc's company. They started with a leisurely lunch in one of the restaurants overlooking the square and did some serious people watching. Marc was charming and funny, keeping her laughing, keeping her thinking, matching her comments with witticisms and astute observations. From there they browsed the art galleries, making a game of choosing original paintings they would buy if they had the money or the place to hang them.

"Oh!" Fiona stopped in front of a picture that could only be set in Greece. A white-washed villa overlooked a brilliant blue ocean beneath an equally brilliant sky. The picture was part photo, part painting, magically surreal. Rustic urns overflowing with bright red geraniums decorated a private terrace and a blue gate led down stone steps to who knows where. Two bright blue chairs faced each other across a small wrought-iron table, waiting for travelers, lovers, escapists from everyday life. The scene evoked in Fiona a longing so fierce it was palpable, to flee the narrow confines of her life.

Marc rolled into position beside her and gazed at the painting in silence. "Those chairs are waiting for us."

Goose bumps rose on her arms as his eyes met hers. She had the uncanny feeling that he not only knew exactly what was in her heart and mind but that in a roundabout way he was suggesting more than simply taking a trip together. Part of her longed to say yes so much it scared her.

"We'd have a glass of red wine on the terrace," he went on in a faraway voice that matched her mood. "Fresh olives and crusty bread. Watch the sun set over the Aegean. Then walk down the hill to the fishing village for dinner. In the morning we'd go for a swim in the sea."

Their only limits were the ones in their minds, Fiona thought dreamily. Wheelchairs could go anywhere—on planes, trains and boats. He could roll along sedate city streets, visit museums and cathedrals, with her at his side. If he was in a wheelchair he could be hers.

But what if he learned to walk again? He would go back to reporting from the battle zone, a place she never could, never *would* go.

In the space of seconds her thoughts went from clarity to confusion. What was she thinking? She wouldn't wish permanent paralysis on him, not in a million years. And yet if he was whole, he'd never be hers.

Marc reached for her hand. "Fiona, are you okay?"

The warm pressure of his fingers helped her shake

off her troubling thoughts. This weekend was meant to be about relaxing and enjoying each other's company, not worrying about what was to come.

"I'm fine," she said. "What do you want to do now?"

Marc turned his chair around until he was facing the exit. "I've already made the arrangements."

"*All* the arrangements?" She eyed him through narrowed lashes. "Where we'll spend the evening? What we'll have for dinner? What we'll do for entertainment?"

He nodded. "Do you mind?"

"Do I mind not having to make decisions for once?" She lifted her arms and spun in a circle. "It's a blessing and you're an angel."

So he'd read her right. That was a relief. He hadn't been one-hundred-percent sure.

Marc led her over the bridge crossing the gushing stream that ran through the Village to the most prestigious resort hotel in Whistler. He'd never stayed here and he'd bet his last dollar Fiona never had, either. It was to be a treat for both of them. She was silent as he checked in, silent as they rode the elevator, silent as he slid the key card into the door of the suite. What was she thinking? Was she wishing she'd gone home?

He shut the door behind them. "I promise I won't jump you before the first course. In fact, I won't jump you at all," he said with a wry grin at the impossibility. "Tonight is about enjoying time together, whatever form that takes. We'll play gin rummy if that's what you want to do."

"I wasn't worried about you jumping me," Fiona insisted even though she'd visibly relaxed as soon as he'd said it. "Oh, you know what I mean." She threw her purse on a chair by the fireplace and kicked off her shoes.

Marc wheeled around the spacious suite, making sure everything was as he'd been promised. Firewood—check. Champagne on ice—check. Separate bedroom with king-size bed—check. Hot tub—check. Fully equipped bathroom with thick terry-towel robes—check. It was all perfect. Luxurious yet cozy and intimate.

When he got back to the sitting room Fiona was kneeling in front of the fireplace, touching a lit match to the pile of tinder and kindling. A crackle and a burst of yellow flame signaled the start of a blaze.

Marc reached for the champagne and began taking off the foil wrap. "I hope you're not disappointed we're not going out on the town."

Fiona rose to her feet, dusting off her hands. "Are you kidding? After spending every Saturday night at the pub I'm delirious at not being in a bar or a nightclub. This is heaven."

"As long as you're happy." He twisted the cork out and tumbled the bubbly beverage into the waiting champagne flutes. Handing one to her, he clinked glasses. "Here's mud in your eye."

"Oh, that's not very positive." She clinked again and

quoted, "'May all your tomorrows be better than your best yesterday.'"

Marc held her gaze as he sipped. "I've never heard that toast before."

"My parents use to say it. I think my mother made it up." She smiled sadly. "Funny the things you remember."

"I like it." He picked up the phone and made a call to room service. "Marc Wilde in Room 514. Could you send up the first course of the meal I preordered right away, please." When he put the phone down she was rolling the champagne glass across her lips and smiling at him. "What?"

"Nothing. Okay, *you.* You're completely different from the drunk who fell on his face in the pub that first day I met you."

One corner of his mouth twisted up. "Maybe I'm just getting better at disguising the jerk."

"I don't believe that." Fiona patted the sofa. "Come here."

Marc wheeled over and transferred to the seat beside her. With his feet resting on the ground he could almost imagine he was whole again, looking forward to an evening with a beautiful woman.

There was a knock on the door. "Room service."

"Come in," Marc called.

A uniformed waiter pushed a linen-draped table on wheels through the door. He placed the covered serving dishes on the coffee table, took off the lids and backed away. "Enjoy your appetizers."

Coconut prawns, smoked salmon, asparagus tarts…Marc barely noticed what he ate but he enjoyed every morsel simply because Fiona was with him. He refilled their glasses and listened as she talked with loving amusement about her pupils at Pemberton Primary.

"I'd better stop yakking and start eating or the main course will be here before I know it," she said, reaching for a prawn.

"Relax. It won't come until I order it. We can eat at midnight if we want and have dessert at 3:00 a.m." He noticed her rubbing the back of her neck. "Sore?" She nodded. "Why don't you get in the hot tub?"

She hesitated. "I didn't bring a bathing suit."

"I'll stay out to give you privacy. Take as long as you want."

Still she wavered. "We're supposed to be spending the evening together. Don't you want—"

Marc stroked a curling lock of burnished hair off her temple, his gaze roving over her face. "I'll admit, when I first met you I wanted to prove something by getting you to go out with me. I wanted to prove I was still a man in spite of being in a wheelchair. Now I just want to make you happy." He smiled. "You've been good for me, Pollyanna."

"No," she protested.

"*Yes*. You didn't let me feel sorry for myself. You

gave me Rowdy. You've been a ray of sunshine to my thundercloud. Thank you."

Eyes bright, she blinked and smiled. "Sometimes I wonder if anything I do makes a difference. I'm just glad I could help."

She leaned over and kissed him. It wasn't a passionate kiss but she lingered and explored, giving his mouth and tongue a great deal of thoughtful attention. Marc tasted coconut and champagne mingled with Fiona's own indefinable sweetness. He could have kissed her forever but she moved her lips to his neck and trailed the tip of her tongue up to his ear where she whispered, "I'm going to get in the hot tub."

While she got ready, Marc picked up a magazine and pretended to leaf through it. Really he was listening to her going about the ritual of turning on the jets, humming to herself through the open door.

"Marc?" she called from the other room. "Won't you join me?"

His heart stopped. Then kicked into high speed. "Sure," he said nonchalantly. "Be right there." He put down the magazine, transferred into his chair and headed for the bedroom and the hot tub, unbuttoning his collar as he went.

The tub was in a small room next to the balcony. The scent of pine filled the steamy air and condensation was starting to form at the edges of the windows. A fat green candle burned in the corner.

Fiona was submerged to just above her breasts, modestly concealing herself in the foaming water. Marc felt suddenly shy of revealing his own battered anatomy. It wasn't just the slack muscles of his legs and buttocks; he had scars, from surgery, from shrapnel. Fearless Marc Wilde, with the invincible body, admired by men, beloved of women, was ashamed of what he looked like.

"I ought to prepare you," he began.

She smiled wryly. "My brother has been paraplegic since before puberty. He was in a car accident, too. Do you think there's anything I don't know or haven't seen? I thought by now you would have learned that appearance isn't important. It's what's inside that counts." Even so she tactfully averted her head to stare out the window at the ski lifts rising up Whistler Mountain. "Did you know we can see the whole mountain from here? There's a dusting of new snow on the peak."

While she was occupied with the view Marc stripped off his shirt and unzipped his pants. The hot-tub rim was slightly raised, with a ledge running around the outside. Transferring from chair to ledge wasn't easy but neither was it as difficult as he'd feared thanks to the workouts he was getting with weights and the handcycle.

He lowered himself into the hot water and sank down, submerging his chest and shoulders. All his muscles went "ahhh."

He must have said it aloud, too, for Fiona's gaze swung to his, her eyes dancing. "Feels good, doesn't it?"

She was lovely, what he could see of her. And what he couldn't see, his imagination easily filled in the blanks. She'd piled her hair on top of her head to keep it out of the water. Her smile was trusting, warm and seemingly willing. The scene was set for romance and Marc was feeling sexual….

In his *head* maybe. As if orchestral music building to a crescendo had suddenly wound down in distorted noise, his buoyant mood deflated. He had a beautiful woman, a hot tub and the evening ahead of him…and he couldn't feel a thing below his waist. His hips were unable to thrust, his penis was limp and useless. He was no longer a man.

"This isn't working," he said abruptly and dragged himself out of the water and onto the edge of the hot tub.

Forgetting about giving him privacy, Fiona sat up in the tub and stretched out a hand as if to stop him. "Marc. What's wrong?"

"Nothing. I just don't feel like a hot tub after all," he muttered. "What are you looking at?"

She subsided, silenced by his ill humor. "Sorry."

Dripping wet and cursing under his breath, Marc dragged one of the robes down and threw it over his shoulders. He slithered sideways into his chair, knocking his thigh hard against the arm of the wheelchair. He didn't feel a thing; later, he knew, he'd sprout a Technicolor bruise.

"Marc, wait, let's talk about this."

"I'm sick of talking. It's all I can do." He gave the wheels a savage push which propelled his chair halfway through the door. Then he jammed his hands down so abruptly his palms burned from the friction. Without looking back at Fiona he said tightly, "Just stay put. Enjoy the tub."

"Are you all right?"

Of course he wasn't all right. He couldn't walk, he couldn't run, he couldn't make love to a woman. Why the hell had he set himself up like this? What had he been thinking? "I'm *fine*."

He hauled himself onto the bed and lay facedown, hating himself for behaving badly, hating himself for just being. He heard the bubble jets die in the other room and Fiona get out of the hot tub. He'd ruined everything.

The bed creaked and sank slightly under her weight as she settled beside him. "Marc?" she said hesitantly.

"Yeah?" He couldn't look at her.

"This isn't easy for me to talk about since I haven't had a lot of sexual experience with men, able-bodied or not." She paused and took in a breath.

Marc turned his head and squinted at her through one eye. Wrapped in a fluffy white terry-towel robe, she was lying on her side facing him. Sweet, sweet woman. What he wouldn't give to make love to her.

"But I've done a lot of reading on the subject so I would know what Jason will have to deal with and be able to counsel him."

"I had sexual counseling in rehab. I know the drill." In a flat voice he repeated, "Sex isn't about getting it up, it's about connecting emotionally, giving pleasure to your partner, experiencing the joy of sensuality rather than the goal-oriented achievement of orgasm."

"You may know all that in your head but you obviously don't feel it in your heart where it counts."

"I'm a man. I'm goal oriented. 'Nuff said."

"Okay," she said patiently. "If you want a goal, you can give me an orgasm." She went pink. "I presume you're adept at oral sex."

"I thought you didn't want the evening to end in intimacy? You said it was too soon." At the time he'd hoped to change her mind. Now he was panicking thinking she had.

She picked at a loose thread in the quilting on the patterned bedspread. "I think we're ready to take our relationship to the next level."

"I'm not interested in mercy sex," he said harshly.

Hurt clouded her eyes and brought her eyebrows together in a tiny frown. "Do you have any idea what a jerk you're being?"

"I *am* a jerk. You're much better off without me."

Understanding dawned in her wide green eyes. "You're scared."

Got it in one. Fearless Marc Wilde. Scared of sex.

"It's okay," she said. "I'm scared, too. You're the first man I've been to bed with in a long, long time. Will I please you, or will I be clumsy and gauche? Will you think I'm sexy, or will you compare me unfavorably to other women? We all have our doubts and insecurities. Look at me, I'm trembling." She held out her hand. A faint tremor shook her fingers.

Marc stared at her hand. Slowly, he reached out and took it.

CHAPTER FOURTEEN

HE HEARD THE EXHALATION of her held breath. Finally he met her eyes. "How long has it been for you?"

"Don't ask," she mumbled. "It's embarrassing."

Marc pulled himself up on one elbow and took a firmer grip on her hand. "You are incredibly sexy. Don't ever doubt that."

She shrugged. Smiled. Lifted her face to be kissed. Marc obliged.

That so much sensual pleasure could be gained from a simple kiss was amazing. Then again, it wasn't all that simple considering the complex emotions surging through his body. Lust, grief for his lost manhood, gratitude, respect, liking, love....

Here his ability to tally inner thoughts and feelings went into a tailspin. *Love?* Was he sure? Did it matter? Why try to label what he felt. For the first time in months he was enjoying a woman's touch. Not just any woman, one he cared deeply about. That much he was sure of.

The kiss ended but the connection held with their

locked gazes. Marc touched Fiona's cheek, marveling at the softness of her skin, the cool freshness of her coloring. Tracing the delicate ridges of cheekbone, nose and jaw, he learned every curve and indentation.

She reached out to him and did the same. The silence grew deeper as they explored each other's faces by touch, plumbed the depths of their hearts with their eyes. Until by mute agreement, their lips met again. The kiss intensified, creating heat. Fiona edged closer. Marc slipped a hand beneath her loosely tied robe to stroke her shoulder. Down, to touch her breast. A shuddering sigh went through him at the feel of her firm, resilient flesh. His thumb found her nipple and an answering moan rose from her curved throat.

Still molding her in his palm he looked upon lips moist with his kisses, eyes dark and full of secret longing. He pushed back her robe to reveal her naked body to the waist and filled his gaze: small firm breasts, the faint shadows of her ribs, tiny adorable freckles dotting her skin, a pink glow that started on her breasts and rose up her neck.

"You're beautiful."

The pink spread to her cheeks. Fiona drew back his robe. "You have such a great physique. Look at those muscles." She stroked a hand down his biceps. "So hard."

He smiled ruefully. "At least something is."

Her hand dropped below his waist and wrapped

around him. "Your muscles aren't the only thing that's hard."

Marc glanced down in surprise. He had a partial erection. It wasn't enough to make love but it was more than he'd expected.

"I've read that when you lose sensation in your genitals other parts of your body become more erogenous," Fiona said shyly. "Like your nipples."

She touched her tongue to the bud of his nipple and an erotic sizzle shot through him.

"That works for me," he murmured.

Fiona nipped gently with her teeth and Marc sucked in his breath. Then he looked down and saw her stroking him with her hand. Even though he couldn't feel it, memory and imagination combined with the very real sensations he was experiencing elsewhere made him feel good. Oh, yes. Very good.

She scooted a little lower and kissed the hollow below his breastbone where his solar plexus lay. "This is a chakra," she said. "A center of sexual energy."

She licked the hollow in a slow circular motion, creating a tingling sensation that spread through Marc's arms and chest and up the back of his neck into his scalp. He'd never felt anything like it.

"I thought you weren't experienced with men," he murmured.

"It's mostly been theoretical…until now." She raised her eyes and gave him a cheeky smile. "I'm grateful to you for the chance to practice some of the techniques I've only read about."

"Oh, so I'm just for practicing on, am I?" he said, grinning. "I'll show you technique."

He dipped his head, took one nipple in his mouth and suckled, gently at first, then harder. She moaned softly and clutched the back of his head as if to drive herself deeper into his mouth. Marc ran his hand over the curve of her hip, down the outside of her thigh then up the inside, brushing the mound of soft hair with the back of his hand. Fiona wriggled and moaned again. He changed breasts and repeated the motion of his hand, pausing between her legs to stroke her up and down several times very lightly. Her hands were moving all over his chest now and he could hear her breathing harder.

He pulled back. Her face and neck were flushed and glowing. "Do you like what I'm doing?" he asked.

"Yes. Don't stop."

He nudged her legs apart and slid his fingers inside her, alternating kisses with gazing into her eyes. He set up a rhythm with his hand and she rocked with him, straining to take him deeper inside. Seeing her so aroused was a huge turn-on for him. "I want to make you come," he murmured urgently. "I want to make your world explode."

Marc found her mouth and thrust his tongue deep, in and out, matching the rhythm of his hand. She was making whimpering noises, clutching him and tightening her legs around his hand. He felt as if *his* world would explode.

"Marc…ohhhh." She tensed, and then a deep quiver ran through her and he felt a gush of fluid around his hand.

He came, too, in a rush and a shudder and an intensely pleasurable release that shocked and surprised him.

Fiona sagged against him, eyes closed, her body limp and damp with perspiration. Tenderly he smoothed back sticky tendrils of hair from her forehead and blew along the hairline to cool her. "Was it…okay?"

"Fantastic." Her eyes fluttered open and she added, "I don't know what *your* criteria are but by my definition, you haven't lost any of what makes you a man."

His arms wrapped around her. Her words were a tonic for his battered ego but more earth-shattering to him than the sex was the emotional intimacy. Even in his present state he recognized how important, how rare this was for him, he who'd always concentrated on the physical side of relationships. At the beginning of the evening he'd tried not to mind that he couldn't get it up—and failed. Now, it didn't matter.

"It was good for me, too. No, make that mind-blowing."

She pulled back. "The same as it used to be?"

He took a few moments to consider that. He thought he'd felt sensation in his groin while they'd been making love but he couldn't be sure with all the other tactile and emotional feelings washing over him. He hadn't had a real erection, nor had he ejaculated. He still didn't quite understand how he'd had an orgasm but hey, he wasn't about to question it.

"Not the same. Different." He kissed the tip of her nose. "Better because I was with you."

"I'm so glad," she whispered with a smile.

"Think how good we might get with a little more practice."

She stretched. "How about the rest of dinner?"

"Are you *always* hungry?" He reached for the phone to call room service.

They watched a movie while they ate grilled salmon, propped up in bed. Fiona, her attention not totally engaged by the film, sneaked sideways glances at Marc. "Fantastic" was an understatement to describe her experience tonight. Her last so-called relationship had been with a ski instructor who knew every position in the book and could perform it with acrobatic ease but had frankly left her cold. She'd stuck with him longer than she should have, thinking the fault lay with her if she didn't respond to his expert manipulations. Finally he'd given up on her, leaving her feeling deflated and certain she was frigid. Also leery of repeating the experience too soon. Now she knew that lovemaking had nothing to do with mechanics and everything to do with how she felt about the man she was with.

She loved Marc. She loved the way he made her feel; womanly and desirable, someone of value worth caring for.

He caught her watching him. "What?"

But she wasn't ready to tell him. "Nothing." She set her empty plate aside to cuddle up to him. His arm went around her shoulders and she laid her head on his chest. "I wonder how Rowdy's doing."

"I was just thinking the same thing. I'm sure he's fine. We'll call in the morning." He grabbed the remote control and pointed it at the TV. "Are you really interested in this?"

She shook her head and he pressed the button to turn it off. Fiona threw back the bedclothes and climbed on top of him, luxuriating in the strength and solidity of his body. "You promised me…" She whispered in his ear.

His mouth curved in a deliciously wicked smile. "I'll get right down to it."

At four in the morning they called for dessert— chocolate-raspberry tart and decaffeinated coffee. Fiona made Marc stay in bed while she served him.

"Your coffee, sir," she said and passed him the cup.

As he reached for it, his hand bumped hers and steaming liquid slopped onto his thigh. "Yeow!"

"Oh, sorry! Ohmigod, that'll burn." She scooped melting ice cubes out of the wine cooler, wrapped them in a cloth napkin and pressed them to the red scalded skin.

Marc was staring, stunned, at his leg.

"Are you all right? Should we take you to Emergency?"

He shook his head, bewildered. "I felt heat on my leg."

"You had sensation? Are you sure?"

He nodded. "This isn't the first time something strange has happened recently."

Elated, she hugged him hard. "Oh, Marc, why didn't you tell me before? What else happened?"

"I've felt pins and needles on and off for a couple of weeks. Val says that's a sign nerve function is returning. One day in hydrotherapy I thought I felt a muscle move in my thigh. Today when Rowdy was attacked by the bear my feet came out of the handcycle stirrups without me being aware of it. I must have moved them. I haven't told anyone all this because I was afraid I'll jinx it, afraid that if I'm wrong I'll be so much more disappointed."

"Definitely you should tell someone now. Get tests done. Do *something*."

"I'll call Val. She'll know what to do next."

"Good idea." Fiona dragged the phone across the bed for him.

Marc started to dial then put the receiver back. "It's four-thirty in the morning. Even for this I don't think she'd want to be woken."

"Tomorrow then. For now let's get some sleep so you'll be rested for whatever is to come."

She stacked the dishes on the trolley and wheeled it into the hall for the waiter to collect. She waited for Marc to finish in the bathroom then brushed her teeth and crawled into bed to snuggle beside him.

"When you're walking again—" she began.

"I don't want to talk about that yet," he broke in, his voice oddly tight. "Not until I know for sure."

"I understand."

Marc pressed his lips all over her face in little kisses that felt like the softest of spring rain. The last kiss was reserved for her mouth, sweet and lingering. He didn't speak but he didn't have to. His tender kiss, his gentle caress said it all.

Or did it?

Fiona lay awake in the dark, unable to sleep. She was completely and utterly full of joy about Marc's recovery. That was a given. So what was bothering her? Was she a teensy bit jealous that it was Marc and not Jason? Maybe. Surely that was natural. Because she knew it was unfair, the emotion ought to be fleeting. Sure enough, simply by naming it she found it was already fading. No, her faint uneasiness stemmed from something else.

Marc's recovery would take the focus off their blossoming relationship and put it on his future. As it should, she conceded. Maybe what was bothering her was that no sooner had they found happiness in his present situation than suddenly they were faced with new unknowns.

She sensed Marc awake in the dark beside her. She wished they could at least talk about it. He didn't have to decide anything, make her any promises. If only she knew what he was thinking.

She yawned and snuggled deeper beneath the covers, one arm across Marc's chest. Tomorrow. Everything would be clearer in daylight. One thing she was sure of, nothing that happened from now on could take this night and all they'd shared away from her.

MARC AWOKE TO the sensation of pins and needles in his legs. His eyes snapped open as excitement surged through him. The pins and needles faded. He pinched the back of his thigh. Nothing. Never mind. The pain of the scalding coffee last night was not a dream; a vivid red burn testified to that.

Fiona's soft even breathing made him turn to her. Tenderness and warmth flooded his heart, insinuated itself into every part of his being. Fiona wasn't a dream, either. The lovemaking, the intimacy, all of that was true.

Sexual healing. Finally he understood that phrase.

Glancing at the clock he saw it was 11:00 a.m. Val would be up. The vet would soon be open. He wanted to bound out of bed, leap into action, accomplish all the things he needed to take care of. Curbing his impatience, he lay still, waiting for Fiona to wake up so he could telephone.

Fiona stirred. Her eyes fluttered open and she looked at him blankly as if wondering what he was doing in her bed. Then her face split in that huge bright smile he loved so much. "Good morning."

"'Morning." He pulled her into his arms, ready to take up where they left off last night. Or try something new. This weekend had taught him that even if he never walked again he could still have a satisfying love life. Correction—*Fiona* had taught him that.

"Have you called Val yet?" Fiona asked, her mind clearly on traditional physiotherapy as opposed to bedroom exercises.

"I didn't want to wake you."

She rolled off him to retrieve the phone. "Do it now. You know you won't be happy until you do."

"I could have waited a *little* longer," he grumbled good-humoredly as he dialed Val's number. A second later he depressed the button. "Her phone's busy. Do you have the card from the vet? I'll call and find out about Rowdy."

Fiona got the clinic's card from her purse and handed it to him. The veterinarian's assistant answered his call.

"Hello? Marc Wilde, here. I brought my dog in yesterday after he'd been mauled by a bear—Rowdy. How is he?"

"Dr. Bannister checked him over this morning," the assistant said. "I've got the report right here. Rowdy's condition is stable. He's eating and drinking normally, no temperature. The vet would like to keep him for a couple more days to make sure there are no complications."

"Fine. We'll come in later to see him." Marc hung up and told Fiona what the receptionist had said.

"Thank goodness. I've been so worried."

"I'll try Val again."

This time Val answered on the third ring. Marc told her what happened with the coffee and described the other incidents that occurred over the past couple of weeks.

"Call your physiatrist and make an appointment to see him as soon as possible," Val said. "He'll want to run some tests to assess exactly how much progress has been made and where you should go from here."

"Does this mean I'll walk again?" Marc scraped his thumbnail along the telephone cord. As the seconds passed and Val didn't answer he became aware he was holding his breath.

Finally she spoke. "It would be irresponsible of me to make a definitive statement before seeing any test results. Even then it would be hard to say. Your physiatrist is the best person to answer that."

Marc tightened his grip on the phone cord at her evasive words and brisk professional tone. "What's your opinion, off the record? As a *friend*."

"Don't quote me but—" Val hesitated, then added in a warmer voice "—I'd say you had a damn good chance."

"*Thank* you." Marc hung up and turned to Fiona who flung her arms around his neck. "Nothing's certain."

"I know," she said, beaming.

"I always knew I'd walk again."

"Nothing's certain," she cautioned him.

"I know," he replied, hugging her tightly.

But he had a hope and a dream, and Fiona. The future was looking good.

CHAPTER FIFTEEN

FIONA SURFACED GROGGILY from a dream about Marc and glanced at the clock. Why was it ringing at 6:00 a.m.?

Not the clock. The phone.

She grabbed the receiver before it could wake Jason in his room next door. "Hello?"

"Fiona? This is Melissa from the school board. Sorry about the short notice but Lillooet Primary needs a substitute teacher. Can you go?"

"Of course." She never turned down teaching work. She wrote down the details and got straight out of bed, trying not to feel cheerful because Ron Thompson had the flu and had to take a day off.

She got dressed and ate quickly, fed the alpacas then came back inside to write Jason a note telling him where she was. Her pen hovered over the paper while she thought of a tactful way to remind him about his interview. Finally she solved her dilemma by putting a ten-dollar bill next to the note and telling him it was for a cab to Electronics Shop.

By seven o'clock Fiona was on the road to Lillooet, singing along to the golden oldies on the radio as her car ate up the miles. Even the prospect of an hour and a half drive each way failed to dampen her spirits after the wonderful weekend she'd had with Marc. Later she would call him and find out when he was going to Vancouver. Maybe she would go with him.

Sunshine, lollipops and rainbows…

MARC RANG DR. SAGAKI, his physiatrist, first thing Monday morning and caught him while he was making rounds at the hospital. Dr. Sagaki's reaction to Marc's news was typically restrained, but he said he would squeeze Marc in if he could get down to Vancouver that afternoon. That was all the encouragement Marc needed to call Nate and tell him he'd be using his and Angela's apartment a day early.

He rang Jason after that.

"H'llo," Jason said sleepily.

"Still in bed? You'll have to get up earlier than this when you have an eight-thirty class across campus."

Jason chuckled. "I'll rig up a robotic arm that will throw a glass of cold water in my face at the appropriate time. What's up?"

"I have to go to Vancouver today instead of tomorrow. Can you manage that?"

"Sure. No problem."

"Have you told Fiona yet?"

"No, but I will right away. She was in such a good mood yesterday I don't think anything will faze her."

"Good mood, eh? I'm glad to hear it." Marc smiled to himself and tried not to feel too smug. "Nate and Angela were able to alter their plans and are still going to drive us down. We'll be by in about an hour."

Shortly before nine o'clock Marc, Nate and Angela pulled into Fiona's driveway. Jason came down the ramp, a sport bag on his lap. He transferred into the back seat next to Marc while Nate folded and stowed his chair.

"Where's Fiona?" Marc asked, noticing her car was gone.

"She's off on a teaching job that must have come in early this morning," Jason said. "She left a note."

"So you haven't spoken to her about this trip?" Marc didn't like whisking Jason away to Vancouver for three days without Fiona's prior knowledge. "Maybe this isn't such a good idea."

"Don't worry," Jason said. "She'll be cool."

"Give her a call," Angela suggested as Nate turned around in the driveway.

"I don't have my cell phone with me. The batteries are recharging," Jason said.

"Use mine." Marc handed his phone across. "She's number five on speed dial."

Jason pressed the button and waited a few seconds. "Either the mountains are blocking the signal or she's got her phone switched off because she's in class. I'll try again later." He gave Marc back his phone. "How come we're going down early?"

Without sounding too optimistic Marc filled Jason in on the recent spate of "incidents" as he called them. "Fiona didn't tell you all this?"

"Only that you'd felt some sensation in your leg. That's fantastic. You'll be walking even sooner than you thought." Jason gave him a big smile.

Even so Marc saw a sadness in his eyes and sensed the news had somehow brought the boy down. "I wish I could wave a magic wand and make you walk again, too."

Jason shrugged. "I know that'll never happen. I'm really happy for you. Honest. Just don't forget to visit once in a while when you're back on your feet."

So that's what was worrying him. "Hey, we're buddies," Marc assured him. "Nothing's going to change that."

Nate slowed as they entered Pemberton and came to a halt at a four-way stop.

Jason looked idly out the window at the shops on their right. Suddenly he said, *"Oh."*

"What is it?" Marc glanced out the window, following Jason's gaze but could see nothing out of the ordinary. There was the deli, the electronics store and a hairdresser's shop. People heading to work. A dog sniffing around a garbage can.

"Nothing." Jason's voice sounded unnatural.

"You're sure?" Marc asked.

Marc noticed Nate assessing Jason in the rearview and met his cousin's quizzical eyes. Marc shrugged and put the matter out of his mind. "Did you bring the transcripts of your high school marks in case we can register you?"

Jason patted his sport bag. "Right here. I brought photos of some of the electronics devices I've built, too."

"Good thinking. That's sure to impress Paul."

Traffic was moderately heavy on the road to Squamish as late-leaving weekenders and commuters made the trip to Vancouver. Rocky cliffs rose steeply on their left, the rushing Cheakamus River tumbled and gushed over whitewater cataracts on their right. A freight train loaded with coal rumbled along beside the river.

Two hours later they were traveling across the Lion's Gate Bridge with all of Vancouver spread out before them.

"Gosh, the city is so big!" Jason said, twisting his neck to look from the freighters anchored in English Bay to the huge white sail-like roof of Canada Place. They passed the big stone lions guarding the entrance to the bridge and he turned to Marc, eyes wide. "Did you see that?"

Marc raised his eyebrows with a bemused smile. "Don't get out much, do you?" he teased. Then immediately wished he hadn't been so thoughtless.

The light in Jason's eyes dimmed. "Fiona doesn't like to drive far, especially with me in the car. We mostly stay around Pemberton and Whistler."

"Right." Marc whistled. Jason needed to get away, almost as much as Fiona wanted to.

They went straight to the rehab hospital. Hospitals everywhere had a sameness about them, Marc thought fighting a flood of bad memories revived by the long corridors, the smell of institutional meals, the metallic clink of trolleys and instruments. A sign asked that cell phones be switched off so as not to interfere with electronic medical equipment. Marc fished in his pocket and turned his phone off. Nate did the same.

Dr. Sagaki had a youthful unlined face despite his iron-gray hair. Just as Val predicted, the physiatrist called for a series of tests to be performed over the next few days.

"You're in luck—the MRI unit had a cancellation and I got you in this afternoon. You'll have an ultrasound in two days time," he added with a calm patience that betrayed no undue optimism.

But then, when had he ever? Marc thought, buoyed by the expectation that the test results would prove what he'd been confident of all along—he was going to make a full recovery. Nothing less would do. "Thanks, doc. I've got a good feeling about this."

Marc went out and told the others he'd be tied up for the rest of the afternoon but that he'd kept tomorrow free to take Jason to the university.

"In that case, I'll take Jason over to the apartment now and attend to my business at the bike store," Nate said. "Jase, will you be all right on your own for a few hours?"

"Sure. I'll call my friend Dave. If he's free, can he hang out with me at your apartment?"

"No problem," Nate said.

"Don't forget to call Fiona," Marc reminded Jason.

"I won't. Catch you later." Jason started to go with Nate then stopped. "Would you rather I stayed with you?"

"I'll be fine." Marc smiled. "But thanks."

THE SCHOOL BELL RANG to signal the end of the day. Fiona dismissed her class of grade-three students, tidied up the classroom and wrote a note for the regular teacher. Then she hurried out to her car in the staff parking lot to check her cell phone for messages. There were two. The first was from Marc saying he was on his way to Vancouver and would call her later that night. She was surprised but pleased; the sooner he saw the doctor, the better.

The second message was from Jason. She pressed the button to listen, hoping to hear he'd gotten the job. What she heard instead made her jaw drop. *He was in Vancouver with Marc.*

She punched in Jason's cell number. No signal. She started her car and headed back to Pemberton. To make matters worse she got stuck behind a logging truck and didn't have the courage to pass. This time when a bouncy golden oldie came on the radio she changed stations.

When she got home she found Jason's cell phone on his desk and his batteries in the recharger. No wonder she couldn't get through. His cryptic note revealed little more than he'd said on her cell phone. *Going to Vancouver with Marc. Staying overnight at Nate's apartment. Talk to you later.* As was his habit, he'd put the day and time at the top of the page. Monday, 8:45 a.m. The brat had missed his interview.

And he was staying overnight! She checked the bathroom. His toothbrush was gone. So was his razor, even though he only shaved every two days. How long was he planning on being away?

She dialed Marc's cell number but it was switched off. Were they deliberately keeping themselves out of communication? Why hadn't they called? Was she being paranoid and overprotective? By eight-thirty she was not only annoyed, she was worried.

At 9:00 p.m. Fiona called Leone. "Do you know the number for Nate and Angela's apartment? Jason's staying there with Marc and I need to talk to him about something."

"Hang on, I'll have to look in the address book. Ever since we got speed dial I never remember anyone's telephone number." She came back a moment later and gave Fiona the number. "Nate called when he got home. Apparently the doctors want to do some tests but Marc is optimistic."

"He's been confident all along. H-have you heard from him today?" Fiona asked, pacing the kitchen. Bilbo, his head resting on his paws, following her with his eyes.

"No, just Nate. I gather Marc will be staying in Vancouver for a few days. I plan to drive down and take him some extra clothes after work tomorrow. I'll be able to tell you more once I've seen him."

"I'm sure he'll tell me all about it when he calls," Fiona said brightly. How could he be involved in something so momentous and not phone her right away?

"Oh, dear," Leone said. "I just remembered. Rowdy's coming out of the clinic tomorrow and I promised Marc I'd pick him up. He's so worried about that dog."

"Would it help if I took Marc's clothes to him? I could bring Jason home at the same time."

"Fiona, you're a lifesaver! To tell you the truth I wasn't looking forward to the trip after working all day. Stop by on your way out and I'll have a bag ready for you to take."

Fiona hung up and dialed the number of Nate and Angela's apartment. It rang four times before the answering machine came on. *Where were they?*

"Hi, guys," she said, leaving a message after the

beep. "Just wondering what's happening. Hey, Jason what about that interview? I'm dying to know about your tests, Marc. Call me tomorrow."

She went to bed but it was a long time before she fell asleep. The two men she loved were a world away, doing things in which she had no part.

MARC CALLED A TAXI the next morning to take him and Jason out to UBC. As they turned off Chancellor Boulevard onto East Mall, Marc pointed out the various campus landmarks. "That's the student-union building. Down that street is the library, over there is the swimming pool, up ahead on your left is Health Sciences."

"This place is huge," Jason said, craning his neck. "How do you not get lost?"

"You'll learn to find your way around quickly enough." Marc smiled. "Engineering and science buildings are clumped together but if you take any arts subjects you'll have to cross campus."

"I had a look at the syllabus and all first-years have to take English. I may be glad of my wheels yet." Jason paused. "That is, if I get in."

"Think positive. If Paul thinks you've got the stuff to make it, you've at least got a chance."

The taxi dropped them at the engineering building and they followed the directions Paul had given Marc over the phone. Classes were in session and the halls empty as they wheeled into reception. Marc told the woman behind the glass window they were here to see the head of the engineering department. She buzzed Paul on his phone and then sent them back into the hall to the office next door.

Paul strode out to meet them, his tie loosened and his sleeves rolled up over well-developed forearms, reminding Marc of the times the two of them had gone rock climbing.

"Good to see you, Marc. It's been too long." Paul shook Marc's hand in an iron grip. His sympathetic gaze took in the wheelchair, then he turned to include Jason in the friendly banter. "Marc has finally leveled the playing field and given other guys a chance by handicapping himself."

Marc grinned. "Not for long. I'm on the road back." He motioned Jason to come forward. "This is Jason Gordon. He's the young man I was telling you about."

"Nice to meet you, Jason," Paul said, reaching for his hand. "It would be highly unusual for us to admit a student this late in the year. Classes are generally full and you've missed a lot of important course work. However, there're always a few dropouts after the first set of midterm exams and Marc assures me you'd be able to catch up. I've got to warn you, though, just knowing Marc won't get you into engineering at UBC."

"I understand," Jason said, swallowing. "I appreciate you making time to see me. I brought my transcripts and some other stuff to show you. I've been studying the first-year textbooks all summer for my own interest."

"So Marc told me. Come into my office and we'll talk. I've invited a couple of other faculty members. They'll be here in a moment." Paul ushered him inside. "Marc, there's a coffee lounge down the hall if you'd care to wait there."

"Nothing I like better than cardboard-flavored coffee," Marc said cheerfully. "Catch you in a while, Jase."

Jason glanced over his shoulder at Marc, surprised and clearly alarmed that Marc wasn't coming in with him. Marc leaned forward and squeezed his shoulder, speaking low into his ear. "Don't worry. You'll do just fine."

Marc left Jason in Paul's hands and went down the hall to an open area where food and beverage machines were lined up across from orange vinyl settees arranged in a U shape. The coffee was just as bad as he expected but it gave him something to do while he waited. He hadn't thought *he'd* be nervous but he found himself worrying as much as if Jason were his own son. He'd pushed Jason to apply. What if the boy didn't get in? Marc would feel partly responsible for his disappointment.

He got out his cell phone and tried to call Fiona. No answer. He and Jason had gone out for dinner the night before and ended up wheeling all the way down crowded, colorful Denman Street. The city was a new experience for Jason and Marc enjoyed seeing it through his eyes.

An hour and two coffees later, Jason and Paul came down the hall to find him.

"Well?" Marc glanced from Jason to Paul.

"My colleagues and I would like Jason to sit an entrance exam," Paul told him. "If he does as well as I think he will, we can accept him into first year."

Jason's beaming grin wiped out any lingering doubts Marc had that he'd done the right thing in bringing the boy to Vancouver. If Fiona had a problem with Jason going to university she would just have to get over it. And if money was a problem, Marc would help pay out of his own pocket. Jason deserved a chance to shine.

"Fantastic." He reached out to shake Jason's hand. "Congratulations, kid. I knew you'd wow them."

"He's built up quite an impressive portfolio of work all on his own," Paul said. "Since there's no time to waste, I've asked him to come back tomorrow to write the exams and we'll be able to let him know by Friday. I suggest you stop by the registrar's office for application forms and also the halls of residence to see what's available for wheelchair-accessible accommodation. The odd room becomes available around this time of year. Otherwise university counselors can advise you about suitable accommodation off-campus."

"We'll do that. Thanks again, Paul."

"Glad I could help. Let's get together for dinner sometime. I don't think you've met my wife, Cindy."

"I'll be in town for a couple of weeks. I'll give you a call."

"Goodbye, Jason," Paul said. "It was nice to meet you."

"Thanks, Dr. Peterson," Jason said. "I'll be here at nine o'clock tomorrow morning, just like you said."

CHAPTER SIXTEEN

FIONA DREW UP IN FRONT of a small apartment building in the West End. So this was the den of iniquity Jason had run off to instead of going to his job interview. Just wait till she gave that brother of hers a piece of her mind.

She carried Marc's suitcase to the front door and after a brief search found Angela's name and rang the bell.

"Hello?" Marc said through the intercom.

His voice sent a flutter through her stomach, which she quickly repressed. He'd led her little brother astray once too often. "It's me, Fiona."

"Come on up," Marc said, sounding surprised but pleased. The buzzer went off to unlock the front door.

Marc was waiting with the apartment door open when she got off the elevator on the fifth floor.

"I brought you a suitcase from Leone." She placed it in the foyer and followed Marc into a bright modern living room with a window overlooking the leafy streetscape.

Marc stopped beside a glass-and-marble coffee table and reached for her hand. "I missed you."

For a moment she wavered in her righteous indignation. This was the man she loved; he was going through a tumultuous time and needed her support. But she made herself be firm. He also needed to understand he couldn't just shanghai Jason whenever he felt like it.

"How could you take Jason away without telling me first?" she demanded. "Not even a phone call."

"It's good to see you, too," he said dryly. "Jason was supposed to talk to you about this trip beforehand. When my physiatrist asked me to come right away, everything got moved up and he didn't have a chance. We did try to call. I hope you weren't too inconvenienced."

"*I* wasn't inconvenienced but Jeff, at Electronics Shop, was. Jason blew off his job interview without so much as a phone call to say he wasn't coming in."

Marc frowned. "I didn't know anything about an interview."

Fiona glanced around the apartment. "Where is he?"

Jason wheeled into the room. "Fiona! I didn't know you were coming to Vancouver."

Telling herself to contain her temper, she began evenly, "Jason, it's nice you were able to give Marc moral support when he went to the hospital. Even if you just wanted a jaunt in the city I would have understood.

But I'm very upset that you took off without even consulting me. We've never been inconsiderate to each other before."

"Sorry, Fiona." Jason's smile faded to nothing and he lifted his hands helplessly. "I...I don't know what to say."

"Obviously. And how about your interview?"

"It was great!" Jason recovered his enthusiasm instantly. "They were really impressed with my electronics projects—"

"*They,*" she interrupted. "What are you talking about? You didn't go to the interview with Jeff."

"Jeff?" Jason looked confused. "I'm talking about Dr. Peterson and the other engineering professors— Oh!" He winced. "I thought you meant...but you didn't..."

Fiona looked to Marc. His painful grimace was partly obscured by his hand covering his face. There was *more* she didn't know? A bad feeling settled in her gut. "*What is going on?*"

Jason swallowed. "I've registered for university, Fi. I'm all but accepted into first-year engineering. I'm going to start classes next week and live in residence."

"You *what?*" she whispered, unable to believe what she was hearing.

"I don't want to work in some piddly little electronics store fixing computers and DVD players. I'm going to university *now*, not some unknown date in the future." Jason's face was white and his voice shook but she recognized the stubborn set of his jaw that meant he wasn't going to back down. "You'll just have to accept that I'm grown-up."

"Grown-up!" she exclaimed. "You've got a long way to go if you think maturity is ignoring your responsibilities and previous commitments. Anyway, the school year has already begun. You can't just waltz in six weeks late."

"Marc's friend is head of engineering," Jason said. "He pulled some strings."

Fiona swung her outraged gaze to Marc. "I should have known you had a hand in this!"

"Jason got in on his own merits," Marc said. "Or he will once he passes the entrance exams."

"And what about the job at the electronics store?"

"That's nothing in the larger scheme of things. It's not what Jason wants to do with his life."

"Oh, and *you* know what that is? You've been on the scene less than two months."

"He's right, Fi," Jason spoke up. "Marc understands."

And she didn't. Like a knife in the back, his words wounded. Then something else occurred to her.

"If you had an interview with the head of the department you must have had this set up for some time." She looked from Jason to Marc. "It had to have been at least last week, in fact." *Before the weekend they spent together.* "You had this all planned and didn't tell me?" she demanded of Marc. "What does that say about us?"

"Jason wanted to talk to you about it so I respected that," Marc replied quietly.

"I was waiting until the night before so you wouldn't have time to talk me out of it," Jason explained. "But then we left a day early and you weren't home...."

"Excuses." She felt utterly betrayed by both of them. Her brother was just immature, intent only on his own wants. But how could Marc have made love to her and deliberately kept such a huge secret from her?

She turned to her brother. "Come home with me now."

"I'm staying here," Jason said mulishly. "I have exams tomorrow. I should be studying."

Fiona took a deep breath. "Jason," she began calmly. "If you apologize to Jeff first thing in the morning he might give you an interview after all."

"I don't want an interview. I'm not going back to Pemberton."

"Listen to him, Fiona," Marc interceded. "He's old enough to make his own decisions."

"Is he? Or is he doing what *you're* telling him?"

"I'm helping him reach his goals."

Tears pricked the backs of her eyes and she blinked them away furiously. "Everything I've done my whole life has been for Jason. We didn't even get in a carer after the accident. I took care of him." She turned to her brother. "Who's going to help you when I'm not around?"

Jason looked at his feet. Marc answered for him. "He'll learn to do things for himself like any other disabled person. You did too much. Instead of teaching him to be independent you've made him so he can't function on his own."

Stung, Fiona lashed back. "He can function at home perfectly well. I made our house wheelchair accessible. I arrange my schedule around him. I hardly ever go out because of him—"

"There's such a thing as being too caring. Your perfect house has become a trap for him. It's a trap for you, too," Marc said. "You're overcompensating because you feel guilty for causing his paralysis."

Fiona froze, as she felt the blood drain from her face. "W-what are you talking about?"

Marc and Jason exchanged glances. Marc looked as though he regretted his last words but grimly he continued. "I know you were driving the night of the accident."

"Jason!" She threw her brother an anguished accusing look. "You promised."

"Don't blame him for telling me," Marc said. "And stop blaming yourself for the accident. Remember what you said to me about my father? The principle applies to you, too."

How was she supposed to reply to that? Her head

was whirling, her heart was aching. She simply couldn't deal with the things he was saying. "This whole university thing is happening too fast. Jason isn't ready for such a big change in his life."

"*You're* not ready, you mean," Marc said. "Sit down, Fiona. Let's talk this through."

"There's nothing more to say." With shaking hands she straightened her jacket. "Jason, you don't need me anymore. Fine. Go ahead—survive on your own. Marc, you were always alone and probably always will be. Good luck to you both."

She walked out and straight into the open elevator, numb with shock. The doors of the elevator shut and the tears she'd been damming for eight years burst forth.

MARC STARED AT THE DOOR Fiona had just closed in his face feeling as stunned as when the bomb blast had thrown him against the wall. Then, as now, his world had blown up around him, leaving devastation and ruin.

"Shouldn't we stop her?" Jason said. The boy looked as shell-shocked as Marc felt.

"No," he said wearily. "You need to study. I need to rest for my tests tomorrow. We'll let her cool down and talk again in a few days."

"Okay." Subdued, Jason retreated to the bedroom to go over his textbooks one more time.

The following day Marc and Jason went back to

UBC. While Jason was writing his exams Marc went to see about accommodation for him. A ground-floor room for the disabled in one of the residences had recently been vacated by a student having trouble coping with living away from home.

"I feel kind of bad getting it at someone else's misfortune," Jason said when they met up later in the student-union cafeteria.

"I know but there's nothing you can do for that person and letting the room go to waste would be worse, right?" Marc said. "How did the exams go?"

Jason brightened. "Pretty good. There were a few questions I couldn't answer but most of them I knew something about."

"Great. I hope I do as well on my tests. I get the results on Friday. Now, what else do you need—new textbooks, calculator, what?"

"Dr. Peterson reckons I can get by with the books I've got and my calculator is adequate, but there are tuition fees. I can apply for a student loan but that'll take time to process." Jason paused. "Fiona—"

"Don't bother her with that," Marc said. "I can lend you what you need."

"Thanks. I doubt she'd even talk to me anyway." Jason sighed. "I feel awful about what happened."

"I do, too. But you've done nothing wrong. Your sister's been taking care of you so long she doesn't know how to stop. It was up to you to make the break.

It doesn't mean you'll never be friends with her again. Blood is thicker than water."

That wasn't true for him, however. He'd said some pretty confrontational things. Would she forgive him? He hoped so. She'd had a significant role in helping him heal, and he didn't mean in just a physical sense.

He didn't hear from Fiona again that week and every time he'd tried calling she wasn't home or her cell phone was off. If Jason was missing her, Marc missed her more. When he got back he swore he'd make it up to her.

"I should go back to Pemberton and get my stuff," Jason said.

"No problem. Nate is coming back for me Friday afternoon. We'll have an early dinner to celebrate all these new changes in our lives, then head out."

By Thursday Marc was exhausted. It had been a grueling week but he was looking forward to the next day and receiving the results of his tests. In anticipation of good news he called and left Fiona a message to meet him Friday evening at the same hotel suite they stayed in before.

THURSDAY AFTERNOON Fiona ran through the pouring rain hunched under the hood of her rain jacket, steaming foam cups of coffee warming her hands. At Liz's wool shop she pushed the door open with her shoulder and stood on the mat, dripping. "What a day!"

Liz rose from her spinning wheel to take the cups

from her. "Hang your jacket over the back of that chair near the heater. Did you just get back from Lillooet?"

Fiona disposed of her jacket then brushed the rain from her hair with her fingers. "Yes. The teacher I replaced on Monday still isn't well. I'm going in tomorrow, too, but it'll likely be my last day there."

"Have you heard from Jason?" Liz returned to her seat and sipped her coffee.

Fiona sighed. "He's left messages but I haven't been able to connect with him. He's coming in tomorrow night to pack his clothes and his books."

"So he's really not coming back?" Liz set her cup aside and started spinning again.

"Why would he? All he's wanted for the past two years is to go to university. Now he's enrolled, thanks to Marc, not me." Fiona paced the tiny shop, running her fingers across the skeins of soft wool. "I'm so ashamed of myself."

"Oh, Fi. You thought you were doing what was best for him. You would have helped him go in another year. Jason isn't the most mature eighteen-year-old around."

"And whose fault is that? Mine, for holding him back."

"Not necessarily. Maybe you were protective because instinctively you knew he wasn't ready."

"How do you tell the difference?"

"That's the trouble with parenting—you can't. You do the best you can and hope it's good enough. The point is, you can't beat yourself up over your mistakes. Learn from them and go on from there."

Tears filled Fiona's eyes. "It's too late. I've lost him."

Liz got up and pulled Fiona into a comforting hug. "Don't be silly. He's your brother. You haven't lost him."

Fiona pulled a crumpled tissue from her pocket and blew her nose. "You think?"

"I *know*. But you'll have to be the one to go to him."

"I *want* to be supportive. I really do." She sat down on the armless wooden rocker and heaved a deep sigh. "For years I've been terrified of being alone. I so very nearly was. Jason almost died in the accident, too. When he pulled through I was so grateful I almost didn't care that he couldn't walk. I know that sounds awful—"

"It's perfectly natural. Far better to be alive and paraplegic than dead. But Fi, the worst has happened. *You're alone.*" Liz raised her hands, palms up. "What's happened? Has a lightning bolt struck you down? Have you collapsed under the weight of your own sorrow?"

Fiona smiled at her friend's exaggeration. "His music used to drive me crazy but now the house is too quiet. I hated doing his laundry but I sure miss his cooking. I miss his conversation and his stupid jokes and crazy inventions. I'm lonely without Jason around."

"Again, that's natural. You've got empty-nest syndrome."

Fiona sighed. "Maybe you're right. It hurts but I'm surviving. It's going to take some getting used to."

"And you will get used to it." Liz handed her the cooling coffee Fiona'd abandoned on her perambulation around the shop. "Now, what about Marc?"

The last of Fiona's tears dried instantly and she smiled, hugging herself. "He'll be back this weekend, too. He's booked the same hotel suite we stayed in before."

"So you're not mad at him anymore?"

"I don't like the way things played out but it wasn't his fault. And he was right about everything. How can I stay angry? I'm just so happy for him that he's getting the use of his legs back."

"And when he takes off again?" Liz said.

"If he really cares for me, and I think he does, we'll work something out."

FRIDAY AFTERNOON Marc sat across from Dr. Sagaki, waiting patiently while the physiatrist read through his file and absorbed the results of the week of tests. Through the half-open slats of the venetian blinds at Dr. Sagaki's back Marc could see Vancouver's north-shore mountains gray with rain. In the city the sun was trying with only moderate success to peek through an overcast sky, shedding bursts of watery sunshine on the nearly leafless trees.

Finally, Dr. Sagaki put down the file and looked up with a smile. "Good news, Marc. I'm very pleased with your test results."

Relief flooded through Marc. "Fantastic. I knew it. Give me the details."

Dr. Sagaki held up a blurry gray-and-white MRI scan and indicated the area of interest with the point of his sharpened pencil. "As you can see on this magnetic resonance imaging scan of the spinal cord, compression has been reduced by almost half in the region of your T10 to T12 thoracic vertebrae where the damage occurred."

Marc was happy to take the doctor's word for it. "So that explains the sensations and the movement I've been experiencing in my legs lately. The pressure is released so the nerves are working again?"

"That's correct. Nerve function has returned in part to the lower limbs. In the coming months you may even experience a small increase over that, which you have now. I think I'm justified in reclassifying you as an incomplete paraplegic."

Alarm bells went off in Marc's brain. "Whoa, doc. You mean I'm still going to be disabled?"

Dr. Sagaki frowned. "Well, yes. Possibly you could be a candidate for gait training either with FNS—functional neuromuscular stimulation—or leg braces, either of which would allow limited walking. There are physiological benefits to an upright position even if temporary. I must warn you, however, that these are not so much a cure as an additional form of therapy."

"But what about the pain when the coffee landed on

me?" Marc demanded angrily. "What about when my legs moved out of the stirrups? Doesn't that mean I'm getting better?"

"You're much improved from when I first took on your case, Marc." Dr. Sagaki removed his glasses and rubbed the bridge of his nose. His head tilted to one side as he regarded Marc with sympathy and compassion. "What you want is a miracle. I'm afraid that as amazing as modern medicine is, it can't fix everything."

"But this FSN—"

"FNS."

"Whatever. It'll let me walk?"

"After a fashion. But it's exhausting and no one uses it full-time for general mobility. A wheelchair is more efficient and less tiring."

"But…but…I'll get more nerve function back, right? I mean, the compression is reduced. It'll go down more and then I'll recover completely, right?" Agitated, Marc gripped the wheels of his chair, shifting it back and forth in jerky motions. "I'll get back on my feet eventually. *Right?*"

Silently, Dr. Sagaki shook his head. "Even if the spinal cord completely decompresses, the damage to your nerves has already been done. You could regain the ability to stand on your own for short periods, possibly even take a few steps with the aid of a walking frame or crutches. But you'll never recover fully. I'm sorry, Marc. I thought you understood this."

He'd been told. Over and over. By every doctor, nurse and physiotherapist he'd encountered. Until now it hadn't sunk in. Frozen inside, Marc stared straight ahead and saw nothing as the blackness crept over him.

He was stuck in a wheelchair for the rest of his life.

Nate and Jason were waiting for him outside the hospital by Nate's Jeep Cherokee.

"How did it go?" Jason asked eagerly. "Were the results as good as you expected?"

Fortunately Marc still had control of the muscles that made his mouth form a smile. "Better," he lied.

"Hurray!" Jason cheered.

Nate grinned broadly and clapped a hand on Marc's shoulder. "Fantastic, dude." He opened the passenger door. "Hop in."

Marc smiled again, this time at the irony of Nate's choice of words. He would never hop again.

He didn't say much on the way back to Whistler; he didn't have to—Nate and Jason did all the talking for him. They seemed to be convinced he would be walking again within the month. And why not? He'd led them to believe it with his own egotistical self-confidence. He would have wept but he was still frozen. Maybe he'd never thaw. Wouldn't that be fitting? Immobilized inside and out.

Jim and Leone weren't home when he got there. Friday night they usually went out for dinner then played cards at a neighbor's house. He'd known that when he'd left his message for Fiona to meet him tonight. The rendezvous would still take place but it wouldn't turn out the way either of them had anticipated.

Marc unpacked his suitcase, put the dirty clothes in the washing machine and turned it on. He didn't want to leave Leone with any more work than necessary. In his closet he found a small backpack. He went to the dresser and opened his sock drawer. Beneath the boxer shorts and gray wool socks he found the vials of pills. They beckoned him like a found pack of cigarettes to a reformed smoker. And he craved them just as much. After only a moment's hesitation he tossed them on top of the clean underwear in his backpack. For some reason he threw in his father's skiing trophy. Then he pulled the drawstring tight.

Rowdy trotted down the hall at his side, prancing and leaping, his intelligent brown eyes darting from Marc to the leash hanging by the door.

"Don't look at me with those puppy-dog eyes," Marc growled. "We're not going for a walk."

At the word *walk* Rowdy's ears pricked forward, the tips flopping over in the cute way they had. His bandages were off but the stitches hadn't been taken out; that was supposed to happen on Monday. Oh well, between Jim and Leone, Nate and Aidan, Rowdy would be taken care of when Marc went away.

Marc leaned over and petted the dog. Rowdy licked his hand with loving thoroughness. With a sob in his throat, Marc pulled Rowdy onto his lap and laid his cheek on the dog's head, holding him close.

A car turned into the driveway. Marc set the dog back on the floor, his eyes blurring. "Good boy, Rowdy. *Stay.*"

Brent, the taxi driver, cheerful as always, lowered the motorized loading ramp so Marc could roll aboard. "Haven't seen you all week. What have you been up to?"

"Spending a few days in Vancouver, catching up with old friends." How easy it was to go through the motions of being alive when all the time, inside he was dead. Afterward he tipped generously. "You're a great guy, Brent. I mean it."

Brent looked surprised and pleased. "Thanks, Marc. I appreciate it."

The hotel suite was just as luxurious as before. Fireplace with firewood—check. Hot tub—check. Terrytowel robes—check. Champagne on ice—check.

He glanced at his watch. Fiona wasn't due for another hour. Plenty of time to get wasted. Picking up the phone he called room service and ordered a quart of Jack Daniel's. Dutch courage—check.

A quarter of the way through the bottle he cried over Fiona. She was too caring a person to let himself be a burden to her. Look how she'd sacrificed her life for Jason. What kind of Prince Charming would Marc be if he saved her only to imprison her with his own disability, and worse, his bitterness?

Before he got too drunk he called the gallery and asked if the picture Fiona'd liked so much was still there. It was. Fantastic. Cool. Awesome. Could they please deliver it to the following address…. Tomorrow morning? Perfect. Timing was everything.

CHAPTER SEVENTEEN

FIONA KNOCKED ON THE DOOR of the hotel suite, nervously smoothing down her dress, touching her hair. Jason had come home and told her Marc's good news. She'd been so happy she hadn't even scolded Jason for not calling her more this week. When he'd told her he was going to pack up his things for the move to Vancouver she'd pretended to be okay with it, but she was glad she wasn't going to be home tonight to watch him do it. He was so engrossed in dismantling his stereo wires he barely registered her announcement that she was staying in Whistler with Marc and wouldn't be home until morning.

Why was Marc so long to answer the door? She'd looked forward all day to the moment she was back in his arms. How foolish they'd been to quarrel when they had so much that was good and true between them. Now that he was getting better maybe they could talk and make plans. She hoped that, like her, he'd want them to have a future together.

She knocked again and put her ear to the door. A

noise, like something being knocked over, was followed by a muffled curse. "Marc? Are you in there?"

The door opened. Her smile died on her face.

Marc's eyes were so glazed over he had trouble focusing and he reeked of bourbon. "C'mon in."

She stepped over the threshold feeling uneasy. Glancing around the room she spotted the half-empty bottle of alcohol. "What are you doing?"

"Celebratin', what else? Wan' some champagne? I'd offer you some o' Jack but I don' think I have enough."

"Marc, are you crazy? I thought you'd stopped drinking."

"Whatsa matter? Worried I won' be able to get it up?" He cackled with insane laughter.

Fiona crossed to the phone. "I'm going to call room service for coffee. You've got to stop this right now."

With surprising swiftness, Marc glided over and depressed the button on the phone before she could speak into the mouthpiece. "I'm not your brother. You can't tell me what to do."

"I don't understand why you're acting this way," she said, scared and bewildered. "I thought we were going to have another night like last time. Romantic and…loving. We have so much to be happy about."

"There is no *we*," he said brutally. "Now that I'm going to be walkin' again, I'm walkin' right outta here."

Oh, no. This was what she'd been afraid of. "I…I could come with you."

For a girl who'd been no farther south than Vancouver and no farther north than Lillooet, the concept of actually getting on a plane to points unknown was daunting despite her pipe dreams of visiting Greece. Yet for one brief, glorious moment Fiona imagined herself taking off with Marc. Then she saw his gaze harden in response to her suggestion and reality came crashing down.

"You *should* get out an' travel," he said. "But you ain't doin' it with me. You'd just slow me down." He took a swig from the bottle and pointed it accusingly at her. "Admit it, Pollyanna, you only went out with me because you thought I was stuck in this wheelchair. Deep down you didn't want me to get better because then I wouldn't need you. You tried to convince me not to count on recovering because you couldn't stand the thought that I'd be able to leave you, too."

"That's not true," she protested. "I *love* you."

And yet she was horribly afraid that at one time there might have been a tiny grain of truth in his accusation. If she'd held Jason back, what might she do to Marc? But she'd gotten past that. Hadn't she?

"You haven't had a serious boyfriend in years," Marc went on. "You gotta wonder why."

"Whoever takes me on, takes on my brother," she said quietly. "Not every man is willing to do that."

"You don' give 'em a chance."

She stared, unable to answer. "Why are you doing this?" she whispered.

He looked away. "Trus' me, it's better this way."

"So you're just going to blow me off after all we've been through together?" she demanded, becoming angry. "You're acting like a jerk."

"I *am* a jerk." Now he stared insolently at her. "I told you right from the beginning but you wouldn't believe me."

Shaking, Fiona gathered up her purse. "You're in no condition to discuss anything rationally. We'll talk about this tomorrow."

"Ain't gonna be a tomorrow," he said. "We're done."

Marc heard the door click shut and his head dropped to his chest. Tears of pain and loss rolled down his cheeks till he could taste salt seeping through his lips. That was the hardest thing he'd ever done.

He must have passed out after that because when he came to nearly an hour had gone by. His head swimming, Marc took a long pull on the bourbon to ease his pain. Tucking the bottle between his useless legs, he went to the bedroom for his backpack. He fumbled open the drawstring and dumped the pack upside down on the bed. The contents tumbled out, the bronze trophy making a heavy clunk among the plastic vials. He picked out two vials at random and let the tablets spill through his fingers. These were his insurance policy and it was time to cash in.

His eye fell on the trophy. *All he wants is to hear your voice.*

The memory of Fiona's words intensified Marc's agony. He tried to banish it by wheeling blindly across the room and ended up crashing into the bedside table. Focusing his bleary eyes, he saw the telephone in front of him.

What the hell. Maybe he should call the ol' man at least once. Just to say goodbye. Now what was the number?

He pressed his eyes shut and visualized the page in Leone's address book. Repeating the number to himself, he reached for the phone and dialed.

A man impersonating Marc answered. Marc shook his head, momentarily confused. "H'lo. Who's this?"

Silence. Then his father said, "Marc?"

"Yeah. Hi." He hadn't realized how much his father sounded like him. Or rather, he sounded like his dad. Nor had he planned what to say. They were both silent so long Marc thought he'd lost the connection.

Then Roland said, "I've been worried about you. How are you?"

"Great. Doin' great. Been to the physi…physi…the speshulist. Sorry, Friday night. Had a few drinks."

"That's okay."

"Anyway, I'm doin' great," he blustered.

"Wonderful. Leone's kept me up to date on your progress but it's good to hear your voice."

His father's naked longing had more of an effect than Marc would have thought. He choked up and before he could formulate another sentence, Roland went on.

"After your accident I went to see your producer here in New York to find out exactly what happened. Why didn't you tell Leone and Jim you were injured because you went back to help a man bring out his wounded child?"

Oh, no, here it comes, the stupid hero stuff. "It's no big deal," Marc mumbled. He was surprised his father had gone to the trouble of tracking down his boss.

"But it is," Roland insisted. "There's nothing worse for a parent than to lose his child. However it happens." He hesitated. "Marc, I'm so sorry for all these years we've spent apart."

You have to forgive him.

Marc was silent a long time while Fiona's words rang through his mind. He was checking out anyway, might as well do one last good deed.

"It's okay. You did what you had to do. I survived." As he said it, he realized he'd done more than survive; he'd had a damn good life. Marc rubbed his forehead. "Did my boss happen to know if the kid in Damascus made it?"

"Both his legs were broken but he lived, thanks to you. I'm very proud of you, son. Your mother would have been proud, too."

"Mom—" Marc broke off, unable to go on.

"Not a day goes by that I don't think of her, Marc."

Roland's voice was barely a whisper. "I loved her and I miss her. I always will."

"Me, too." Tears streamed down Marc's face. A wrenching pain seemed to rip his chest apart. "I—I miss you, too, Dad."

A muffled sob met his ears then Roland spoke again. "Once you've fully recovered and are back at work I'd like to see you the next time you're in New York. You could meet my wife and your stepbrother and sister. I guess you heard that Belinda had a baby boy."

"Yeah, we'll all get together." Marc choked on the lie. He took a deep breath, clearing the way for the truth. "The thing is I just found out today I'm not going to recover. I'll always be in a wheelchair."

There was another long silence. At last Roland said, quiet and calm, "No problem. We'll come out there."

Marc's gaze fell on his father's trophy, lying on its side on the bed. Rightly or wrongly his dad hadn't been around during his childhood because he'd had the drive and determination to pursue his dream. Marc had inherited his father's strength of will; he'd always been proud of that.

You've got to forgive yourself.

Marc didn't want to be a hero; he just wanted to know that when it counted he'd done the right thing.

"Thanks, Dad. I'd really like to see you."

He hung up and dried his face on his shirtsleeve. Then he scooped up the pills. They made a tidy lethal handful. Fearless Marc Wilde or spineless coward?

Ha, ha, spineless. That was a good one.

Spinning in his chair, he wheeled into the bathroom and flushed the pills down the toilet.

FIONA STRUGGLED THROUGH the next few weeks in a haze of pain, taking one day at a time. Some days were easier than others. With the onset of colder weather she got more subbing work as teachers came down with colds and flu. The pub was the same as always, noisy and crowded, both social life and social death, as Liz had taken to pointing out with increasing frequency.

More snow fell on the mountains, blanketing the peaks down to two thousand feet and reminding Fiona that winter wasn't far off. She would stare at the picture Marc sent and dream of bright clear light and two chairs waiting for lovers who would never arrive.

Occasionally she saw Marc in the distance riding his handcycle and once at the library reading to his group of seniors. She visited Rowdy and saw for herself that his scars were healing. She had tea with Leone and taught Marc's golden-haired niece, Emily, who never spoke above a whisper. From Leone she learned Marc was spending a lot of time in Vancouver, staying at Nate and Angela's apartment and doing intensive physiotherapy. Progress wasn't as fast as initially expected but Leone spoke optimistically of Marc's future.

When Fiona called Marc to thank him for the picture he was distant and terse. She never approached him in person. His cruel rejection of her still hurt.

Nor was she in contact with Jason. Although she missed him desperately she decided she wouldn't under any circumstances beg him to come home again. She'd gone to Electronics Shop to tell Jeff about Jason's new plans only to find that Jason had already done so. He was growing up and taking responsibility after all.

She took a night-school course—as if she didn't have enough to do—a photography class purely for enjoyment. Just in case she ever got the chance to go traveling she could take some memorable photos to hang next to the picture of the waiting chairs.

One evening as she was eating her dinner and feeling particularly solitary—one lamb chop, one potato, one roasted tomato and one stalk of broccoli—the phone rang.

"Hello?" She poked her fork into the tomato and watched the juice flow out.

"Fi? It's Jase."

"Jason!" Her heart picked up tempo and she sprang to her feet, unable to sit still. "How are you? Is everything all right? How're you doing?"

"Fine. How are you?" His voice had that wistful quality she remembered from when he was a small boy.

Something was wrong. She was about to demand he tell her what it was, but she controlled herself and sat down. "I'm doing okay. Keeping busy. How're classes?"

"The work is pretty hard but not too hard. Except for English 101. I have to write essays."

Fiona laughed. "That's good for you. Do you like your room? Are you meeting people, making friends?"

"My room is fine." There was a long pause. "I'm kinda homesick, to tell you the truth. I'd like to come back to Whistler if that's okay."

Fiona's spirits leaped for joy. "Oh, Jase, I miss you, too. Of course you can come home. I'll drive down Friday night and take you back Sunday."

"Uh, Fi? I meant I'd like to come home for good. You know how you said I could do classes by correspondence. Maybe that's not such a bad idea."

Fiona felt a moment of euphoria—this is what she'd wanted—then she sat down abruptly. It was all wrong for Jason. Even she could see that now. "Why? What's the problem? Are people being mean to you?"

"Not mean, just kinda thoughtless. Some stare, most look right through me." His voice wavered. "It's too hard. I don't want to do this anymore."

"You've got Dave."

"He's not always around. He's into scuba diving every weekend. I haven't made any new friends."

Her heart bled for him. It would be so easy to tell him he could come home, but she loved him too much to do that. "I'm sure it is hard, but you've got to stick it out. At least finish the year."

"Why?" Jason cried. "You've never pushed me to do anything I didn't want to before."

"I was wrong." Fiona shut her eyes and told herself to be strong. "I'm not going to let you bail on this. Think of how much trouble Marc went to to get you into university. How could you let him down?"

"He's always telling me I've got to make my own choices. This is my choice," Jason said stubbornly.

Jason was right; she was telling him what to do again. Finding the correct balance was hard. "Okay. Let me tell you what I think before you decide. I don't think you're really a quitter which is exactly what you'd be if you left university now. Who cares if you haven't made a lot of friends? You just haven't met the right gang yet. Try joining some clubs with activities that interest you."

"I don't have time what with trying to catch up with my school work. You don't know what it's like being all alone with no one to talk to day after day."

"You think not?" she said dryly.

"Most of the guys on my floor have girlfriends," Jason went on bitterly. "Girls aren't interested in a boy in a wheelchair."

Fiona cast around for inspiration. Her gaze fell on the picture of the chairs on the terrace. "Somewhere, someone is waiting for you. You might not meet her today or tomorrow, but someday you will. You're a lot more likely to find someone special on a campus of nearly thirty thousand young people than in Pemberton."

"Fi, can't I please come home?" he pleaded.

Torn, Fiona jammed her fingers in her mass of hair

and tugged. Part of her wanted more than anything to go back to their cozy situation. But if she gave in now neither of them might ever reach out again. *Neither?* When had she pushed herself beyond her comfort zone? Who was she to advise Jason to follow his dream unless she was willing to do the same?

Taking a deep breath, she said, "You can come home—"

"Thank you." His relief was palpable. "I knew you'd understand."

"—but I won't be here."

"What!"

"I've decided to take a trip." She looked at the blue waters and whitewashed walls and the sunlit terrace and smiled. She needed this. She *deserved* it. "I'm going away for a while. To Greece."

"But…you can't. Who's going to look after me?"

"You'll be fine, Jase," she said and found she really believed it. "You can stay in the house. It's yours, too, after all. I don't think Jeff has found anyone to work in his store yet."

"But…but…" Jason sputtered. "How will I cope on my own? Who'll help me with my exercises?"

How was it she'd never heard that faint whine in his voice before? Truly, she hadn't been doing him any favors by being so accommodating. It hurt to be so tough on him, but she knew she was finally acting in a way that would benefit him in the long term.

"Who's assisting you now? A physiotherapist at the

university, I suspect. You could make much better use of Whistler's excellent social services than you have in the past. Marc used to go to Val right here in Pemberton. Groceries can be delivered. Or you could get hand controls fitted for my car. It's about time you learned to drive."

"Gosh, Fi," he grumbled. "I just want to go back to my old way of life. You're making me do all sorts of new stuff."

"You thought they were great ideas when Marc suggested them," she pointed out.

"That was before I knew how hard the real world is."

Fiona sighed. "It *is* hard, Jase, for able-bodied folk, too. That's what growing is all about at any age—pushing yourself to reach your full potential."

"So what am I going to do?" he wailed.

"Instead of coming home this weekend how about if I visit you on Saturday and we talk some more. I've never seen your place and I'd love to."

"Okay," Jason said reluctantly. "See you then."

MARC WIPED HIS forehead across his shoulder to take the sweat from his brow. Every muscle in his body burned as he strained to keep himself upright in the walking frame. The knowledge that his legs and not his arms were doing the majority of the work kept him going. He never knew anything could be so painful or so frustrating. If he could last just five minutes he would let himself... He tried to think of a suitably enticing reward. A slice of Leone's chocolate cake, a cold beer, a *rest*. Yeah, a rest sounded good.

But not very productive. His reward would be *another* five minutes in the walking frame. The stronger he got, the more he practiced, the closer he'd be to walking again.

The minute hand of the wall clock ticked over, launching him into the final five minutes. His breath came in deep rasps now and he no longer had the energy to wipe the perspiration away. It dripped into his eyes, stinging them with salt until he couldn't even see the clock.

Clunk; he thrust the frame before him. *Drag*; with excruciating effort he lifted his right foot a fraction of an inch off the ground and slowly moved it forward, leaning heavily on the frame. Time lost meaning. His goal now was to make it across the room.

Clunk, drag, clunk, drag...

From the other room he heard the phone ring. A moment later Leone was calling him. "Marc? Are you in there?"

"I'm here," he tried to say but it came out as a gasp.

Leone knocked and opened the door. "Marc? Oh, there you are. The phone's for you."

"Tell them...call...later..." he wheezed.

"Okay." Leone started to leave. "I'm sorry, Fiona, he can't talk right at the moment. Can he call you later?"

Fiona. Three weeks had passed since that horrible night in the hotel. Surely he could do her no harm with a few words. Somehow he found enough breath to speak. "I'll…talk…now."

Two more steps. With Herculean effort he advanced the walking frame and threw his leg forward. Ignoring the stabbing pain he did it again.

Leone hovered anxiously while he laboriously turned himself around with his back to the bed. "He'll just be a second," she murmured into the receiver.

Finally, the mattress rose to meet him. Leone couldn't stop herself, she ran over to lift his legs onto the bed. Marc didn't have the strength to protest as every cell sighed with gratitude at being relieved of forced labor.

Leone handed him the phone and also the towel lying on the bed. Marc smiled his thanks and mopped his face.

"Hi," he panted. "Fiona?"

"I hope I haven't caught you at a bad time."

She sounded courteous and distant, not the woman he'd made love to only a few weeks ago. "Just… doing…my exercises." He took a few deep breaths. "That's better."

"How's it going?" she asked. "Will you be leaving for New York soon?"

He deserved to squirm after what he'd done to her but this was so hard. And she deserved the truth. "I lied when I told you I was going to fully recover."

"But the tests— I thought…"

He cleared his throat. "I've made progress but the doctor believes I'll never walk unaided again."

"And now you believe it, too." Her voice was flat.

"I've faced reality. But you know me. Never say die." He paused. "I'm sorry the way things turned out. You're a good person, Pollyanna. You deserve a whole lot better than me."

She said nothing.

"Rowdy's recuperating well," Marc went on. "The bandages are off and he's licking his scars which Leone tells me is good for healing." From his basket in the corner, Rowdy heard his name and looked up, thumping his stubby tail against the cushion.

Marc ran his fingers through his hair. "How have you been?"

"I'm working through some things. It's been kind of a difficult transition with Jason gone."

"I'm glad he decided to stay at university."

"You knew about that?" She sounded surprised.

"We get together when I'm in town."

There was a long pause during which Marc debated whether she would shoot him down in flames if he asked her out for dinner. It would be a crazy thing to do after the pain he'd put them both through breaking off their relationship. But he *missed* her. He missed her bright clear eyes and unfailing optimism. Most of all he missed her glorious smile. He was about to speak when she did.

"I'm going away for a while. To Greece."

The magnitude of what he'd lost hit him. He pressed his fingers into the inner corners of his eyes and felt the moisture against his skin. "I'm glad for you. Have a wonderful trip," he whispered. "Take care of yourself."

"Thank you. You, too." There was another long pause.

Marc couldn't bear to hang up first. Finally he heard the click of the receiver in the cradle and knew she was gone.

MARC LEANED BACK in his wheelchair on Jim and Leone's patio and lifted his face to the late-October sun. A faint breeze carried the scent of wood smoke up the valley and an unexpected feeling of peace and well-being washed over him.

In truth, he had much to be grateful for. He was alive, for a start, with all his mental faculties and the ability to get around independently. Strange as it seemed he was almost grateful for his injury. He'd learned that he wasn't immortal and that each day was to be savored. His home, his family and friends, were more important to him than playing a bit part on the world stage.

Only one thing was lacking—Fiona—but at least he could rejoice that she was finally fulfilling her dream. One day, maybe, she would see him in another light.

Rowdy raced about the yard, chasing birds. When he was tired Marc wheeled inside to his room and went back to revising his interviews of people of war-ravaged nations. He'd tried to sell them to a magazine. The editor had rejected them but suggested a book publisher who turned out to be very interested.

As Leone said, at least he wouldn't get blown to bits sitting in front of a computer. A time would come, he knew, when he would get the urge to travel again. When that time came he had an idea for more articles that would take him to foreign lands. Not every country in the world was at war.

He heard the doorbell ring but ignored it knowing Leone was home. The familiar voice in the hall was impossible to ignore. He'd turned his wheelchair toward the door when the knock came. "Come in."

Fiona entered. She looked more heartbreakingly beautiful than ever with her clear gray-green eyes, small lively features and fresh skin. And that mass of burnished hair he loved to bury his face in.

His heart began beating furiously though he strived to appear calm. "I thought you were going away."

She pulled an airline folder out of her purse. "I booked a ticket to Greece, Air Canada Flight 801."

For a moment he couldn't speak. Striving to sound normal, he said, "Who will look after your animals?"

"Liz is taking Bilbo and Baggins and my neighbor will feed the alpacas."

Marc nodded. "Then I wish you a good journey," he said. "Have a glass of retsina for me."

"There are still seats available," she said, coming farther into the room, bringing with her the faint scent of roses. "If you want to go, you shouldn't delay because they're filling up fast."

She wanted him to go with her. Marc tried to laugh for joy but his chest was so tight with emotion the sound he made could have just as easily been a sob.

Fiona's smile wavered when he didn't answer. "I'll go alone if I must but I really would enjoy it more with you." She pursed her lips and frowned at his continued silence. "I thought you wanted to find those chairs."

"Fiona—" he choked out.

"Hear me out. It's irrelevant to me whether you're in a wheelchair or not. I'd been thinking all along I didn't want to be responsible for another disabled person although I was so ashamed of that I didn't want to say it aloud. Then you implied I wanted you tethered to me by need, like Jason, and I was really confused. Until it occurred to me that neither view is right. Everyone, able and disabled, has certain abilities and lack of abilities. Even in a wheelchair you're way more independent than I am in some ways. Oh, I don't know quite how to say it."

"Fiona—"

"So I'll just say, I love you. *That* is the truth. Whether you're in a chair or running a marathon the basic facts are the same—you're the man I fell in love with. A man who makes me laugh and think, who challenges me and supports me. A man who cares about people even when he claims not to, a man who's tough on the outside and a marshmallow inside, who lives his dream and encourages others to do the same." Tears sprang from her eyes but she brushed them away impatiently. "I'll push you up Mount Parnassus if need be. Will you come with me?"

Marc placed his hands on the sides of the chair and bore down, using his arms to help his still-weak leg muscles bring him to his feet. He heard Fiona's gasp and remembered she'd never seen him stand. With halting, painful steps he slowly covered the distance between them, his gaze fixed on her, his greatest reward.

She didn't run to him. She didn't try to help him. But suddenly she was laughing and crying both at once and holding her arms out to him. "You're so tall. I didn't realize you were so tall!"

He wrapped her in his embrace, his chin resting atop her head as they swayed slightly. Marc had no fear of falling. Small and fragile as she seemed, she was his rock. She would anchor him when he threatened to disintegrate. She would be his light when the blackness overcame him.

When his heart slowed its thunderous pounding enough to hear himself speak he drew back and kissed the tears from her eyes. "Greece with you sounds wonderful. Shall we make the trip our honeymoon?"

Her eyes shone. "We'll sit on the terrace and eat

olives and bread, and walk through the gate to who knows where. Together."

"We'll do all of that, and more." He held her close again and whispered in her ear, "And when we're done wandering we'll come home to the mountains by the sea where we belong." He paused. "Did I tell you I love you?"

"Not in so many words." She looked up at him and with a small smile, lifted an eyebrow. "Well?"

"I love you."

Her smile grew.

"I love you, I love you, I love you…" He took a breath. "I *love* you—"

"Okay, you can stop now."

Grinning, he continued, "—I love *you, I* love—"

Standing on her tiptoes, she pressed her lips against his and shut him up with a kiss. Marc grinned to himself; it's what he'd been angling for all along.

* * * * *

Read Aidan Wilde's story in the final book of
THE WILDE MEN *trilogy,*
A MOM FOR CHRISTMAS (SR #1236),
available in November 2004.

HARLEQUIN *Super*ROMANCE®

Two brand-new Superromance authors make their debuts in 2004!

Golden Heart winner Anna DeStefano
The Unknown Daughter (SR#1234)

On sale October 2004

Seventeen years ago Eric Rivers left Carrinne Wilmington with more than just a broken heart. So Carrinne decided to leave her stifling hometown and make a new life for herself and her daughter. Now she's returned to get help from the one man who holds the key to her future. Running into Eric again was never part of her plan.

Pamela Ford
Oh Baby! (SR#1247)

On sale December 2004

Annie McCarthy and Nick Fleming were married briefly and then divorced. Annie moved to Bedford, Wisconsin, and told a little white lie—that she was married. The problems begin when Nick shows up to tell her they really are still married!

Available wherever Harlequin books are sold.

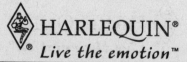

HARLEQUIN®
Live the emotion™

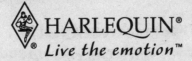

If you enjoyed what you just read,
then we've got an offer you can't resist!

Take 2 bestselling love stories FREE!

Plus get a FREE surprise gift!

Clip this page and mail it to Harlequin Reader Service®

IN U.S.A.	IN CANADA
3010 Walden Ave.	P.O. Box 609
P.O. Box 1867	Fort Erie, Ontario
Buffalo, N.Y. 14240-1867	L2A 5X3

YES! Please send me 2 free Harlequin Superromance® novels and my free surprise gift. After receiving them, if I don't wish to receive anymore, I can return the shipping statement marked cancel. If I don't cancel, I will receive 6 brand-new novels every month, before they're available in stores. In the U.S.A., bill me at the bargain price of $4.69 plus 25¢ shipping and handling per book and applicable sales tax, if any*. In Canada, bill me at the bargain price of $5.24 plus 25¢ shipping and handling per book and applicable taxes**. That's the complete price, and a savings of at least 10% off the cover prices—what a great deal! I understand that accepting the 2 free books and gift places me under no obligation ever to buy any books. I can always return a shipment and cancel at any time. Even if I never buy another book from Harlequin, the 2 free books and gift are mine to keep forever.

135 HDN DZ7W
336 HDN DZ7X

Name	(PLEASE PRINT)
Address	Apt.#
City	State/Prov. Zip/Postal Code

Not valid to current Harlequin Superromance® subscribers.

Want to try two free books from another series?
Call 1-800-873-8635 or visit www.morefreebooks.com.

* Terms and prices subject to change without notice. Sales tax applicable in N.Y.
** Canadian residents will be charged applicable provincial taxes and GST.
All orders subject to approval. Offer limited to one per household.
® are registered trademarks owned and used by the trademark owner and or its licensee.

SUP04R   ©2004 Harlequin Enterprises Limited

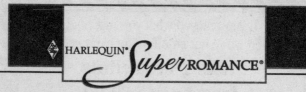

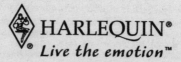